A Sky Littered with Stories

RD Pires

For all who care to take a look inside

CONTENTS

LUCINDA'S GHOST

Lucinda dragged an arm across her eyes, moisture soaking through the black lace sleeve. With one last glance, she waved at the dark windows of the silver Lexus, hoping her family couldn't see through the brave smile. Maybe from that far away the glimmer of tears wasn't noticeable. She could fold the veil back over her face, but no—then they'd definitely come back to comfort her.

The facade proved to be enough. Tailpipe exuding a puff of vapor, the vehicle took off and with it went the last of the mourners. They could gather in solemnity at their hotel. Lucinda would have the peace she desired. The solitude to wade in her own grief that she'd sought all day. God, if only the reception could have ended sooner. She'd nearly been unable to stand on her own when they lowered... when they...

She opened the front door and rushed inside, fingers trembling. This wasn't how things were supposed to be. They were meant to have had a long and happy life together. Lucinda slammed the door shut, frantic, barely holding

1

herself together. She turned to flee into the bedroom and—

She screamed.

"For God's sake!" he bellowed, recoiling from her howl.

Panting, Lucinda backed up against the front door. No! The exhaustion and grief were affecting her. She had to get a grip on herself.

"Harold?" she gasped. "It can't be. Harold?"

"I think so," the visitor said. "Ta-dah."

"But how is this possible? I just… I just buried you!" she said, blinking furiously and wondering if she'd gone mad. The translucent figure before her refused to vanish, and even seemed to grow more solid the longer she stared.

"I'm not really sure—"

"You're dead!" she screamed. "I buried you— Are you… are you a ghost?" She placed a hand over her chest. "Have you come here to haunt me?"

He snapped his fingers. "You know, I was asking myself what was going on here. Now that you say that though… yeah—yeah, that does make a lot of sense."

"No, it doesn't," Lucinda hissed. She grabbed the sides of her head. "What is going on? I have to be dreaming or having some sort of hallucination. Perhaps if I called an ambulance—no. This is just like you, Harold. You can't just go popping up in someone's home as a bloody ghost. You'll scare them to death."

"Well, that'd be missing the point of the haunting… their being dead, I mean."

"Bloody hell, Harold." She collapsed into an armchair and sank with a slight *squick*.

"I'd sit too, but I'm not really sure… I am standing on the ground right now, but chairs—"

"Oh, will you sit," Lucinda said, entirely not in the mood.

He sat, but nothing sank or *squicked*.

"I would've thought I'd be gone longer…"

"I just buried you. I was supposed to come home and grieve in silence," she muttered, her gaze fixed on the china cabinets.

"Well, if it makes you feel any better, I really thought I'd be floating through space right now on the way to face some higher power." Harold chuckled. The stare she flung could've pinned him to the wall.

"So what happened?" she asked. "Why did they find you out there on the road? Where were you going so late at night?" This had been the lingering thought plaguing her through all the services.

Harold stared down at his folded hands. "Well, you see… funny story, actually."

"I can't wait to have a laugh."

"You remember I'd finally got that do-it-yourself mouth guard? The one where you boil it then press it to your teeth for a brief spell and it takes on the shape of your gob?"

"Yes. *Jesus*, Harold, what has that got to do with it?"

"Well, I think I did it wrong. I think I pressed too hard when I was forming it and it got too thin at the front, see."

"That made you leave?"

"No, no." Harold shook his head. "So then, when we went to sleep, it must've broke in half in the middle of the night from me grinding away and I swallowed it, or at least attempted to."

"You what?" Lucinda asked, eyes widening.

"Yeah, yeah. I woke up all choking and such."

"And you died? How did you end up on the road?"

"No, I didn't die yet. I couldn't breathe, so I realized I needed to get the pieces out of my throat."

"Did you try to wake me?"

"Well, no—"

"Harold!"

"You looked so peaceful sleeping and I know how hard you work. I didn't want to be bothersome, you know? I didn't want to be a burden—"

"A burden? You were choking to death!"

"Yes, but I didn't want to wake you. You looked like you were having a pleasant dream."

Lucinda clapped her hands to her face. Inside, she could feel the warning signs of irritation burning, but she counted to ten like she'd read in that one issue of *Living Stress Free*.

"So, you made the mouth guard incorrectly, it broke in half and got lodged in your throat. What did you decide then, Harold? Enlighten me."

"I had to drive myself to the hospital, didn't I?" he said, as if this were the logical next step. "But I realized it was rubbish night, and we hadn't remembered to put out the bins."

"Oh, that's tonight, isn't it?" She took out her mobile and tasked it to remind her later that afternoon. "Thanks."

"No problem. So, I couldn't leave without doing that. If I had to stay overnight at the hospital and you wouldn't be awake in time... I gathered the rubbish and went out to put it in the bin, only the bag broke as I was going through the back door."

"Is that why the ground was filthy?" Lucinda asked. "I thought the cat had gotten into things."

"Sorry about that. I tried to pick it all up."

"You got most of it, it's alright. Go on."

"Well, I scrambled to get it all in the bin by hand, but then carrying it to the front was a real bollock—"

"You carried it? Why didn't you drag it like we normally do?"

"It was late. I didn't want the neighbors to—"

"*Harold!* You were choking to death and you were worried about the neighbors hearing you take out the *bins?*"

"Lucy! Lucy!" Harold chanted her name softly, trying to calm his widowed wife. "What would they think if I'd woken them at that hour? Forgetting the chores and all that."

Lucinda's head fell into her hands again. "My God," she murmured, "I'm married to an idiot."

"*Were* married, love," he offered.

She rolled her eyes.

"So I went on my way—I was severely lightheaded at this point, mind you, lack of oxygen and whatnot. I noticed the car smelled rather disgusting." His nose wrinkled as if the odor were still present. "It didn't take long to realize that one of the salmon skins from dinner a few nights before had got stuck to my shoe."

"Oh, Harold," Lucinda sighed.

"Well, you know how I get with smells."

"Yes, quite. We've been married for thirteen years."

"I tried and I tried to ignore it, but I just couldn't stop thinking, you know? If I didn't get that off my shoe then it was going to forever smell like rotting fish. And the longer it was in my car, the more likely my car was going to smell like rotting fish and—"

"You didn't."

"I tried to get it off my foot."

"You're the thickest man alive."

"*Was* the thickest man alive, dear." He clapped his hands together with finality. "I don't remember much after that. I got the skin off, went flying into the air, next thing I know

I'm back home with you sending off the relatives after the what-to-do with my *corpus obsoletus*." He chuckled again. "Still got the mouth guard chunks in my throat though—look, you can see them protruding…"

"I'm going to take a nap," Lucinda said. She stood and straightened her skirt.

"A nap? Since when do you take naps, Lucy?"

"This has all given me a rather bad headache."

"And what am I to do now?"

She looked at him, still sitting on the sofa, floral prints showing through his lap as if faded in the sunlight. "I don't know, Harold. Find a way to keep yourself busy. What is it ghosts do? Learn how to turn off the lights or something. You never did it when you were alive."

"Right-oh then." Eagerness painted Harold's translucent features.

Lucinda sighed and rubbed her palm across her forehead, attempting to counteract the imminent migraine. This was going to be a long death.

ONE LUMINARY CLOCK AGAINST THE SKY

Ice swirls and glasses tinkle under mood lighting. Bar mirrors catch the reflection of the crystal chandeliers, magnifying the opulence twofold. Black tabletops with gossamer speckles line the boundaries of the indoor veranda. Chatter is kept politely low.

Dress it how you want, Audrey thinks, *it's still a bar.*

Yet she waits, listening to idle chatter. Snippets of conversations enter her ears, but never more than that. Never enough to know what the voices are saying. Mostly, she just makes sure the glass of Diet Coke on the counter is never empty. The bartender eyes her suspiciously at first, but soon stops wondering. Bass thumps carry muffled through the wall across the carpeted hallway, coming from the hotel's ballroom. Well-dressed wedding guests wander past the entrance to the bar.

Then one enters.

She is petite. Dark skin with a sleek, low bun at the base of her neck. She's wearing a violet taffeta dress. Black high heels. The woman stares around, black clutch at her stomach, surveying all the booths. A few of the patrons glance up at her, but most take no notice. After almost thirty seconds of scanning the tables, she steps up to the bar instead and sits beside Audrey.

"Manhattan," she says. Her voice is high, but smooth.

"Couldn't get one in there?" Audrey asks, tilting her head toward the thumping ballroom.

The woman smiles. "He doesn't make 'em right. Plus, I wanted a breather."

"They're having a fun time?"

"Oh, definitely," she says, and laughs. "Everybody sweatin'. Girls got their shoes off. I don't do that though. My mama told me how she got a foot infection once takin' her shoes off at a club. It's too grimy."

They both laugh at that. Under the bar, Audrey crosses her ankles. "What's your name?" she asks.

"Larissa." The woman reaches out a hand to shake. Audrey obliges.

"I'm Audrey."

"And what do you have in there? Rum and Coke?"

Audrey stares down at her tumbler of dark liquid. The ice swirls as she tilts the glass this way and that. "Just Coke." She smiles but quickly closes her mouth when she sees the woman falter. Larissa has probably seen her missing teeth.

The girl clears her throat as the bartender hands her a Manhattan. "Just Coke? Are you waiting on somebody to get started?"

They both take a sip before Audrey responds. "This is as *started* as I get, I'm afraid. But I am waiting on someone, matter of fact."

"Ooh!" Larissa clasps her hands together. She probably expects a date. "Who is it?"

"My daughter, actually."

Larissa scans the bar patrons again, but nobody new has entered. "Isn't that fun? Mother-daughter night. Hanging out, just the two of you. I do that with my mama sometimes when I go back home for a visit, but she doesn't like going to bars. She's all about Olive Garden, so that's mostly where we end up going."

Audrey can't help smiling again. "Nothing wrong with Olive Garden."

"I guess," Larissa says.

"That's great—that the two of you go out regularly, I mean."

The younger woman nods. "I was raised a mama's girl. Daddy gets his love too, but I've done everything with my mama ever since I can remember. She taught me how to play basketball, and cooking, dress shopping when I'd go to the dances. You know? She's done everything for me."

Audrey chuckles lightly, taking another sip instead of answering. She drops her eyes.

"So, are you on vacation together?" Larissa asks.

"What was that?"

"I asked if you were on vacation together?"

Audrey shakes her head. "No... no, I'm just visiting."

"That's good too. It means you get to stay in style. This place is beautiful."

"I'm not the one who chose."

"That's a good mom. Coming out here to—"

"Don't." Audrey slams her glass down a little too harshly. The clink quiets the bar for a moment. A few heads turn, then conversations resume when nothing dramatic ensues. The bartender, in the midst of taking a request from another customer, glances cautiously in their direction.

"I—I'm sorry," Larissa says. "I didn't mean to—"

Audrey lowers her voice. "Don't call me a good mother."

"I was just—"

"I am anything but." Audrey's voice quivers, and when she raises her glass to her lips again, the sleeve of her dress falls away from her arm, revealing a glimpse of deep red dots on the pale skin.

"I'm sorry," Larissa says. They sit there in silence, each nursing their own glass. The window behind the liquor display stretches to the furthest city lights. Then, when Audrey doesn't say anything for a few minutes, Larissa speaks up again. "Are you alright?"

The glass shakes in Audrey's grip. She's not swirling the drink, but struggling to hold it steady.

"I shouldn't be bothering you," she mumbles. Blonde strands fall across her eyes. They've escaped her ponytail.

"No, it's alright. It's alright," Larissa coos. She may have shrunk away without realizing, but now scoots her stool closer to reconcile her initial reaction. The gesture releases some of the tension in Audrey's shoulders.

"How do you think we atone for our greatest faults?" Audrey asks with a croaking voice. She purses and unpurses her lips several times. "I've been a terrible, terrible mother."

"Ma'am, Audrey, I'm sorry to hear you feel that way." Larissa lifts a hand, which spends an inordinate amount of time hovering in empty space before coming to land on Audrey's hunched spine. If the contact is unwanted, both women hide it well.

"I abandoned my baby for twenty-three years," Audrey continues. She doesn't cry, but there are heavy lines on her face like canyons carved by long-flowing rivers. "I should've been a mother like the one you got, but instead I left my child."

Larissa is silent now. She doesn't do anything but watch Audrey speak.

"I cast her aside for a man and an addiction—several, if I'm honest," Audrey says. "She should hate me. If she hates me then it's right, because she should. If she doesn't, then she ought to. I had only to be a good mother, but instead I spent my time high. Didn't even fight for her when the time came. I only woke up a year ago. It took losing everything else, but I woke up."

Audrey's hand goes to her mouth, but the glass is empty. Minutes pass in wordless conversation. Ice swirls, glasses twinkle. The lights above seem to shimmer like stars.

"That's good," Larissa says. Her voice is hoarse. "That's a start."

Audrey nods and lifts her head to look at her acquaintance. "I had to find her—my girl. I let her get taken away, but I knew I had to find her. That girl was going to keep me alive even if she didn't know it. And I had one hell of a time tracking her down. Courts don't like giving up a person's whereabouts even if she is your own daughter, especially when you were in trouble as deep as me."

Audrey stops speaking again. She asks the bartender for another Coke and he obliges. Larissa glances down at her Manhattan, barely touched. She puts her fingers on the glass, but doesn't raise it. Another full minute ticks by. The pounding rhythm from the wedding continues to waft through the doorway.

Then Audrey sighs.

"It took a year, but it was worth it," she says. "I found out that shortly after she was put in foster care, she was adopted.

She had a real family. She went to school. She was loved and cared for. She had siblings. She was… successful. That was more than I could have hoped."

"That's good, isn't it?" Larissa asks.

Audrey nods. "It is. It's so, so good. She didn't need me after all. I hadn't broken her."

Larissa doesn't say anything.

"How do we atone for our greatest faults?" Audrey asks again.

Larissa reaches out and places a hand on Audrey's. "You're here now," she says. "That has to count for something. She mustn't hate you if she's come to see you."

Audrey smiles through closed lips. She cranes her neck, staring through the doorway beyond Larissa. "She's not meeting me," she says. "She's not ready to meet me, and I'm not certain that I'm ready for her either. I only came to see her happy."

Larissa turns, following Audrey's gaze. Through the doorway she can just see her friend, adorned in her elegant white bridal gown, emerging from the ballroom. At her side is her new husband. The two are laughing, holding hands, oblivious to everything else around them. Larissa watches them until they round the next corner and disappear.

When she turns back to her drink, the other woman has gone.

CHICKEN OLYMPICS

Summer? Kinda boring. Friends? Total flakes, but that's alright. I do it too.

Waking up at four in the afternoon? Priceless. Pure. Fucking. Bliss.

I roll onto my side, opening my eyes and gazing out across my room. Sunlight is streaming through the blinds. I guess Mrs. Welder was wrong when she said I was "incapable of adapting to changes." I've rebelled against my diurnal instincts and managed to sleep soundly through broad daylight. How's that for evolving?

But I may as well get up now. I've proved my point. I push myself into an upright position, my tangled hair falling to my shoulders. My 'do must look ridiculous; hairspray'll do that overnight. I need to get a look.

I slip out of my covers and skip over to the mirror on my dresser. It doesn't take long to see what's going on. Rad! My shit is fucked! I should take a pic so I can prove to Ms. Le the laws of physics can be broken. I laugh, seriously contemplating the idea. But no, I cannot be seen like this by anyone in the general public.

My phone starts vibrating on my nightstand. Patting the craziest parts of my rat's nest down, I pick it up. Mom.

"Hello," I say.

"Hi, Kimberly. It's Mom."

I roll my eyes. She hasn't caught on yet that caller ID is a thing all humans use now.

"Yeah, what's up?"

A pause. I can hear road noise in the background.

"Just letting you know I've got your father from the airport. He's safe—"

"Hi, Kimbo!" my dad says. God, my parents can be so lame.

"Anyways, we should be there in about thirty minutes. Okay?"

"Okay," I say. Thanks for the updates on your whereabouts, guys—insert eyeroll.

"Your dad wants to barbecue the chicken tonight. How does that sound?"

Shit.

My stomach does a triple backflip inside me. Immediately I can feel myself begin to sweat. Jesus Christ, I was supposed to take the chicken out of the freezer this morning! I totally forgot. Shit. Shit. Shit. Shit. Shit.

I laugh nervously at the tail end of some joke Dad's told that I didn't catch any of. "Sounds good," I say. "See you soon."

I don't wait for a response. I hang up and bolt downstairs, my feet flying over the carpet. Dammit. I knew I should've set an alarm to take the chicken out. Mom is going to flip if it isn't defrosted. She cannot handle that sort of thing. Last time

I forgot, we nearly had to have her committed—she kept going on and on about how I can't handle simple responsibility and I'm going to die if I'm ever out on my own because defrosting poultry is essential to domestic life.

I jump the last few steps, landing catlike on my bare feet. I leap into the kitchen, snatch the bag from the freezer, and slam it on the counter top. It nearly breaks the tiles, the chicken is frozen so solid. If anyone ever broke into our house and I needed to defend myself, I could always just grab a decade-old bag of something from deepfreeze and the burglar wouldn't stand a chance.

But in this instance, a five-pound block of ice is not going to save my life. It's going to end it.

Hot water! I spin and flip the faucet on as high and as hot as it will go. I dump the bag in a bowl (it nearly breaks the glass) and shove it under the water.

I need to clean myself up. If the chicken isn't thawed, I'm in trouble. If the chicken isn't thawed *and* I'm a mess, I might as well dig my grave out in the backyard. I run to the bathroom, wet my comb, and start fighting with my spray-paralyzed locks. What was pretty rad a few minutes ago now feels like a death sentence. It fights me every step of the way, but a mixture of comb and brush gets it into a decent ponytail.

Back to the kitchen.

Water is now overflowing the bowl, pouring over the sides of the bag with coils of steam coming off. Good, it's hot. I tap my toes impatiently for a few seconds, then dart forward to pull the bag out.

Dammit. I don't think the hot water has made a dent in the ice block. What is this? Heat-resistant freeze? Is the meat so frozen that even high temperatures can't bring it back?

What am I going to do now? I look at the clock. It's been ten minutes since she called. My mother has the most accurate internal sense of time estimation known to humankind. Google Maps could hire her as the ETA proclaimer and they'd never receive another complaint. If she says they'll be here in thirty minutes, they'll be here in thirty minutes.

The microwave. Wasting no more time, I open the bag and slap the chicken on a plate. Into the microwave the pink, rigid breasts go. I slam the door shut and jam my finger against the DEFROST button.

"Come on," I mutter. Inside, the yellow light illuminates and the plate starts rotating at an excruciatingly slow pace. It's like the kitchen is trying to get me killed. If this is because I don't like doing dishes, I'm sorry, but that's why we invented the dishwasher.

The timer is set to five minutes. Back to the bathroom I go.

I don't bother showering. I know at this point I won't have time. Instead, I start rubbing off last night's makeup. My foundation comes off, my lipstick, then I grab the Vaseline to do my eyeliner. I'm pretty pro at this part, but because I'm rushing so fast, I do end up getting a glob in my right eye. I shove my face under the sink to rinse it.

The microwave starts beeping at me downstairs.

"Crap!" Trying to get ready in-between checking on that stupid chicken is like competing in the Olympics. And I'm sucking right now.

I sprint back downstairs and open the microwave.

The tiniest flutter of hope stirs in me. The permafrost has begun to give way. I can see actual fleshy meat showing through. I can poke it and feel it squish some. I may have a chance after all! I may not have to die today.

Eleven minutes on the clock. The chicken's going back in for another spin. Quickly, I rinse my hand in the sink. No salmonella, thank you. Now for my clothes. To my room!

My feet are pounding on the stairs. My heart is beating a rhythm David Guetta would be proud of. I can do this. My parents will never know that I slept until four and didn't even take the meat out of the freezer like I was supposed to. I'm going to be fine. I'm going to get away with this.

Some might say I have problems choosing an outfit. I will admit that I've fallen victim to an hour plus of wasted time staring into the void that is my closet and coming up empty-handed. Today, this is not the case. I plow into that mob of clothing—half of it hung on cheap plastic hangers, the rest of it piled on the floor—and emerge like the motherfucking swan princess. I even have time to step back in front of my mirror and commend my efforts. Not only do I not look like I just got out of bed thirty minutes ago, I look like I've accomplished things. I look like a productive member of society.

The microwave beeps again. The chicken has to be thawed this time, and with six minutes to spare.

I run back out of my room, heart still racing, mind just beginning to calm down. I get to the stairs, thinking maybe I'll have time to call Andrea and brag about what I got away with, when I feel it happen. My bare foot reaches out for the next step and clips the edge. Then there's nothing but air. I tip backward in slow motion, my body tilting as if I might be carried up through the roof and into the sky to the place where self-centered teenagers go. Teenagers who've failed their moms. All the wasted time. All the things I could have accomplished, or meant to have accomplished before my time was up. I'm leaving them all behind while I sail away. At least the chicken will be ready for my parents when they get home. That will be the legacy I leave.

Then I hit the ground and start rolling down the rest of the stairs.

Two. Three. Five. Seven.

I hear family photographs come crashing down as I knock them off the wall.

Then I stop, spread-eagled on the ground. I stare up at the ceiling wondering if this is what it's like to be dead. Every part of my body is sore. My back, my legs, my arms, my butt—everything hurts. The wind has been knocked from me and all I can manage is a pathetic moan. Realization slowly dawns, though, that I can't be dead. Not if I can feel. Not if I'm breathing.

I don't want to move. I don't want to risk angering my body. I'll be lucky if I don't have a black eye after that. My left eye socket comes to the forefront of painful anatomy. I must have hit it at some point. I don't remember.

Drip. Drip. Drip.

Slowly, so very slowly that I can't tell if I'm really moving or not, I turn over onto my side. The sound is coming from the kitchen and is gathering speed as if ramping up. I don't want to know, but I have to know.

Drip. Drip. Driiiiiiip.

I crawl over to the kitchen, though it's more of a drag than a crawl. As I round the corner, my worst fears are realized.

Water is seeping out of the bottom of the microwave. It runs over the edge of the counter and drips to the floor. Raw chicken water. Disgusting.

I roll my eyes. I don't want to deal with this. I shouldn't have to deal with this—I just fell down an entire floor's worth of stairs. I defrosted the damn chicken. This shouldn't be my job.

But I brace myself on the refrigerator door and pull myself up. Miraculously, neither of my ankles are broken. I can stand. I grab the roll of paper towels and start mopping up the water. Then I open the microwave to see how much is left inside.

"No!"

I actually scream it in a long, drawn-out note that wavers between hysterical and operatic. My hands may actually clench into fists and shake ruefully at the empty air about me—I can't be certain. I nearly collapse.

The rotating plate and the dish I used for the chicken are filled with water, yes, but this is not the worst part. The worst part is that the center of each chicken breast is still obviously frozen, while the rest has started to cook from being defrosted for too long. White and pink and gray all over.

I can't present this. I can't show this to my mother; she'll never accept this as passably thawed poultry. We can't eat this for dinner now. I'm finished. Over. Ended. There's nothing for me here.

Defeated, I sink into the kitchen chair and stare at the water that continues to drip out of the microwave.

As if on cue, the garage door opens.

I don't react. I don't move a single muscle. I just sit there and wait for my judgment to come.

My parents enter the living room. They're halfway through calling out a greeting to me when my mother gasps. She's obviously seen the fallen photos. I wonder if I've left a pool of blood behind. That would feel appropriate, and it might give cause for some mercy, but I don't think I'm bleeding.

"Kimberly?" she calls. She comes rushing into the kitchen, Dad one step behind her, and gasps again when she sees me.

They both take in the sight, confused. Paper towels everywhere. The microwave open with a pile of half-thawed meat inside. Water dripping out onto the floor. Me sitting slumped in one of the chairs. "What the hell happened here?"

She doesn't sound angry, just concerned.

I shrug. I don't even care anymore. "I forgot the chicken."

"What?" she asks. Her voice is hoarse.

"I forgot the chicken, alright? I'm sorry."

Mom and Dad are speechless, their mouths gaping. They keep looking from me to the microwave and back to me again. Dad still has his backpack on and his rolling suitcase at his side.

"Well—well, honey," my mom stutters. She shoos my father out of the way. "I left it in the refrigerator this morning to thaw. What—"

"In the refrigerator?"

She nods and opens the refrigerator door, pointing at a gallon Ziplock with three fleshy, pink, completely thawed chicken breasts inside. And you know what? I actually don't care about that either. Zero percent. I even start to laugh. Perhaps a little afraid, my father nervously joins me.

"Well, you usually forget," my mom explains, "so I didn't bother asking this time."

"I usually… I do usually forget, don't I?" I mutter. Then I stand. It's painful—in fact, all of me is still in pain—but I manage, and stumble over to one of the drawers. I pull out a fresh Ziplock bag, then amble over to the microwave and grab my darlings from the whirly plate, shoving them inside.

"Kimbo?" Dad says. "What are you doing?"

"I fell down the stairs," I say. "I'm gonna go ice myself."

"With chicken?" Mom asks.

"Yeah," I say, waddling past Dad and out the door. I don't even bother washing my hands first, even though I just touched the pseudo-raw meat. "Don't worry, they're still frozen."

OCTOBER

Night did fall. He locked the door.

She picked the sheets up off the floor.

Darkness filled the room, enough that she couldn't see. But there were not so many things in the room that she couldn't place them all by memory. In that corner was the table. Over there was the little dresser she could stand on. And in the shadows, by the lamp, was her stuffed bear, Mrs. Frederick. She gathered the comforter in a bundle and hugged it to her chest, feeling exhausted. The blanket was cool even if it was damp.

Back onto the mattress she crawled, and lay down in the dark.

A ribbon of silver light flicked through a gap in the curtains. She wanted to ignore it, finally halfway to rest, but a toothy grin found its way to her face without her doing. The light was dancing, and how could she ignore that? At once, she slid off the mattress to the floor and crawled like a cat to where the wisps of silver shone on the rug. It made the red stains look gold.

What beautiful light.

Giggling to herself, she followed the ray from the rug to the curtains, which she tugged open tentatively. A halo of light came crashing through the window and she had to squint until her eyes adjusted. The moon shone in. *I found you*, it said. And she giggled again, obliging its game. The silver light was cool on her skin and she spun, letting it bathe her in crystals. She put her hands on the sill and gripped tightly, gazing up at the big round moon with longing.

Then she gasped. She'd noticed the stars.

Down from the window fell the bars.

What funny little things those twinkling dots were. They stretched out their arms of light and joined hands across space. A net! They made a net! So she reached out her hands into the sky, slid her fingers into the holes of the net, and pulled herself up, up, up out of the dark room.

Here was a view to remember! The girl climbed into the sky, the moon lighting her way and the stars in her hands. Exhaustion slid from her skin, entangled in the window frame. She climbed until she couldn't tell the trees apart. She climbed until the room was just a dot underneath her. Then she stood on a cloud…

… and ate a piece.

She was right. They tasted like cotton candy, and she was so hungry. *I can't eat too much of it*, she thought, *or I will fall*.

She fashioned a skirt of starry thread.

And wove a shirt to pull over her head.

Now she had clothes! Clothes like she'd seen the little girls wear in the magazines in his bathroom.

What fun this was. She danced with the moon as her spotlight, the stars on her skin and the clouds whipping foggily around her. She could stay here forever. Here in the sky. Here where every thought was a story that could take her away to places she'd never seen or even imagined. Laughter escaped her again and again. The night wasn't so scary after all.

Then a thought occurred to her. Why not stay? Maybe she wouldn't go back. After all, she felt so exhausted in that room so often, and now she felt nothing but energy. Her skin was unbruised under the moon. Her head clear. Why not stay here forever? Who knew what would happen when the moon set and the sun rose? Maybe she could grab hold of the stars again, and when they fled from daybreak they could take her with them. She would love to see where they went after the sun rose.

Her dance coming to a close, she walked to the edge of the cloud and sat, dangling her feet over the ground. She was not afraid. Not now. Not ever again.

She looked down at the trees she could not tell apart, and the streets with their yellow lights that looked like stars but were nowhere near as enchanting. She looked at the tops of the houses like dollhouses she'd never owned, and she found the room. It was easy to spot. The only one with bars on the window. Somewhere in there was a table, a little dresser she could stand on, a lamp, and Mrs. Frederick too. Oh, and of course the calendar on the wall that always read October. She couldn't change it because she was much too short, but she'd never minded that bit. She liked the name October.

Swinging feet. The moon shone on.

The sun arose and she was gone.

BOXES

One was labeled *CDs*. Inside it was everything from Elton John to The Clash, The Isley Brothers to Three Dog Night, Duran Duran to Cher. Cher was undoubtedly the odd one out, but the hands had eclectic tastes and *CDs* held them all without question. The plastic cases stacked neatly inside, one against the next. Two rows side by side and a second level right on top. There were the perfect number, almost as though *CDs* knew how many compact discs the hands had and had sized itself appropriately.

The other was labeled *Misc*. *Misc* had a dozen felt-tipped markers, a tape dispenser, watercolors, a few paint brushes, tacky gum, masking tape, a pencil sharpener, thirty-six paper clips, Elmer's glue, five colored marbles, a pack of pipe cleaners, googly eyes (of course), and a framed four-by-six photo with lots of smiles. The contents slid and slumped against each other but *Misc* held them just as harmoniously as any of the albums in *CDs*.

They were packed on a Friday night, and on Saturday hands carried *CDs* and *Misc* one by one out to the truck where they sat together in the bed. The engine rumbled to life and they pulled out of the drive, sunlight beating on their paper lids. The air was crisp.

At the first stop sign, *Misc* bumped *CDs*, letting out a giggle of rattling marbles.

Not to be one-upped, *CDs* bumped *Misc* at the next turn. The compact discs inside clattered with delight.

This became a game, sliding around on the corrugated plastic bed, bumping each other back and forth to the beat of the road. When the truck stopped at the red light, *Misc* slid forward one final time, making just enough contact with *CDs* that an onlooker might say they were nuzzling. They stayed like this together for the rest of the journey, watching the boxy houses pass them by. Browns and tans and blues and pinks, the sun beaming down on each of them.

Then the truck stopped in front of a gray roll-up door in an aisle full of other gray roll-up doors. Behind the door was a room filled with shelves that held all sorts of things. Not just boxes. There were lamps and a couch, shoes, Christmas decorations, and a bulky box television with bug-like antennae on top.

The hands put *Misc* on a bottom shelf, but *CDs* was placed two shelves above. They were much too far apart to nuzzle and no amount of sliding would allow one to bump the other. The marbles did not rattle and the plastic cases did not clatter.

With a deafening crash, the metal door came down and the truck rumbled off. The only light came through the gap underneath the door, but not much was needed to see that *Misc* and *CDs* were two shelves too far from each other.

Hours turned to days in darkness. A felt-tipped marker shifted, the photo frame settled, but *CDs* could not reply, for its contents were too neatly stacked. Only the creak of the couch or a mourning howl of the wind answered. They could do nothing to help. Softly, the paper clips dripped to the bottom of *Misc* until there were none left to fall.

One morning, rumbling grew in the darkness. Was the truck returning? Were the hands coming back to take them off the shelves? Could it be? But the rumbling only grew louder and louder, and instead of the door rolling up with a blast of sunlight, the entire room began to shake. The television rattled on its table, the lamps articulated on their hinges, the door bounced up and down, knocking the cement ground.

Misc slid an inch, but *CDs* pitched forward, sliding over, over, over the edge of the shelf. The fall lasted less than a second, but contained minutes, hours, days. On the way down, *CDs* and *Misc* crossed paths and for the briefest of instants they were level.

Then came the crash.

CDs hit the concrete with a heavy finality. Out came Elton John, The Clash, The Isley Brothers, Three Dog Night, Duran Duran, and Cher. Plastic cases were strewn everywhere, thrown far enough to land beside the couch. Shattered compact discs clattered on the floor, their reflective undersides catching the light from underneath the door. And when everything came to a standstill once more, *CDs* lay spilled and spent before *Misc*.

Silence held the storage room captive. A paint brush in *Misc* settled, tapping out a questioning knock. Marbles rolled to one side in a call for affirmation. And finally, paper clips trickled until none were left to fall. There came no answer.

Another rumble. An aftershock. *Misc* slid forward enough

to tip off the bottom shelf, enough to lean down onto the concrete, enough for the boxes to make contact. Just enough to nuzzle.

When the hands found them the next day, *Misc* and *CDs* were still on the ground. The hands flew up in frustration, then came together in sadness, then sat on hips in thought. They reached out for the shattered discs and paper booklets thrown everywhere, but instead of gathering the pieces to discard, they poured them back inside *CDs*. Then they grabbed both *CDs* and *Misc* and loaded them in the back of the truck.

At the new house, the hands took the reflective shards and Elmer's glue. They took the colorful booklet inserts and paintbrushes with watercolors. On a large sheet of cardstock, the hands used the felt-tipped markers. They glued the shards. They patterned with patches of colored paper. They even used a few googly eyes and stuck the whole thing on the wall with tacky gum.

Then the hands put away the marbles and paper clips. The leftover pieces from the broken album cases—the few much too small to use—were swept into the bin. They put every last piece and particle away.

For the finishing touch, the hands took the frame and set it on top of the dresser. They positioned it just so, so that the photograph full of smiles gazed across at the collaboration on the opposite wall.

When the hands were finished, *Misc* and *CDs* were folded up neatly. They were taken out to the garage in the new house and slid together between two shelves. Touching enough to nuzzle.

THE QUIET THINGS STAY HIDDEN

Concrete pillars block my view of the sun, sentry towers where a pair of patrolling guards look down on my vehicle suspiciously. They've seen me come and go four times a week for the past three years without giving me the benefit of the doubt. I suppose that's what's going to save us in the end. Lax security would ease my apprehension, but preventing weakened defenses is more important than my weak constitution.

I can't tell if we make eye contact due to their dark lenses, but I nod as if we do anyway. I coast up to the gate, reaching into the glove compartment for my papers. Amrit is on duty.

"Morning, Kellen," she says as my window sinks. I hand her my bundle of tri-folded sheets.

"Morning, Amrit." We never say *good morning*. That wouldn't feel right.

"Joan says you're up for renewal soon." Amrit's eyes scale the length of each sheet, front and back, making sure everything is in order. Of course it is. The only time those sheets ever leave my glove compartment is when I'm handing them to her.

"We'll see," I say. "That may not be good news if something doesn't happen soon."

She nods at first, still scanning the last page. Then shrugs. "Isn't that true for everyone? They'll renew you. They're not going to stop caring even if they make it sound that way. He's too interesting."

I nod and take my papers back, stowing them in the compartment.

"Yeah, but maybe they'll find someone cheaper to do it. Someone without a degree." I hold out my left hand next as she pulls out a scanner from the booth. Routine, all of this.

"Maybe," she says. "I hope not. I'd hate to see you replaced by the usual hotheaded prick that hangs around this place."

"Me too." I smile and the scanner flashes green. My facial profile pops up on her screen; I can see it reflected on the glass behind her.

"You're all set," Amrit says, pressing a button to lower the barricade and open the gate.

I raise my window and wave at her as I drive through.

She's wrong, I think. The boy is interesting, but he's not *that* interesting. Not to them. Not enough to keep funneling money into our sessions while I try to teach him language so that maybe he'll talk to us. The fact of the matter is, at this point, I don't exactly know what he'd have to say that would help us. What I think they want—and maybe this is just my cynicism finally maturing—is his consent. Everyone knows about him. God, he's so beloved. People treat the kid like their own son, hanging up photos of him on their mantlepieces. Never mind that absolutely none of them have met him. Never mind that he does nothing but stare vacantly at the camera any time the demand gets high enough for the feds to sanction a new television segment on him. I think their hope was that me teaching him to speak verbally—to verbally give them consent to run tests on him—would sate any uproar over making him a lab specimen. That patience is wearing thin after three years. They're prepping to test other methods of securing that consent.

Once parked in the garage, I hustle over to Building C, a sun flare reflecting in my glasses. I use my thumb print and retina to gain access. Then I'm stalking through the pristinely kept hallways with my head low. I don't like talking to most of the people in here. They look at me as if I'm some sort of joke, which I suppose I am in some ways. Everyone's aware of my dismal track record and how it compares to nearly every other project on file. Whereas Amrit hopes I'll stick around, most of the others wouldn't bat an eyelid were I to vanish.

On the other side of the building is the smallest wing: 505. It contains only two segments: 505A and 505B. I enter A and am greeted by the low, deep hum of machinery. The lights in this room are kept to a dim blue, which I've never understood. Along the back wall is said mumbling machinery, which controls all the utilities in segment B—lights, temperature, water heater, etc. Along the right wall are a pair of raised bleachers. The entire left wall is an observation window—except for a glass door and square security panel—looking into 505B.

505B is where he lives.

505B is his apartment complete with a living space (the observable area), a private bathroom, and a private bedroom (although "bed-sized closet" would be a more appropriate name). Currently, he's not in view. The rectangular room

31

shows only his scattered toys, a small coffee table, and a pair of armchairs. I step up to the glass door and press the intercom button on the security panel.

"Jack, it's Kellen," I say, hearing my voice projected on the other side of the wall. "I'm coming in."

I hold my badge up to the scanner, causing a green light to flash. The door unlocks. I step into 505B. The beige carpet is clean and soft and prevents my shoes from making any noise as I cross the threshold. When the door falls shut behind me, the hum of the machinery is cut off and I am left with silence. As I walk over to the pair of armchairs, I look over to my right, staring through the glass at the empty observation room on the other side. There used to be a time when he would rarely use the living room because he didn't like being watched, afraid of the people—personally, I don't blame him. But he doesn't shy away from playing out here anymore, especially since the observation room is empty most of the time. Old action figures and building blocks collect in scattered piles. Once a week he's removed so the place can be cleaned, but he purposely leaves them out in organized piles. Why, I've never understood.

I sit down and wait.

A toilet flushes and I hear Jack washing his hands. Those two habits were the talk of the town when he first started doing them. I got smiles and pats on the shoulder back then. It validated me both as a scientist and as a father of some sort—at least in my mind—even if the boy isn't biologically mine. The bathroom door opens.

As far as we can tell, Jack is about ten now—prepubescent, small. He has hazel eyes and almond skin. After his first bath—an incredibly taxing affair—we were able to determine he had dark brown, wavy hair. For sixteen weeks, he wouldn't make eye contact with anyone, not even me. For thirty-one weeks, he wouldn't voluntarily let anyone touch him, not even me. But after fifteen months, he would come out to see me without needing to be coaxed. We lost a lot of chocolate bars before reaching that milestone.

Now, I think he likes me. During each my visits, he'll come out and play with his toys in this room. I talk to him and he looks at me. When he wants me to sing—which I do in a low voice because I don't think he knows what good singing sounds like—he touches a fist to his chest and then his throat. We go through math workbooks, which he completes with relative ease, and language workbooks, which he fills out sometimes. When I go to leave, every once in a while he gives me a hug.

I sometimes bring him books. He either sits at my feet and listens to me read or stares at the pages himself. I have the notion that he understands them. The only cause for uncertainty is *he never speaks*. When I ask Jack questions, he never responds. He will write words to answer his workbook problems, but never full sentences. I've tried to teach him sign language, but he refuses to use it.

That is the crux of my problem, and why I don't believe I will be renewed.

"How's it going, Jack?" I ask. He smiles in response. I don't wait for anything else. "How are you feeling today? Should we start with some play time? I see you've left your figures out from yesterday."

Without saying a word, Jack gets on the ground and grabs a pair of miniature robots. He makes them fly through the air on some mysterious errand. He doesn't even make sounds for them, although I don't know why he would considering he's probably never seen a robot in his life. Hell, I've barely seen a robot.

"You know, we're coming up on your third birthday— well, the third anniversary of you being found." I speak while he plays, our usual routine. Sometimes I join him. Sometimes I sit here and do other work while he's off in his own world. Most of the time he'll stare at me, waiting for me to talk before he starts playing. I don't know that he hears anything I say. He just likes the noise, I guess.

The robots land on a building of connectable blocks he keeps constructed.

"I think that's rather special, don't you? I'm going to see if I can find some of that cake you really liked, the dark chocolate one. We could both have a piece, because I have to admit, I liked it too."

When he reaches up, his shirt lifts to reveal a portion of his lower back. I glance at the scars and see that they're mostly gone, though the line is still visible if you know where to look. *If you hadn't had those marks, they wouldn't have cared nearly as much.*

"I found the last book in that fantasy series," I continue, going back to tracing the seam in the armrest with my thumb. "I forgot to take it with me this morning. I left my house and was in the tunnel before I realized I'd left it on the counter. I was so frustrated I almost turned around once I'd made it past the sector wall, but I didn't want to be late. It takes so long to get past tunnel security, I never would have made it in time. I'll bring it on my next visit, I promise."

He sits on the ground now, cross-legged, and stares at one of the robots in his hand. The other one lies forgotten on the ground. His fingers brush over the face and the boxy torso, then each of the foldable legs.

"I'll have to stem my curiosity though." I

laugh. "Otherwise, I might read it myself."

"Have you been outside?"

My heart nearly stops. My jaw drops open and my eyes dart to him, half disbelieving that the words came out of his mouth. Someone else must be in the room. But no, it's just us two.

"What? W-what did you say?" I ask.

He looks back and forth between me and the robot, and I wonder for a moment if I was hearing things. He couldn't possibly have... There's no way he...

"Have you been outside?" he says again. His voice is husky, unpracticed. "En-clo-sure," he says, as if repeating it after someone. He's probably heard me say that word a couple dozen times.

"Enclosure. Yes, enclosure," I say encouragingly. "Have I been outside the enclosure walls? No, Jack, I haven't. Why do you ask?"

"How find me?" he says.

I'm so excited, I nearly crap myself. My heart has gone from stopping to hammering so hard in my chest it hurts. I wonder if he can see my change in state. He must be attuned to these things. I should probably press the alert button on my badge clip, but I don't want to do anything that might dissuade him from continuing the conversation.

"Well, Jack," I stammer, "we have cameras all around the outside of each enclosure-town, to watch for infected, you know? The mean people. The ones with the red eyes who attack—"

"I know," he says.

"Yes, sorry." I clear my throat. "Of course you do— we saw you on one of the cameras, walking through the forest. We had never seen a child survive out there, usually they get eat—they can't compete with the larger infected. We could tell you weren't one of them because you didn't have the spasms. You moved so *normally*. People were sent out to rescue you."

"Not you?"

"Not me. I'm not trained to go beyond the enclosure."

"Trained?"

"I—I haven't been taught how to fight the infected."

This is incredible. Not only is he showing clear signs that he's understanding complex, multi-faceted ideas, he's inquiring more about them. He's holding a real conversation! I can barely believe what's happening. Someone else should be witnessing this, I know, but I also don't want to share this moment. This is a moment between the two of us.

"Fight them," he says. Then he sets the robot down next to the other one. For a while, he just sits there, staring at the two action figures.

"Jack," I say cautiously.

He looks over at me, those round hazel eyes connecting with mine in a way they haven't before. Now I *know* there is understanding behind that gaze.

"Yes, Kellen." He says my name and something inside of me stirs. I know right now that I will do whatever I can to protect this boy. I never want them to tear him away from me. I cannot glean a consent for experimentation from him. Not with good conscience.

"May I ask you a few things about your life before we found you?" Either I can now hear the machinery humming in the next room or my mind is buzzing.

He considers the request, never breaking eye contact. He sighs. I almost want to take back my question now.

"Yes," he says.

I nod. "Thank you." Where do I even begin? I don't want to overwhelm him, but my abundance of curiosities is held back by a dam that's beginning to fail. I want to know everything. I want to know all the details: where he slept, what he ate. *How you survived after being bitten.* "Were you alone?" is what I settle on. "We were trying to find your companions but found no one."

He looks at the floor by my feet. "I was alone."

"For how long?"

He shakes his head. "Don't know."

"Do you remember anyone? Parents, maybe?"

He shakes his head again. "I see faces sometimes. My head. Don't know who they are. Don't remember when gone."

"So who taught you how to find food? Who taught you how to avoid the infected? Where to sleep?"

He lifts a hand and holds it over his narrow chest. "No teach. I hid when heard them coming. I found eat. Sick sometimes, but I get better. Slept in trees. Infected not good at climbing trees. Be silent. No noise, no find."

I realize I'm sitting on the edge of my seat, my hands clasping the cushion beneath me. Jack is squinting, no doubt remembering what life was like before he was brought to Building C in Enclosure-Sector Kappa. He was so young—is still so young. But to have survived like that out on his own, with nobody to watch after him or teach him how to stay alive—that is truly remarkable indeed.

"Akamu."

My breath hitches. "What did you say?" I can't have heard him right.

"Akamu."

"Why would you… How do you know his name?"

"You started story, once," Jack says, unaware of how constricted my chest feels. I used to think that name in my head every single day. It would echo non-stop until I was so frustrated alone in my home at night that I would sob. "Interrupted. Tell me. Please. Finish."

I stare at the boy. Jack. I want to sink to my knees on the beige carpet, but I refrain. As it is, the static friction holding me in place is barely enough to keep me up. How can he remember me mentioning Akamu? I don't even remember mentioning Akamu. Had I babbled so much during our sessions when he would play? I would say anything to keep talking because I thought he didn't hear the words. What else have I told him?

"I can't," I say. "I'm sorry."

Jack looks at me and then at the floor. He feels betrayed, I can tell. He expected us both to share. He doesn't understand how painful my memories are. He is too young, perhaps, or has never developed that intimate a relationship with another human being.

"I'm sorry, Jack. I can't."

"Not trust anymore?"

"No! No, it's not that. I do trust you. I trust you more than anyone."

"But, no?"

My jaw clicks shut and my eyes close. "It just hurts too much to talk about."

"Fight hurts, bitten hurts. Not memory."

"Memories can hurt just as much as either of those, Jack. Just in a different way."

He contemplates what I've said for a moment, staring off into the space above my head. Then he lifts a hand to his heart and tilts his head inquisitively. I nod.

"Hurts here sometimes. Please?"

I sigh. I haven't spoken to anyone about this. Never. But if I say nothing now, if I betray his trust, how can I expect him to keep sharing with me?

"Akamu and I were very much in love." My throat is dry. "We were living together in Denver when word of the outbreaks first reached us. Watching the news reports was one of the most terrifying things I've ever seen. The chaos... the—the bloodshed was mortifying."

One instance in particular had been a live feed by a news crew who hadn't yet understood the dangers surrounding the infection. I remember seeing panic in the reporter's eyes when the infected individual leapt onto her, the scream as teeth punctured her shoulder. I remember standing frozen in fear in our living room while Akamu held me. His embrace had always felt so strong.

"We bought weapons—guns in case the outbreaks reached Denver, which we knew they would. Every day was filled with terrible reports of the bedlam engulfing the world. The virus was everywhere. Nobody knew how to stop it or how to cure it. We'd seen horror movies about this sort of thing, but they'd never seemed real. This *was*. Nobody knew how to react.

"Akamu's parents had a cabin out in the woods in the Rocky Mountains. Very isolated. Perfect for hiding. We decided to go out there and maybe we would have a better chance. Cities were falling every day."

I can still see the sun flare created by the windshield, the evergreens passing overhead. The radio came in heavy with static, but we didn't dare turn it off, afraid of missing some key development—which eventually came.

"Reports emerged of safe zones, the first iteration

of enclosure-sectors. They urged everyone to get to a safe zone if we could. There was no other way. The likelihood of surviving outside a safe zone was next to nothing. Nobody lived.

"But we knew we'd never make it. If you didn't live right next to one, or weren't picked up in a military extraction, the trek was impossible. The infected overran cars. They burst into homes. They were unstoppable. Akamu and I... we decided we didn't want either of us to become one of them. It would be better to die first than risk becoming one of those *things* who could potentially lead to more spread and more disease. We decided to kill ourselves."

I wipe away the tears that have collected on my chin. My lips taste of salt.

"Akamu decided the best way would be to shoot each other. It would be quick, simultaneous. We would be together." I can barely get the words out, but I *have* to. My eyes flick to the window, the observation room, but nobody is watching. Nobody has come to check on us. Why would they? "We kissed. I held my gun to his head and he to mine. We counted down together.

"And then shot."

Jack is crying with me now. Perhaps he does understand emotional pain, perhaps he is already capable of empathy. I cannot fathom a guess at the moment. I'm too busy looking down at a crumpled body with a pool of blood collecting around the head.

"His gun jammed. Mine did not. I lived. He did not." Akamu. I miss Akamu. My head and my heart ache for him.

"Not your fault," Jack says.

"That his gun jammed was not my fault," I say, "but I am

still the one who shot him. And to make matters worse, I fled. I made it to an enclosure-sector alive."

"If you died," Jack says, "how taught me?"

He stands, crosses the room to where I sit, and wraps his arms around my shoulders. I hold him too. He cannot know how much any of this means to me, but then again, how can I continue assuming things he doesn't understand? He has already demonstrated an emotional intelligence I would've never attributed to him. Perhaps I'm the one who doesn't understand. I let my head rest against his. He's so small. I would expect him to be fragile.

I don't want to go. I don't want them to decide my meetings with Jack are over. Neither do I want to reveal this recent development to them, though. If they know he has begun to speak, that he has shown cognitive capabilities we thought were ages away, they will not hesitate to have me press him harder. Or worse, to have others press him harder. But how soon will they remove me if I hide his speech from them? If I pretend no progress has been made?

I don't let go of Jack for a long time, and neither does he let go of me. When our embrace finally does end, we exchange a silent agreement to proceed with our session the way we normally would. He sits on the floor at the coffee table and I produce the workbooks from a cabinet in the observation room. He answers all the math problems without issue, but approaches the language questions with vague, singular responses. Perhaps this is another area in which he understands more than I gave him credit for.

Meanwhile, my stomach has clenched and will not unclench as my mind lingers in a dark place. I hate the thought of them invading Jack. I hate the thought of him spending years, maybe the rest of his life, as a lab rat while they poke and pry or possibly mutilate him permanently. But what of his immunity? The bites on his back were confirmed to be from infected, yet he has never shown symptoms. That immunity cannot be ignored and maybe holds the key to our survival. Do I have a duty to humankind to report that he now shows the ability to consent? Millions might be saved, but will the cost be this boy? Jack, my son? And is a cure possible, or a stab in the dark? I lower my head in my hands while he works silently. My boy. My son. And the rest of humanity. I know what duty means. I know the agony of loss, too.

The session finishes and he gives me another long hug filled with all the things he's yet to say aloud, or may never say aloud. I'm not yet sure.

UMBRELLA

When dawn broke, so did the clouds. Rain washed away sidewalk chalk and dirt. It cleared the pollen from the hoods of the cars and the windows on the buildings. Upturned flowers collected water droplets in their petal cups. Cats shook the rain from their fur and took cover under bushes and vehicles.

As he left the house, he drew the collar of his coat tighter around his neck and opened the yellow umbrella. The weather changed from a feeling to a sound, drumming a soft beat on the nylon skin. He walked away through the apartment complex to the bus stop, listening to the tap, tap, tap just above him.

Someone was already there, standing under the poor excuse for an awning. What use was a trellis when it came to rain? The person was unprepared, wearing blue jeans and a black jacket with no hood. They hovered by the pole on the left side of the bus stop, blinking each time the water drip, drip, dripped onto their head. Their hair was black, eyes brown, and freckles dotted their face like paint splatters.

He with the yellow umbrella and the other someone
nodded to each other, and then he went and stood by the
other side of the awning, listening to the rain tapping and
wondering when the bus would arrive. It could be late or on
time; there was never a pattern. If he leaned forward to
peek—sometimes standing on tiptoes helped—he could peer
down the street and watch for it to approach.

Rain made the tall grasses wave in the field across the
road. It made the cement sidewalk darker. It turned the
gutters into water highways and made the stoplights that
much brighter. Cars drove past, their headlights reflecting off
the shining pavement. Windshield wipers bounced back and
forth, back and forth. Puddles collected in the potholes.

"I think we're early," the someone said.

"Yeah?" he with the yellow umbrella replied, coming
down off his toes.

"I forget the schedule's different on Sundays."

He'd forgotten too, and wished now that he'd taken a
closer look at the red-and-gray pamphlet he kept by his keys.
The umbrella kept him dry but the air was cold and his nose
was threatening to run. His ears were going numb. "Have you
got Sunday's schedule?"

"I haven't." They smiled.

He smiled.

"This is a pretty useless bus stop," he said, gesturing at the
awning above them with his free hand. "No benches, no
roof, and no schedule or map."

The other someone nodded. Water was now running from
their hair over their face, joining the freckles like connect-the-
dots. They had their jacket zipped all the way up under their
chin, so the droplets fell over their collar instead of down
their shirt. He realized they had a small backpack under the

jacket. Maybe that was why they hadn't pulled the jacket up to cover their head.

"There's a bigger stop four streets down with three walls and a great big map if you wanted," the other someone said, nodding to a place further down the street. "But you'd have to get there before the bus came."

He stood with the yellow umbrella, considering this option, but thought better of it. Knowing his luck, the bus would pass by when he was halfway to the other stop and he'd have to wait for the next one alone. "I'll take my chances."

"It might take a while," the other someone said.

"And it might not," he replied.

They laughed politely, hands stuffed in their jacket pockets. They must be cold. Enough water had collect in their hair to plaster the strands to the top of their head. "It might not," they agreed.

Still, the bus hadn't come. The petrichor filled the nostrils, calming and sweet and fresh. Above, the rainclouds blanketed the sky as one converged gray being sliding across the atmosphere. Rain continued tap, tap, tapping over the umbrella, telling him things that he should know. The other someone didn't speak, and neither did he, but he wondered if he shouldn't say something. If he shouldn't ask them if they minded the drops dripping down on them. If they were cold and if they wished they'd brought an umbrella like his. And maybe ask them why they hadn't? But he decided that he didn't have the right words to say and wouldn't trust them to come out properly even if he did. He decided the other someone must be cold because he could see their chin quivering while they shoved their hands deeper into the jacket pockets as though searching for some warmth hiding there.

He decided the storm was lovely, but perhaps best enjoyed under some shelter. And he decided also that the yellow umbrella might be big enough for two.

A PLACE OF PEACE

My name is Yearning.

***

When I was born, the lights were off and the curtains were closed because my family didn't want anybody to know that my mother was giving birth. My father was too proud to have anyone know that I was to be born in a living room, because we didn't have any medical coverage for my mother to give birth in a hospital. I think it was pointless for them to try to hide it, because every time I've ever seen a woman give birth she's always screaming, and our walls were much too thin to hide it.

They laid out layers of blankets on the floor and that was where I was born: straight into my grandmother's arms. She was the first to hold me, the first person I saw. And she said that it was so strange because I never cried.

***

My first memory is of our house being robbed.

When I was four, we did a play in preschool for Christmas where we dressed up and danced around the biggest tree I'd ever seen. Somehow it fit on the small stage where we performed, but I was a teddy bear and that's what mattered to me. There was a surprise visit from Santa Claus. He was a big man dressed in a red coat who appeared out of the sky. He told us all to behave and that he was watching to make sure we were all being good people.

The man who broke into our house stole the necklace my father had given my mother on their wedding day. The man who broke into our house took my father's watch and even my Mickey Mouse piggy bank. I cried when I saw the shattered front window. I cried when I asked my grandmother why the robber would steal. Why didn't he care when Santa was watching?

She replied that "Sometimes coal isn't enough of a punishment to make people good."

***

My father was the best baseball player I knew. We used to go out into the backyard, in the grass that ran the length of the house, and play catch. When he bought me my first glove, it was much too big for my hand, but my father said that was okay because I'd grow into it.

Even oversized, I loved it because it was mine. I liked to imagine I had some of his skill. I was a pitcher standing on the mound in the center of everyone else, and with all eyes on me I'd throw the ball as hard as I could toward the catcher's glove.

But it *was* too big for me, and once I didn't catch the ball and it hit me in the eye. I cried and my father took me back into the house and we put ice over it. The ice stung. It was so cold.

When my father asked the next time if I wanted to go into the backyard to play catch, I told him no. I didn't want to.

"Why don't you want to play catch?" he asked.

"Because I can't," I said. "I'll miss the ball."

"Don't you like playing catch?"

"Yes."

My father told me that sometimes everyone misses the ball, even him, and that it's no reason to stop playing. Nobody could ever tell me that I couldn't do something I wanted to do, not even myself.

I grabbed my glove.

***

I used to take a nap every day after lunch. My parents were both at work and so my grandmother would sit by my side and tell me a story before I went to bed, or sing me a song to lull me to sleep. I would lie with the covers beneath my chin and listen to her soothing voice. Soft, serene. I was lying in a boat, rocking gently on the ripples of a silver lake, her voice drifting across the wind and blowing gently across my face.

One day she told me that I made her so jealous.

"Why are you jealous, Grandma?" I asked.

"Because whenever you sleep, you are always smiling," she said. She told me that when you smiled in your sleep it meant you had found the place of angels. You were at the most peace. She wished she could find that place.

I asked her how she knew she did not smile when she slept.

She replied, "I would know if I was at peace."

***

One day, when I was five, my mother took me to an old park next to a lake by her work. We played on the jungle gym for a while, then threw torn pieces of bread out into the placid water and watched the floating birds dip their necks to eat them. When the birds came onto the land, I would chase after them with my arms out, trying to grasp one. My mother asked me what I was doing and I told her I wanted to catch one so that I could fly.

She told me that all I had to do was spread my arms out like wings and I could. I threw my palms apart as far as they could go and gave a great leap. I was flying! The ground fell beneath my toes and I was in the air with the wind on my face. I flew around in a circle and then back toward the water. I came to the shore's edge and looked down into the glassy surface at myself as I flew. But when I saw my reflection I realized that my mother was carrying me. I hadn't flown after all.

***

After kindergarten, my grandmother would pick me up and we'd stop by the cemetery on our way home. The cemetery was where my grandfather lived, buried in the ground where the wind couldn't kiss his face any longer. I didn't remember him, but my grandmother would stand there for a while every day, staring into his picture with tears in her eyes. Sometimes the tears would fall and sometimes she would just close her eyes, say a prayer, and then we would leave. I wanted to know where he had gone, but she would only tell me that he had found peace.

***

When I was six, my father started working late. I would see him early in the morning before I left for school, but often he would not be back by the time I went to bed. Now that I was in school, my mother would tell me, he had to work a little bit harder.

On the nights when he wasn't home in time, I would put my glove up on the shelf in his room, hoping that when he came home he would see it there before he went to bed. Maybe it would make him want to play catch again. My hand was big enough to fit into it now.

When he did come home before I slept, I would ask him if he wanted me to get his glove. He always replied in the same way.

"Not tonight, sport. Your dad's a little too tired."

He was always too tired.

***

One night, our house was broken into again. This time, they stole our television and my grandmother's wedding ring. She cried and cried all night, but all the policeman said was, "We'll do our best to find whoever did this."

My father swore a lot that night. He promised my mother that he would get us out of "here." Whatever "here" was.

***

The next year, my grandmother started coughing.

It sounded normal at first, but then it got harsher and drier and pretty soon she could barely finish a story before she'd develop into a fit. Her stories grew shorter, told only at night before I went to bed since I was too old to take naps anymore. She no longer sang me songs.

"Grandma," I asked one night, "when are you going to get better?"

"I don't know," she replied, her finger tracing a seam in my blanket. "Your grandma's getting old."

"Well, don't they have medicine for you to take?"

"I don't think they have medicine for this," she whispered.

"Then when I grow up, I will become a doctor. And I'll take care of you."

She began to laugh, but it quickly turned into coughing, one hand to her mouth and one to her heart.

That night, I dreamt I was flying.

***

One day, my mother picked me up from school. We went straight home while she asked me everything about my day. What I'd learned, what we'd done. I showed her a picture I'd drawn of a bird flying high in the wind over a green lake. My mother told me it looked like a bird she'd seen before. I gave her the drawing and she hung it on the refrigerator.

I told her that I wanted to go back to the lake and the park. The one we'd gone to years ago. She told me that it had been closed. The play structure was too old and so they'd taken it down.

***

At night, I used to awaken to hear my grandmother coughing. She was always coughing, and it never seemed to stop. Sometimes, I was surprised that I would drift off again, since the sounds she was making were so sharp.

***

When I was eight, my father came home before dinner.

My family was so happy that we went out to eat at a restaurant, where we sat down and they took our orders. I asked what was happening, and my mother told me that my father had gotten a promotion. We stayed at the restaurant until my grandmother started coughing again and we had to go home.

***

Later that month, we were moving into a new house that was bigger and had a backyard that stretched around both sides. My father and I would play catch almost every day after he came home from work. And nobody ever broke into our home again.

***

When my grandmother died, I was at school.

My mother came to the door during class. She took me home, but this time we rode in silence. When we got to our house I saw that only she and my father were there. My grandmother wasn't with us, and she wasn't asleep in her bed.

My father said my name and then he told me what had happened.

Tears fell down my face for the remainder of the day. I had failed her. I had promised my grandmother that I would take care of her, but I hadn't been quick enough. I don't think I stopped until I had cried myself to sleep.

***

On the last day I saw her, we stepped up to the doors of the funeral home with the wind against our backs and the cold on our lips. Inside, a small fountain trickled. We crossed the room between endless rows of pews. There weren't that many people there to see her go, but I didn't want there to be. I didn't want anybody there; I didn't want them near me. I didn't want to look at them. I didn't want to look at her.

They murmured with my parents, acting as though they didn't see me.

It was so strange. They said, "Her death was strange."

When my parents went up to the coffin, I stayed behind in the pew, staring at my feet. Then staring at my hands. I closed my eyes and sat there in the darkness.

I don't know how long I was there, but when I felt my father's hand touch mine, I knew they were ready to go.

I wasn't.

We left the way we had come, my tears welling up but refusing to fall. *I will become a doctor. And I will take care of you.* My words rested in my chest. I wanted to say goodbye to my grandmother—I wanted to run back to the coffin and hold her hands in mine, to hug her like I used to every night before I went to bed. My head wouldn't let me.

When my father pushed the door open, the air rushed into the room with an icy ferocity. The tears were lifted from my face and carried on the wind. I turned my head to look at her. My last chance to say goodbye.

And I saw that she was smiling.

ANNIE GOING HOME

The sun has vanished behind the horizon of skyscrapers by the time I hit the city limits. One minute I'm in the orange glow of dusk, long shadows and hazy light, and the next I'm plunged into darkness. Colors mute. I switch on the headlights, which fan out across the dusty dunes on either side of the road.

"Sweet Annie" by ZBB comes on my mixed CD and I raise the volume. I like to pretend they're playing for me, like the titular name is intentionally mine. Zac's voice fills each of the seats in my Outback.

Five miles out, I turn onto an unmarked dirt road. I haven't seen this one before. I wonder where it goes. I'm about to find out, anyhow. Did I leave the window in the bathroom open? I hope I did. I left a pile of cat chow out for Gina, but she's going to need to get out sooner or later— when she realizes I'm not coming back, at least. I did leave it open. I can see the gap between frames in my mind. The dry plastic tub beneath. Yes, I did. She might have already left.

The Outback jumps. I shouldn't be going this fast on dirt. My rear lifts off the seat for a moment before I bounce back down on the cushions. This is kind of fun. Why haven't I tried this before? All-wheel drive. Isn't that what this thing was made for?

That's when I see it.

At first, it doesn't look like more than another boulder peeking out of the ground. But my car swerves a bit coming down off another bump and the headlights flash over the surface of the protruding object.

And the surface reflects.

Rocks don't reflect much unless they're wet, and it doesn't rain much out here so I'm sure that's not the case. It must be something else. I slam my foot on the brake and skid to a stop on the side of the road. The road must've climbed more than I'd thought because I can see the city like a patch of grass off in the distance. Funny, it looks so small from over here. The only thing that makes it any special are the lights the buildings emit.

I get out. The air is still hot and dry even though the sun's fully down now. Dust kicked up by my sliding tires drifts past me in a cloud. I cross over the road and walk back a ways over a small hill. Cresting, I see the protrusion is still there, sticking out of the packed dirt and sand. It looks like it's a solid gray, but that might be the night. I amble over, meandering around tumbleweed and rock—real rock.

This thing has got to be made of metal. At first, I'm wary, but I haven't got much to lose. I run my hand over the side. No doubt about it, the object is metal of some kind. Warm from sitting in the sun all day, possibly longer. Maybe it's been out here for several days, or weeks even. I can't tell in the dark. The thing is at least five or six feet wide—oblong, like a really stretched oval—without a sharp edge to be found. The sides converge and round at the top. This thing could be part of a massive statue, hidden by the geology.

I know better though. I know what this is. It's an alien spacecraft. A genuine, undeniable, indisputable U—F—O. Well, a crashed one anyhow.

I gasp, the hand I was touching it with covering my mouth. Instinctually, I step back even though nothing has threatened me. When did this get here? How has nobody seen it and reported it? It should have been all over the news. Michelle Greenwald on Fox 10 would have been all over this. My conscience buzzes. I have an obligation, don't I? I can't follow through with my plan tonight because then this thing will go undiscovered for another who knows how long. Weeks could go by before another human being comes this way—and I specify human being because whatever flew this could be back at any moment.

I freeze, then sit down on a boulder behind me. Realization hits. The pilot could be back at any moment. Do I call now? I know what happens next. I've seen them all: *War of the Worlds*, *Independence Day*, *Invasion of the Body Snatchers*, *Signs*, and so on. Widespread chaos. I know what's coming.

But maybe I don't.

My pulse is racing. *Annie, you'd better calm down before you have a heart attack.*

I have to remember that movies aren't real and I can't let them dictate my response. Think about it. In all those movies, what's the government do when they find out about the aliens? They *always* attack. They come in with tanks or helicopters. Sometimes bombs get involved. Then again, that's usually because massive spaceships are coming down from the sky. This is one little spacecraft. One little ship that could probably only carry one guy at a time. What if he's not like Hollywood makes aliens out to be? What if he doesn't have violent plans? If I get the government involved, the first thing they're going to do is catch him and destroy his ship.

I want to know if he's friendly. I want to know if I can talk to him, or communicate in some form. See what his planet is like and how far away it is from Earth. Why is he here? What does he hope to find?

So I stay sitting on the boulder. The moon is getting pretty high in the sky now; I can see its distorted reflection on the side of the UFO. If the visitor landed today, they might be on their way back. I could be the first to make contact. I could be the one who greets them. Wouldn't that be something special?

I wait. And I wait. And I wait.

A few times I catch myself nodding off, my head slipping from my hands. I jerk awake each time my chin hits my chest, immediately glancing up, startled. But the ship is still there, unmoved. Waiting for its captain to return. I haven't missed anything.

I wait until the sky starts to lighten again. Overhead gets all pink and orange and the city lights start to flicker off. Nobody comes that night, but that doesn't mean they won't be back today.

When the sun shows itself, I decide I can't sit here forever. My stomach starts making harsh noises; I feel like an animal is clawing against my insides. *Remember me? You need to feed me.* Plus, I should probably go to work. My boss will call and I don't have much of an excuse. Hopefully, Gina is still home. If I leave now, I can close that bathroom window before she figures she can get out. I can shower, go to work, and get back here right away. Hopefully my visitor won't have returned yet. Something tells me he moves around at night.

Something tells me it'll be safe to leave now.

I get up and stumble back to my car.

***

The day stretches on forever. Work is how I imagined it would be. I drag myself to my desk and do all the things I'm supposed to do. Writing reports and answering emails about reports I've finished. Mind-bogglingly boring is the only way I can describe it. Every time I look at the clock I'm surprised by how little time has passed. All I can think about is the UFO I'm hiding and whether I'm right about the alien's nocturnal habits. The worst thing would be driving out there after work to find the place empty. The very idea makes my heart race.

"You look distracted," a chiding voice says. I look around. Lupe is leaning against the wall of my cubicle, a smirk on her full lips. I notice she got a haircut over the weekend—with highlights. The change is nice on her. I don't say anything about that though.

"Didn't sleep a lot last night," I say. I turn back to my computer screen.

"Was it your cat?" she asks. "What's the name? Tina?"

"*Gina*," I say. "After Gina Torres? You know, from *Alias* and *Firefly*—never mind." She never gets my references. I'm too much of a geek and she's probably never watched much besides *America's Next Top Model*.

"Oh, right. Did Gina keep you up?"

"No. I just couldn't sleep."

"Sorry to hear that."

"Yeah, me too." I have a lot of emails to get through and they pop up faster than I can respond to them. Apparently, a typo in my last report is leading to confusion. Of course. This kind of thing is constant. I grunt and type faster. When I glance back, Lupe is gone. I'm glad she didn't stay to ask more questions.

As soon as the clock hits five, I bolt from my desk and hop in my car. I have enough mind to pass by the Wendy's drive-thru on my way out of town and inhale a double cheeseburger and chocolate frosty while I wait in traffic. I know I've said that I should stop going to Wendy's, but I don't really have time to go home and make anything. The sun will be going down soon and I wouldn't make it in time.

The Outback shouts in protest as I fly along the desert road, bouncing over the unpaved trail. Gravel beats the underside of the vehicle, but the car can take it. All I focus on is the sight of the spacecraft sticking out of the ground. I know it has to still be there. It *has* to be. I don't know why I know this, but I can feel it inside me. The visitor wouldn't leave during the day.

At last, I crest the steep bump and on the other side I see the metal artifact sticking out of the sand. It's a bit earlier in the evening this time than when I arrived last night, so I can see a few more of the details, like the fact that this was definitely recent because the dirt cratered by the impact is still loose in some places. The material is a dull metal, like steel, painted a storm-cloud gray—although this could very well just be the color of the material, not paint. I can't tell.

I can see the seams separating the panels, with trails of rivets lining the edges. This is most definitely a spaceship. I can no longer doubt it, not in the light of day. My heart surges with excitement. No alien would willingly leave their ship in the open like this—he's got to be coming back.

I park the Outback and hustle over to my rock again, plopping down to watch the sun set over the city. From way out here, the city doesn't seem so bad. You can't see the miles of traffic, or hear the hum of thousands of horns, car alarms, and sirens. From out here, the city looks like a picture: peaceful. It doesn't seem so isolating. I sit beside my spaceship, staring at the desert valley. Every few minutes, I glance over just to make sure. It sits there unchanged.

I wait all night again. This time I let myself nod off, but wake up pretty often. Nobody comes along. Silence until the sun rises again and I have to get in my car and go back home.

On the drive back, the thought occurs to me that maybe my alien friend *has* been to visit his vehicle. Probably to make sure I'm not doing anything to it. I'd do the same thing if I were on a foreign planet and saw some native creature coming to visit my craft. I'd wait off to the side, making sure they were peaceful and trustworthy before I revealed myself. After all, if his goal is to make contact with humans, he has to make sure we're not dangerous. Come to think of it, I may have felt like I was being watched last night. I was trying to play it off like I wasn't paranoid, but I definitely might have felt eyes on me some of those times I woke up.

My apartment is quiet. Gina makes an appearance to purr and rub herself against my leg, so I give her some wet food. My ears are ringing from complete silence, so I talk to her a bit, just to use my voice. I shower and decide to check the mail, but all I've got are a few ads and a bill. Then I look around my silent apartment before shutting the door and going to work.

The office is the same as it was yesterday. I spend my day answering emails and reading people's notes so I can write up reports. My mind rarely strays from my UFO waiting for me out in the desert. I wonder how many nights I'll have to go before my alien friend decides I'm trustworthy enough to approach. Maybe if I bring him food or something, like an offering? That sort of thing usually helps. If I saw someone leaving things beside my spaceship, I'd definitely take it as a positive sign. Now, I'm almost certain I felt like I was being watched last night.

"Any more sleep problems last night?" Lupe again. Why does she feel obligated to come talk to me every day? I know she likes to know everyone in the office, but if she wants to skip me, I won't take offense. I'm used to that kind of thing. It's more awkward that she forces conversation like this.

"No, I feel a lot better today," I say, trying a smile.

"That's good to hear."

I nod and go back to my work, but this time she doesn't go away.

"Listen, I was wondering." She folds her manicured hands, all except for her index fingers, which she leaves extended, tapping together. "Do you want to get a drink after work?"

I have to admit, I'm a little surprised by the request, but I don't have time to contemplate her motives. I recover after only a few seconds and shake my head. The UFO is clear in my mind. "I can't. I've got plans."

"Oh." She almost looks surprised that I refused. Maybe she didn't expect me—lowly Annie Espinosa—to have a life outside work. "How about tomorrow then?"

"Sorry, Lupe," I say. "I'm pretty busy right now."

I do feel a little bad, because she looks crestfallen when I say this, but then I imagine a short little green man coming around the moonlit protrusion and I know I've made the right decision. Besides, she's probably not really disappointed; she's probably going on a date with some meathead who's got an ugly friend she needs to keep busy. I've more important things to do.

When the clock hits five, I run out to Wendy's to get my usual, then dip into a grocery store for a loaf of French bread from the bakery and a couple of the reddest apples I can find. I book it out to the spot again, managing to scrape the bottom of the Outback on a rock as I come off a particularly bad moment of airtime. The scrape sounds expensive, but nothing about the car's driving changes afterward, so I've probably just left a scar.

I breathe a sigh of relief. The spaceship is still there. I set the bag at the foot of the protrusion then get to work on my own meal, staring out at the city while I eat and the sun sets.

Nothing again. No visitor emerges as the moon rises and falls. I don't feel discouraged though; this sort of thing takes time. I was foolish to think Mr. Alien would join me for dinner. He needs privacy to examine what I've brought him. Was French bread the right thing? I tried to bring some tasty but pretty mild selections. Who knows what kind of taste buds he's got.

Wake up. Go visit Gina, shower, head to work. Mind-numbing computer screen. Lupe makes small talk. Wendy's. Then drive back out to my post.

The grocery bag and all the food are gone. This is a good sign. I can't find any indication that they were blown away by the wind, and I can't find any animal tracks. Does that mean my alien friend can levitate? This is a ridiculous possibility, but I can't rule it out. Imagine if he could. Imagine if he emerged on some kind of hovering chair or something. That would be incredible. He might let me have a spin once we got to trust each other. Of course, he might just be really light and that's why there aren't any footprints, but I'd prefer the first possibility.

No luck with any visits in the night though.

Wake up. Gina. Shower. Work. Lupe. Wendy's. Out to my UFO. Repeat.

First, it's four nights. Then it's six. Then eight. Then twelve. I can't give up though, because I know that if my alien is shy, he just needs another night to get comfortable with me being around. He wouldn't leave his ship here forever, because eventually he's going to have to go back home. Right? If his planet is far away, he'll probably need the ship to make contact. If he's got supplies, he's most likely not carrying them all around with him. No matter what, he's going to need to come back eventually. Yes, the excitement does wane some, but every time I come over that crest and the wing—I've decided it's probably the wing—comes back into sight, I feel my heart leap and I know tonight is the night. Patience is going to be what saves me. Us meeting was meant to be. If I *had* killed myself that night before finding the spaceship, I would've missed the chance to meet my alien friend.

So, on night eighteen, I drive out to my post yet again. I don't take the trail nearly as fast anymore. The gravel grumbles under my tires. On the seat beside me, peaches roll around in a basket. I crest the hill, holding my breath for just a second, and there it is, sticking out of the ground and reaching for the stars it left behind. I wonder how I would react at this point if I came out here and it was gone. I wonder how disappointed I would be if he came back while I was at work and flew away. Or maybe I would be angry. No, probably not angry, I think. I might feel a little uplifted. After all, I would like for him to get home if he wants to. It would prove I was right after all this time. It would prove that aliens don't necessarily have to be aggressive.

But I'd be sad as well. I'd regret never having the chance to meet him. To learn how to communicate with him. To get him to tell me about the worlds out there and if this is the first planet he's visited or one of many. Are there planets where everyone gets along? Where people don't start wars against their own species and there isn't starvation or discrimination or loneliness? Is suicide only a human contemplation? Did he seek out other worlds because he was missing something in his own?

I'd be sad, because maybe a part of me is hoping if I made friends with him, he'd take me too. That's a silly thought, I know, but wouldn't that be incredible? I'd be the first human to visit another planet with sentient life.

The sun has disappeared, and the city illuminates itself.

Then something new happens.

Light appears behind me and the rumble of an engine resounds in the desert silence. My heart nearly explodes out of my chest, my breath catching in my throat. I turn around to face my UFO, prepared and unprepared to see it coming to life, but it remains sunken in the ground and immobile. Confusion spreads within me, but then I realize another car has arrived. Everything inside me sinks. We've been found out, me and my alien friend. I'm no longer the only one who knows, and this probably dashes my chances of seeing him tonight.

The car shuts off and Lupe gets out. She's wearing jeans and a sweatshirt. She carries a bag over her shoulder that's too big to be a purse. My pulse is quick again, even if this isn't the surprise I was hoping for.

"What are you doing here?" I ask.

She walks all the way until she's standing beside me on my rock, then lets the bag sink to the ground.

"I could ask you the same," she says.

"I was first."

"I followed you," she says, grinning apologetically. She shrugs. She is very pretty. The moonlight is so soft on her brown skin.

"Why would you do that?" I ask.

"You said you were always busy. I see you run off after work like you've got a fire under your ass—I just wanted to know why, I guess." She shrugs again. "I saw you come here yesterday, but I was too afraid to come out and let you know that I'd kind of been stalking you. So I went home. But I thought tonight... hey, maybe you'd like some company."

Her face is expectant, so I move over on my rock enough to let her sit down. The rock isn't exceptionally wide, but she's much smaller than I am and she perches beside me just fine.

"I brought some wine and arroz con pollo, but I forgot we wouldn't have a microwave out here, so we're going to have to eat it cold." She laughs. The loud sound is new out here, where I usually spend the entire night in silence. It seems almost wrong for the laugh to radiate out into the hills like that. I look around, but there's no sign of my alien friend shrinking back into the shadows in fright.

"Will you eat with me?" she asks.

I nod, even though I've already had my usual Wendy's double and a milkshake.

She pulls out a pair of plastic containers. One for each of us.

"This is a pretty view," she says.

"Why did you follow me?" My voice is a little harsher than I mean it to be.

Taking her time, Lupe opens the lid of the container, grabs a fork from the bag, and takes a bite. She chews and I wonder if she's purposely making me wait for her response. "I told you, I wanted to see where you were going in such a rush all the time. I wanted to see what you were doing out here."

Then, when I don't respond, "What *are* you doing out here?"

Reluctantly, I look over at the protruding wing of my UFO.

She follows my gaze but doesn't say anything, instead grabbing a fork out of the bag and handing it over. I'm not hungry, but I know it would be rude at this point to refuse her food, so I open my container and take a bite. It's delicious. The best arroz con pollo I've had since my mom was alive. Even cold, the flavor fills my mouth like a blessing. I'm no longer hesitant to eat more of it.

Eventually, Lupe gets out a pair of plastic cups and pours us both a glass of red wine. I've never had wine with arroz con pollo, but if that's her drink of choice, I won't question. She doesn't ask me anything more, just eats in silence. We both laugh when we can't find a place to balance our cups. We just end up setting them on the ground. I want to ask her if she's the one who made the food or if she got it somewhere, but I can't find the right time to say the words. Much to my surprise, I don't mind her being here. I'm actually enjoying us eating together, having some company.

"So, what do you think it is?" she asks.

I look over at her, startled. She's staring at the spaceship, cup in hand. I think it's pretty obvious, but maybe she hasn't seen this sort of thing before. Like I said, I've only ever heard her discussing reality TV and telenovelas with the other women at the office. But people don't like to be told they don't *get* something easily—it makes them feel stupid—so I won't point out that the answer is obvious.

"Do you want the truth?" I ask. She'll probably think I'm crazy. People can be so close-minded about things sometimes.

"Yeah," she says. "Tell me what you think it is."

I shouldn't tell her what I really think. She'll definitely leave if I do. There's still a chance that this is some ploy to get dirt on me. Then she and all our other coworkers can laugh about me. I have a sneaking suspicion they already do, but there's no reason to fan the flames. I know how ridiculous the truth sounds.

"Come on, I want to know." She takes a sip.

"I think it's a UFO that crash-landed," I hear myself say. The cat is out of the bag.

Lupe laughs again, but when she sees the look on my face she immediately stops. "Are you serious?"

I just let my eyes sink to the dirt.

Lupe doesn't respond for a very long time. She watches the protruding wing, and now I'm not so sure that it's a spaceship at all. Now, the entire thing seems so ridiculous to me. I'm embarrassed about how many nights I've been out here, swallowing burgers whole and forgoing sleep in my own bed to sit in the darkness on a rock. I could've actually done what I came out here to do in the first place instead of letting my thoughts run rampant with every slightest shred of forced evidence that upheld my claims.

She turns to look at me again and I can see pity in her brown eyes. My heart sinks.

"Have you been waiting for someone—some*thing* to come

back?" she asks, almost in a whisper. "Annie…"

I want to cry. Instead, I stare up at the stars above us, no longer wondering which one is the home of my alien, but in sheer awe of how unimaginably far away each of them is. My thoughts cannot even grasp the concept of this distance. The thought of our separation had never occurred to me. Never on any of the nights I sat here waiting. If I feel far from the city now, how many millions of times farther is that closest glowing speck?

"I just thought, maybe…" I don't finish my sentence either.

We stare up at the stars, the two of us. I try to find the constellations but I can't remember any of them besides the most common: the Big Dipper and Orion's Belt. I'm sure the sky is littered with stories but they've all eluded me. I don't believe in an afterlife—at least, not the one where we sail up into the heavens on a white cloud. I'd be no closer to those stars dead than I was sitting here waiting for my alien friend.

Lupe surprises me one more time. She hooks her arm into mine. Without looking at me, she says, "I'll wait with you."

"What?" I'm not sure what she means.

"I'll wait with you," she says again. "Maybe tonight will be the night."

So we wait by my spaceship until the rising sun colors the sky orange and pink.

PARTY FAVORS

My strong belief is that people who cloud themselves in excessive amounts of perfume should be forcibly submerged in the substance until they spill their darkest secrets. After all, they have to be hiding something if they'd rather you couldn't stare straight at them without your eyes watering and your nose starting to dribble blood. I'll admit that I treat myself to Lancôme La Vie Est Belle Eau De Parfum at most release parties, but I limit myself to a tasteful amount. Good heavens, dearie, is your natural body odor so repugnant?

Laureigh Dumont is, unfortunately, one such person. God, I love her films, but the woman couldn't sneak up on me if I had a sinus infection. On occasion, I've wondered if supernatural powers *do* exist, in which case hers is to exude whatever floral, aromatic assault she's got on her mind in nauseating amounts.

We kiss at the door while she exalts my earrings. I compliment the pairing of her honey gown with her chestnut plait.

"Marie, darling, I'm so happy you could come!"

"I wouldn't miss it."

"Have you decided whether to get that dog or not yet?"

Then I escape to a corner of the ballroom where I don't find myself losing consciousness.

Cocktails seem to be in order.

And immediately Mitch Fleeker finds me. I could bury myself in an uncharted cave system beneath the eastern seaboard and that man would somehow walk up to me as if nothing at all had happened. He wears last season's Tom Ford three-piece in charcoal with—God, of all things— a monocle beneath his furrowed brow. Yes, that was not incorrect. The man actually wears a monocle as if he were some 1900s landlord in a capitalist board game. He smiles at me by way of sneering, but that can't be helped. That's just his face.

"Miss Champeaux," he exclaims, and almost loses the monocle by raising his eyebrow. All he needs now is a black cane.

"Mr. Fleeker," I reply, sliding my martini off the counter.

"Such a surprise to see you here." A wry smile curls his lips.

I roll my eyes. "You say that every time we meet at one of these things."

A black man joins us as well, Gavin Chard of *Making an Entrance* fame. He chuckles. "Well, Mitch doesn't show much variety in his films. What makes you think you can expect any different from his greetings?"

I *love* Gavin in that instant. We all laugh, though Mitch does so with a deadness in his eyes.

Gavin doesn't miss a beat. "Mitch is just mad because Toronto neglected him this year."

Were I ten years younger, I would have laid Gavin on the bar then and there. "Did they really?" I ask. I hold up my martini glass to cover my smirk. I don't like Mitch Fleeker, but I have to keep in his circle of friends. Favors are the currency of my business.

"Haha," Mitch says. "Let's not pretend we don't all think Toronto hasn't fallen out of step some."

"That was a triple negative, Fleeker," I say. "I'm going to need a minute to unpack that."

"Come on, Mitch," says Gavin. "Don't be that way. There's always next year."

Mitch ignores the comments. Instead, he drops the monocle into his breast pocket, then turns around and hastily waves someone over. His enthusiasm is apparent. Obviously, this is his big subject of the party. "Has either of you met Chardonnay?"

Gavin and I snort. Was that someone's name? Pretention is the cheapest form of idiocy.

"Yes, quite frequently," I say. "In fact, we met just last night over a candlelit bath."

"I'm partial to darker varieties myself," Gavin says with a wink, "but you can pour me a glass anyway."

Mitch sneers at us. We go quiet in the next instant though, when the most gorgeous woman I've ever seen tiptoes over. Her stilettos come up to my shoulders and I'd bet my left ass cheek her real name isn't any kind of fermented beverage, but there is no doubting her stunning looks. She must be an aspiring actress, or otherwise has a heart of gold to be attending parties with a person as acidic as Mitch Fleeker. She smiles coquettishly and I nearly have to shield my retinas.

"I'm Chardonnay," she says with a European accent I can't place.

Like hell you are, I want to respond, but it comes out, "Marie Champeaux."

"Gavin Chard."

We both shake her hand.

"You are all making the movies?" she asks.

"Films, darling. *Films*," Mitch corrects.

She giggles. "Oh, excuse me. I did not mean offense."

Gavin bows. "None taken." Instantly, my to-lay list seems to have erased itself. "I'm the director of *several* award-winning dramas."

"Yes!" she says, suddenly recognizing his name. "The—the—the... *Making an Entrance* film."

Very good. So, she has done some homework.

"I'm a critic," I say.

"A very prolific critic," Gavin adds.

"Most directors and producers run from her if they know what's good for them." Fleeker raises his glass and his eyebrow. We all laugh, myself included. Rarely do I shy from my own reputation. Doing so increases the face wrinkles.

"She is tough?" Chardonnay asks.

We laugh again. Gavin extrapolates. "She once reviewed *The Curious Case of Benjamin Button* and delivered the following quip: 'What the film lacks in plot, it makes up for in length. The filmmakers have failed to realize that unlike the titular character, we in the audience aren't getting any younger.'"

We howl with laughter again, including our adequately lost Miss Pretty. I fake a curtsey.

"You are terrible," Mitch says, "but brilliant."

"Oh, stop it. I'm nothing of the sort," I reply with a dramatic wave. People have an easier time swallowing false modesty if they can't tell whether you're joking. Of course, I'm aware of my standings—the Guiseppe Zanottis don't pay for themselves—but how else would I be here? What Fleeker has said about most film directors isn't entirely untrue, especially in the greater Vancouver and Los Angeles areas where I spend most of my time. Either they befriend me with invites to soirees and dinners—although I have *never* given a dishonest film critique—or they stay away from me and hope for the best.

"Whose film is this?" Chardonnay asks.

"Laureigh Dumont," Gavin says. He points to the head of the room, where our hostess is sharing a word with a large entourage. The honey of her dress deepens in the light of the crystal chandeliers.

"Oh, the smelly lady," Chardonnay says before clasping a hand over her mouth. Airhead.

Gavin and Mitch chuckle.

"So you've noticed," Gavin says.

"It's impossible not to," Mitch guffaws. "I'm surprised they're all standing so close."

"I know I can't. I start to gag," Gavin says.

"She came to me and I had to choke," Chardonnay says.

Mitch sniggers. "At least you can see her films without having to smell her."

"She's rather nice," I say.

A moment of quiet follows. An awkward quiet. I roll my eyes inwardly. Where the hell had that nicety come from? If I keep that up I'll be writing Hallmark cards soon. I can see Gavin and Mitch glancing at me and then at each other, smirking.

"Oh," Chardonnay squeals, suddenly very excited. She jumps up and down, Mitch and Gavin tracking her every bounce and jiggle with voracious stares. Even in my prime I could never command the attention of men like that, but I suppose that's why I now have a successful career. "I just remembered, Mitchy"—I vomit just a tablespoon in my mouth— "you said you would introduce me to Lee Anderson!"

"Of course, darling. Let's go see him now." Mitch places a hand around her petite waist. With a sneer, he leads her away into the party.

"I have never envied Mitch Fleeker before," Gavin states, "but this might qualify. Maybe he's got a wonderful personality somewhere deep, *deep* down."

"I guess it's just you and me now," I say.

Gavin straightens his jacket. "Actually, I only told Laureigh I'd stop by tonight. I'm going to another party in North for a friend's thirtieth. Sorry, Marie, you'll have to go back to whoever you came with."

I laugh, patting Gavin's arm affectionately. You can only trust anyone in Hollywood, anyone at all, to stay at your party for as long as your friendship is worth to them. There's always another party. Endless parties. That's why I had to stop living in this smog-ridden town. I was going to party myself to death—a much more attainable outcome than you'd expect. Who had tied Gavin's tie? It's crooked. I resist the urge to fix the damn thing myself; his suit is tailored so poorly anyway, nobody will care about the tie.

We exchange cheek kisses and then he's gone. I finish my martini and leave the olive. I look around but don't immediately see anyone I want to strike up a conversation with. Maybe there isn't much of a reason to stay longer after all. Besides, the chill-hop emanating from the DJ is threatening to sour my stomach with its bland, melody-less void. I head for the door.

I've almost made it out unscathed when one of the attendees by the exit sticks out a gloved hand.

"Party favor, ma'am?" he asks.

He holds out a minute bottle of perfume. I grab it out of obligation.

HAPPY, HOPEFUL MADDY

June 21, 2004

Noll Whitcomb,

I haven't sung so loud since my friend Liam Derringer popped the '57 single malt on my wedding night. Can it really be true? I haven't heard or seen your name in over fifty years. I almost can't believe it's you writing to me now. You sure this ain't one of the girls playing prankster with me? I guess it couldn't have been, seeing as I don't think I've ever said anything about you to them. Good thing I was already sitting down when my daughter handed me the envelope or I would've found myself on the floor. Would've knocked me off my feet, it would've, seeing your name scribbled all unruly on the envelope. The address almost made me think it was a trick too—I didn't recognize it even though you're still in the same town. But then I suppose you would have moved from the Corner House since we were kids. In my mind, I guess I always thought you'd stay there forever.

Well, now. That's a lot of questions for me to answer, Noll. How do I start?

You said you got my address from Lisa Garner? Yes, her mother and my mother were friends until the end. Then I suppose you know I didn't stay in Indiana after the move. As soon as I married my husband, we ended up settling in Maine, closer to his family. I always did want to be by the ocean. Don't you remember? Boats all in the water and the tide coming in all nice. It attracted me back then as much as the forest did. Still does, matter of fact. I go down to the water most days in the morning.

I guess you could say I've done well for myself. I'm not ashamed admitting my life has been good. I wouldn't have things go differently even if that was the way the world worked.

After the move, I started school right away. Some of the kids were nice, some not so much. I missed you terribly, so I was still in a state of grief. I kept pretty much to myself at first, but you know me. I can't stay quiet for too long. I took up ballet and piano, which kept me busy until I was done with high school. Then I got myself a job at the deli, standing outside the door passing out meat samples to the people walking by.

Betty, who danced with me, was going with Liam at the time, and Liam had a friend named Jack Keane. They were both part of the Knights of Columbus, who had a chapter at St. Mary's church a town over. During the summer of 1962, Betty invited me to a social the Knights were hosting, saying that their friend Jack needed a date and I should go with him. Well, you don't need to know the rest. I fell in love and we married a few years later—probably because he promised to take me to Europe, though that's yet to happen. Go figure! Moved out to Maine to a summer-blue house in Stockton Springs. Marne, my daughter, came first, and Neil followed not too long after. I had the time of my life raising them. Of course, they're long out of the house now with little ones of their own, but I never get tired of showing them off. I'll send you pictures if you'd like to see (and I'll probably send them anyway whether or not you ask!).

I want to know how the boy Noll Whitcomb turned out. You know, every once and a while you'd cross my mind. I'd be practicing pas de bourrees or sitting down to eat and I'd think of you and wonder what other kind of mischief you must've gotten into after I left. To be fair, I was mostly the proprietor of the trouble that went down behind the Corner House, but I liked to think you carried on in my honor.

I'd think about coming home with foxtails in my hair and clinging to my ripped stockings. The whippersnaps that were always waiting on the counter or in one of the lighthouse cookie jars your mother liked so much. If I concentrate real hard, I think I could still taste them. I really do.

And you running after me because I was always faster. That I'll never forget. Sprinting through the tall grass and hearing nothing but the hiss of the stalks rubbing together and our feet stomping that ground like the devil was coming to chase us. I didn't need to look back, but sometimes I did just to be sure. Just so I could glimpse you on my heel with that ridiculous, straw-colored hair getting in your eyes. You were always right behind me. Just a few paces back.

Makes me think of my mama too. You know how frustrated she got. Every time I came back all out of breath, braids half undone and more dirt than skin, she'd roll her eyes and draw up to her full height, puffing out her chest because she was holding back from knocking me across the head.

"Another pair of stockings?" she'd say. She'd throw up her hands and I'd flinch, feeling bad and promising myself I'd never ever rip another pair again. "Just where have you been that you're coming home looking like you've been living the first years of your life in the jungle?"

She knew where I'd been. At the Corner House with Noll Whitcomb. Saying your name lessened the intensity of her irritation.

"Noll," she'd sigh. "That happy, hopeful boy."

I wonder sometimes why we never took up writing each other. You were my best friend back then. I planned every day around running with you. I guess we parted ways before either of us was old enough to fathom a pen pal. Hearing from you now is something special though, I'll tell you that. Please, Noll, tell me all about you.

Best,

Madeline Keane

***

July 2

Noll,

You've got me laughing! I know that isn't my name according to *you*, but I haven't gone by Maddy since I was in high school at least! Seemed too girlish after that, and you know I wanted only to be sophisticated by that age. You would be right though; you've never called me anything but, and so I can't really ask you to start with Madeline now. Come to think of it, I can't imagine you saying anything but my nickname. It wouldn't feel right. Though that's in a little nine-year-old voice that I'm sure isn't yours no more.

I hope I can meet Kate someday. She sounds like a lovely woman. We get to a certain age though, where traveling doesn't feel like a privilege anymore, do it? Jack still gets to bugging me about a trip every now and then—bless his heart, he's still a romantic—so maybe I can hop on board for a trip down to Tennessee if my joints will allow. Wouldn't that be something?

I've been awaiting your letter since the day I sent mine. Almost convinced myself that it didn't happen and I was acting like a fool thinking I'd get a response. The girls at the book club kept teasing me, talking about how I was head over heels again for my first crush. They laughed on and on, poking fun at me.

"Hasn't Jack kept you smitten these last forty years?" they were saying.

They don't know.

I loved you. You weren't my first crush. You were my brother. Is that a strange way to feel, seeing as we only knew each other the first nine years of our lives? Nine years playing in a lone house at the end of a cul-de-sac. A house made of corners where the rooms didn't have four walls—they had six or seven or a hundred. They folded around themselves until you couldn't be sure if the other side of that wall you were knocking on was the kitchen, the study, or another world entirely. I know we knew our way around that house, but thinking on it now, I'm not sure I remember which rooms led to the others. I had it in my head, if you ran fast enough, you'd catch one of them doors leading toward Beyond. And who knew what would happen then?

Anyway, I'm writing this while Jack is driving us to Neil's house. We're going to have dinner with him and his family tonight. I'd better stop though, we're almost there. Can't wait to hear from you again.

Best,
Maddy

***

July 8

Noll,

Now wait just a minute, that isn't fair! You can't just send all those embarrassing pictures in the mail and go addressing the envelope to Jack Keane! What about the bond of trust we're supposed to have? What about the unbreakable code of childhood friendship? Come back half a century later and the first thing you do is go besmirching my name. Jack went straight to Marne and Neil to show them the pictures and now I can't hear the end of it.

I guess the word's out that Miss Book Club spent her youth in a disheveled state of ratty tangles and dusty skirts. I couldn't outrun my past even moving a thousand miles away. Couldn't leave behind that bewildered little girl if I wanted to. She was a fast runner, wasn't she? I will say, I didn't know those photographs existed, Noll, so I've got to thank you for that.

Speaking of the photos, you know the one you sent me where I've got my arm hung around your neck and I'm missing one of my front teeth? The one at your birthday party? Do you see what's on my mama's armchair behind us? It's the box! You know the one I'm talking about, right? Oh, you have to. There's no way either of us could forget. Color me surprised, seeing that thing sitting on the chair behind us—brought back a flood of memories, came straight up behind my eyes.

You know sometimes how you think back on your childhood and there were things you knew had to have happened, but now you're sitting there wondering if maybe they weren't just dreams after all? Or maybe your imagination was a lot more convincing in your youth than you gave it credit for? I think something about that when I get that box in my head. It's been a while since my mind last brought it up but I can remember debating real hard whether or not the whole thing wasn't just us dreaming.

Being the little girl I was, I know I wrote it all down somewhere. I had a notebook where I documented the whole ordeal just in case it needed telling someday. Knowing me now, I'd bet my left arm that I kept it and it's tucked away somewhere in my house. I think I'm going to spend some time finding it. I'll get back to you.

Thanks for the pictures, though, Noll. Despite you revealing my unkempt stages to my entire cohort and family, that was a real treat to see us again. That was a pretty place. Happy fourth, by the way.

Well-kept,
Maddy

***

July 10

I found it!
I was going to wait until your response but I knew I

couldn't hold it back another day. The journal was tucked neatly into my bin of old writing and things I kept from grammar school. The pages are stiff as boards and yellowed as all hell, but my nine-year-old penmanship is as legible as ever. I even did a big curlicue with the *y* in my name to make it look all prim and proper.

The whole thing's there, just as I remembered it and a bit more. You have to give a hand to us—it was something. And the images came back to me as real as they did back then. I even got the conversations down in what must've been somewhat verbatim. Looks like it, anyways.

Do you remember it all? Would you mind if I told it to you? It would be something: writing it to you, maybe there are details you recall that I didn't get down. When my mind was going a mile a minute, I was apt to skip over something.

Eternally as Journal Keeper,
Maddy

***

July 16

Noll,

Well, according to me, it began on a summer afternoon the week after school let out. We were thinking up games to play at your birthday party which was coming up and stealing cherry tomatoes out of old Mr. Durant's yard up the street. If we walked along the path between his house and the next one over, it was easy not to get caught since the vines peeked through the diamonds in the chain-link fence.

Old Mr. Durant had the best apple trees in his yard, but it was harder to pick those without being seen.

Anyways, you were thinking about bobbing for apples like you'd seen kids do at other parties, but I was trying to convince you we should cut down the field behind your house so we could play ball. Kids liked playing ball more than they liked bobbing for apples, after all. I had already turned nine a few months earlier—with a shiny new wristwatch to prove it—so I had experience planning such things.

My convincing was starting to take hold, so I suggested we head back to the Corner House to scope out the land prospects.

"Here is where the backstop would go," I said. I drew a circle in the air to help visualize the location. "It's got to face away from the house so if anybody hits a real good one, they don't go breaking your windows and make your daddy upset."

It was logical, so you agreed. Then you saw something flashy falling out of the trees at the edge of the woods. "What was that?" you asked.

I hadn't seen it because I was too busy mapping out the infield, but you started pointing and raising a fuss. Something shiny had fallen out of the trees. Fell right to the ground and caught your eye.

We were in the business of nosing in everything that was worth exploring, so we decided we needed to see what it was. Our mamas didn't know we ever went into the woods since it was strictly forbidden, so every time we got close I always got that exhilarating rush, knowing I was getting away with something I wasn't supposed to. We both were good at keeping hush about it—so as long as we didn't go there too often and didn't stay too long, we wouldn't get caught. What

you saw had fallen right at the edge, came right out of the last
trees where the green-gray foliage gave way to the tall grass.
Technically then, we wouldn't have to go into the woods at
all, but I still got the rush all the same.

"It was probably a bird's nest. Some birds got those shiny
eggs, you know, with the patterns all over them," I said to
you. And you nodded, not wanting to say you didn't know
about shiny-egg birds and needed clarifying.

We trod right across that field. I think I hypothesized a
few more causes of the falling flash by the time we got to the
trees. But when the first branches were hanging over our
heads, we could definitely see it wasn't a bird's nest.

"It's a treasure chest," you said.

That wasn't quite the correct language. "That's not a
treasure chest. It's not big and heavy enough."

"They don't all have to be big and heavy."

"Yes, they do. If it's full of gold it's gonna be heavy
because gold is heavy."

"That's true. It's a box, then," you said.

I nodded. "It's a magic box. It gives you what you need."

I don't know how I knew that, or why I said it. But my
answer was definite and there was no questioning. The box
looked like it had been made out of a map. Painted
continents in faded hues stretched across the faces with
dotted lines marking trade routes through the great seas.
Calligraphed names sprawled everywhere in variant scripts,
giving the impression that somehow this magic box had been
to every location it bore. The sides were flat and the seams a
plated metal—the source of the flash of light when the sun
caught it—but the front and back edges on top were
rounded. I admitted later in my journal that it *did* look like a
treasure chest, albeit a small one, but light as it was there

could hardly have been gems inside.

Since you had seen it, it was only fitting that you got to pick it up first. After turning it over and over in your hands, brow furrowed like you were trying to figure out a puzzle that you just couldn't solve, you grabbed the latch on the front and tried to pull it open.

The latch wouldn't budge.

It was shaped like a brass hook, like something you'd catch giant fish with while out on the sea, only the tip wasn't so pointy. It slid through a hole in a metal knob that stuck out of the bottom half, pulling the lid tighter the farther the hook slid in. As far as we could tell though, there wasn't a way to lock it. It was nothing more than a hook and a hole.

You got your couple minutes of trying and then I took my turn, grunting and huffing as I pulled here and tugged there. Rosy patches were darkening on my thumbs the more I went at it, and then my fingers actually started turning sore. Still, the lid had not budged an inch. It was sealed tighter than a mason jar after brining.

When I was sufficiently hot in the face, I collapsed back against a tree, sinking down next to where you sat.

"That thing's useless," you said.

"It probably ain't opening because we don't need anything right now," I said, still squeezing the box in my arms.

"Alright, alright," you sighed.

I was looking all around, my eyes combing the thick branches overhead. Light peeked through the gaps in the leaves. It seemed like such a long way up to those first branches. These trees weren't like the ones farther in with twisting roots that folded up out of the ground like knees and arms hanging low enough to swat your head if you weren't looking where you were going.

"Where d'you think it came from?" I asked.

You took a second to reply. I almost thought maybe you hadn't heard me.

"It didn't need to come from nowhere," you said. You were drawing lines in the ground with a stick, I remember that. I didn't write it down in my book but I remember that clear as day for some reason. "It's a magic box, it probably came from one of those places on there."

And that was what it was and how we came to have it. Eventually, we got up and started playing some game right there at the edge of the woods. We didn't think any more about bobbing for apples or mowing down the field for a ball game. We played until the sun touched the top of the Corner House and we knew it was going to be time for supper. We decided I'd keep the box for that first night and we'd figure out how else to try to get it open the next day when we'd had some time to sleep on it and brainstorm.

That suited me just fine. Holding the needful box, my mind was already buzzing with a hundred things that might come out of it. How we'd sail oceans and fly like superheroes all because we had this unlimited magic in our possession.

Wielder of Magic,
Maddy

***

July 25

Noll Edgar Whitcomb,

You cannot tell me that I'm the one who saw the box fall.

I'm the one reading it straight out of my journal entry from that very day, you old fool. Knowing the proud girl I was, I think I would've taken ownership of seeing the box first if that's how the events had sorted themselves. I very specifically wrote that you were the one who saw the box. That's probably something that disappointed me, but I was not afraid even then to give credit where credit was due. If you're trying to blame this whole ordeal on me—I will tweak your ear. Now I'm laughing again.

Marne has seen some of your letters now. She likes the way you write. It makes her want to know you more. She says, "Mama, why haven't I ever heard you talk about Noll before? It sounds like you were good friends."

I told her sometimes you forget about people in your life when it's been a long time. You don't mean to, but you do. All it takes to get them back though is a little nudge, then everything comes pouring into your heart and your mind. She was silent for a time. She's the thinking type and I can never seem to read her thoughts—I stopped trying when she was a teenager (didn't stop trying soon enough though, Lord knows). After a while I says to her, "Baby, what are you thinking so hard about?"

She says, "Trying to remember if I've forgotten anyone."

Isn't that something to say?

Well, this one's going to be a long one. I had a lot to say about what happened first. It comes back to me as I read it, but the details sure get rusty, don't they?

Anyways, so I took the box home with me, and every day I looked at it. It was probably as much an obsession as my nine-year-old mind could keep. I woke up in the morning and looked at it. When I was supposed to be doing my reading, I'd glance up every few lines just to check that it was still sitting on my window ledge. And at night, before I fell asleep, I watched the moonbeams silhouette it against my shutters. Try as I might though, it would not open. And while some would have given up on it, this impenetrability only made me more obstinate. See, we tried wedging it open with screwdrivers and rocks. You pulling on the lid and me pulling on the base. We thought about busting it with your daddy's sledgehammer, but we didn't want to ruin it getting it open. It was too pretty to damage, too mystifying. I think we even figured that the sledgehammer couldn't have busted through the shell anyway. The magic would protect it. So I got to obsessing instead.

Finally, the very day before your birthday party, things changed.

I woke up early in the morning, with the sun peeking through the wooden slats at my window, and looked over at the box as usual. To my surprise, the latch was undone! I nearly jumped out of bed, euphoria taking over me. My heart raced, blood pumping through my ears, my feet dancing across the floor. The hook was out of the hole, was resting outside it instead. The box was ready to be opened.

I had half a mind to flip the lid then and there, but I knew you'd be disappointed if I did it without you. So instead, I dressed myself real quick, ran downstairs to eat the grits and sausage my mama always had ready for me, and bolted out the door with the box hugged to my chest before she could get in a word edgewise.

We'd figured out before that if I booked it hard the whole way, I could sprint to the Corner House in three minutes. That morning, I did it in two flat, I swear. And there wasn't no huffing and puffing when I got to your porch, neither. I was shouting to you to get down as quick as you could.

Probably scared your dear mother to death in my haste. She asked all kinds of questions, but when I told her something about the box she must've figured it was just kids being kids.

"What's wrong, Maddy?" you asked as you were coming down the stairs.

"It's open," I said.

We hurried out through the backyard.

I remember us crouching by the shed where the bougainvillea came tumbling off the roof and made a little cave we liked to hide under. We waited for your mother's ever-watchful eye to wander away from any of the windows where she might see us running off toward the woods. The sun was sliding off the shingles and blanched the fence boards at our backs. I was all energy and you were still part asleep but getting there too.

"How'd you get the lock?" you asked.

"I didn't," I said. "When I woke up this morning, the latch was undone."

"It must mean it's ready."

I nodded.

With a deft flick of the wrist, you opened the gate along the back fence. Golden stalks raised their thin, feathered heads to greet us. Waving us back in. We chased our shadows into the day, the magic box hugged to my chest. Under the branches of the first trees we stopped. This felt like the right place, right where we found it.

You urged me, "Do it." I had the strange inclination to let the moment hang there, holding the box out in front of me. I was afraid of what it would mean when the box was open because I'd spent so many days staring at it, dreaming about what would be waiting for us inside. But contemplative moments like these are fleeting for children. I hadn't yet learned how to hold on to them, or how to let them take root.

So I opened the box.

Oh, Noll, I don't know if you remember how disappointed we were.

"What is that?" I asked, the first to unclench my jaw.

"It's a plant," you said.

"A tree," I corrected, but more specifically, it was a branch from a tree. Still-green leaves sprouted from long scales of bark. Pliant scales that frayed like rope ends. The piece was small enough to fit in our box, but still it was gnarled, bending this way and that every few inches. At one end it split off into two.

"Why'd it give us a tree?" you asked. But I knew just as much as you.

I tried not to let disappointment show, secretly crushed that it hadn't been a bottle of glowing potion or a wispy fairy dancing on spindle legs. Still, I knew I couldn't be wrong about it being a magic box, so I snapped the lid shut and hugged it back to my chest defiantly.

"It's not done yet," I said. "It starts as a tree branch but it's changing into something else. Like a butterfly."

You nodded, but also didn't want to make it seem like it bothered you too much. I could always count on you for that, couldn't I? You knew just how to act to make things not bother me like they did. That's how you got that nickname from my mama. You always had a laugh hidden up your sleeve or a smile tugging at your mouth. I don't know if you did that by choice or not, but I appreciate it now.

We decided to run from bandits then. They were hiding in the trees, plotting their next moves, waiting for us to slip up. My treasure was mighty fine, and not a dirty soul in town was going to pass up the opportunity to steal the chest. You were the sheriff trying to find me a place to hide while helping me ward off the most daring of outlaws. I laugh thinking about how we ran around like that: imaginary hats pulled low over our eyes, finger-pistols cocked and at the ready.

Every chirp was a bandit sending a signal to another, every falling leaf had been knocked loose by an errant foot. We pushed our way through the woods, scampering over every boulder, crouching in the big roots, crawling beneath bushes. The edge of the forest was clear out of sight and still we didn't notice. Before that day, we'd never gone so far beyond the field.

I realized the shine on my watch must've been giving us away, so I snatched it from my wrist and shoved it into the breast pocket on my shirt.

"This way!" I called, and you sprinted across a narrow gap in the underbrush, an arrow missing your ear by mere inches. We leapt over a stream, crashing down into the bushes on the other side. I rolled over first and helped you up. The bandits were closing in. There was only one place to lose them and that was against the massive trunk up ahead.

I took you by the hand and we spun around the side of the trunk, looking to press ourselves into a wide pleat.

In the journal, I describe it as sliding in, but in all honesty, I think it was more akin to falling. We screamed in spite of ourselves.

Then we were on all fours on a dusty ground. Dirt simmered slowly out of the air. My hands stung from scraping and I'm sure I'd never had stockings with holes so large before. At first, I was petrified of what my mother would think, but then the thought occurred to me that I had no idea where we'd fallen into.

I looked up. The best I could describe it was that we were in a room made out of tree. Rings circled the ceiling and I noticed that beneath the dust, the floor had them as well. The walls bore the marks of carving. It wasn't possible though— the tree hadn't been this large on the outside. Along one end was a kitchen, for there were counters and cabinets all the same dark brown as everything else, and against the far wall were book shelves and a table sculpted right from the floor. Flames from numerous lamps lit the space with a dim glow that was just bright enough to cast shadows.

To our right, the tree room had a bed that rose up out of the ground. I could just make out a lump beneath the thick wool blanket. A body immobile.

"Just who do you think you are?" a high, childish voice said. A woman came out of the darkness, although *woman* was a generous word. She had the air of age, but she couldn't have been above my shoulder, and her skin was as taught as a drum head. She had round pearl eyes and wore a blue apron tied at her waist.

You stuttered something. I'm sure between the body beneath the blanket and the miniature woman, you didn't know what to say. So I spoke. "We were being chased—"

"By the Palakostos?"

"—by bandits. We just meant to hide and fell in here."

Her face fell. "Oh. I was hoping you'd come to help me."

The woman—I didn't know what else to call her— immediately went to the kitchen corner and began cutting up things, bringing out a large copper pot as though maybe she were making soup. Now that we had somewhat explained our circumstances, however vaguely, she seemed too busy to show us much interest. I wrote that she kept glancing back at us as if making sure we were there, but didn't say anything.

"What's wrong with him?" you asked after a few minutes of listening to the click of her knife. You were staring at the body beneath the blanket.

She sighed and slid the vegetables she'd been chopping into the water, then turned to face us. "He's incredibly ill," she said, "and I can't seem to reverse it. It's my husband. He's been that way for weeks."

"What happened?" you asked.

"I don't know. He caught fever, started to swell, and then passed out." She avoided looking at the bed, eyes darting here and there while she spoke. Worry racked her brow. "I don't know what else I can do, I—"

She stopped, gaze locked at a spot on the ground by the entrance. "Is that—is that what I think it is?"

I was afraid she was going to cry. I also realized then that since we'd fallen, I didn't have the box in my hands. It was lying on the floor by the small wooden steps descending into the tree room. The crash had opened the lid and now it was sitting wide, the leaves on the branch emitting a faint green bioluminescence.

"It's our box," I said.

She clasped her hands over her mouth. "You brought it here? That's—that's a yew branch. That's got magical healing properties." And when we didn't answer, "Have you come to help me after all? Why didn't you say so?"

I looked from her to the box and back again, bewildered. "Are you sure that's what it is?"

"I'd know yew if I saw it anywhere," the tiny woman squeaked. One thing was clear to me though—I had no use for the disappointing tree branch the box had provided, but if she wanted it, that was fine by me.

"You can have it, if you'd like."

She nodded wordlessly, then rushed over to the box and grabbed the branch. "You're cured, Gabriel," she said, placing it on the counter by her boiling pot. Then she ran back to us and squeezed us each in a tight hug, tears streaming from her eyes. "I think you saved my husband. I can't thank you two enough. What are your names?"

"I'm Maddy and this is Noll."

"He's going to be alright?" you asked.

She nodded. "I think so."

"What's your name?" you said. I hadn't even thought to inquire.

"I'm Mrs. Akeso, but you can call me Tabitha."

With deft hands, she peeled the bark from the branch and crushed the leaves, adding them to the boiling pot, which began to give off tendrils of green light like vapor. While the soup brewed, she pulled a loaf of bread from her oven and cut us each a few slices in thanks. Not knowing what time it was, but that we'd been out long enough, we figured it was time to head home. We waved, mounting her small wooden steps while Tabitha bowed and thanked us again and again, and when we turned away from her doorstep, we found that the entrance to her tree home had vanished.

Quite the happening for our first time opening the box, wasn't it? I never wondered again how Tabitha Akeso and her husband, Gabriel, turned out. I think her utter certainty and boundless thanks put me at ease.

Yew-bearer,
Maddy

***

July 29

Noll,

Don't you go getting a swell head now. Marne's just at that
age where her babies aren't babies anymore, and that changes
the way you think about life. It's not because you're some
Shakespeare that she's hankering to hear more. You got me
laughing.

I will say though, even her brother is interested now. She
told him about you writing and how you're my friend from
way back and now they're asking me all sorts of questions.
You're lucky Jack ain't a jealous man, or all this fuss might've
put an end to our communication. But he knows. Maybe I
told him once about the Corner House. Maybe I don't
remember it, but I told him.

Anyways, you're right. That wasn't the end of our troubles
that day. We left Tabitha's home and found ourselves a new
problem.

"I don't suppose you know the way back?" you asked.
You were already tearing a piece off one of the bread slices
she'd given us.

I realized then that I didn't and held the box out in my
hands. "Maybe it'll give us a map." I went to open the lid, but
the box had shut itself again, the latch as sealed as it ever had
been. Try as I might, it wouldn't budge, and I sighed with
discontent. How come it had opened to give us something
for the nymph but it couldn't open to give us something for
ourselves?

We wandered for what might have been minutes but felt
like hours, walking back and forth through the underbrush

and stumbling over rocks and a stream. I didn't want to tell you, but I was beginning to worry that we were lost for good and nobody was ever going to find us because we weren't supposed to be out there in the first place. All the things my mama had said about the woods came rushing back to me and I had to swallow the lump in my throat to keep big, fat tears from rolling out.

You were a little calmer, though, when it came to those things. You probably hadn't even considered the possibility that we might not find our way back.

When it was getting harder to keep my composure, you made a suggestion that turned our fortune around.

"How about I climb one of these trees and look for the chimney peeking over my house," you said.

That's just what you did. We found the tallest tree and you climbed it. Didn't falter one step, you just scurried right up like a chipmunk. Up until I could barely see the bottoms of your shoes.

You said you could just see the top of your chimney, but that was enough. Every once in a while when we weren't sure if we were keeping a straight line, you'd hop back up to check. And eventually, the field came out before us just as the sun was waning over the rooftops. I might've gotten a stern question or two, but my mama didn't find out about us being in the woods, even with my stockings torn to shreds.

Your birthday party was the next day. In-between cake and ice cream and games of tug-o'-war (our team won every time, of course), we kept stealing knowing smiles at each other. When it was over, we grabbed hold of one of the yellow balloons, climbed out onto the roof of the Corner House, and tied it to the top of the chimney. That way, we figured, it would be a little easier to find our way back if we ever went in again. I imagine we were pretty proud of ourselves for that.

Balloon Bower's Keeper,
Maddy

***

August 8

Noll,

The picture you sent of your grandson is adorable! I can't believe how much he looks like you did at that age. Isn't that remarkable, how all this turned out? I'll bet he's just like you too—running around getting into things he shouldn't because he can't help trying to figure out how they work. I'll bet he's smart. You were smart. There wasn't anybody who could think about things the way you did.

You told me once that stars were burning balls of energy just like our sun, only billions of miles away. I hadn't thought much about what the stars were up until that time in my life, and to hear you say that—and to say how far away they were—changed the way I thought about the universe. I hadn't thought in spaces so large before. I don't think even after that I still had a grasp on that measure of size. Maybe I still don't.

I talked to you about stars after that. About the universe. We wanted to claim a star then, you and I. We proclaimed it. We were each going to get a planet going around that sun. Isn't that just like children, to claim things as their own? Now that I say it, I suppose some people never grow out of that.

I've got to run now, Noll. We're going to Neil's tonight for dinner again and I still need to put my face on. Hear from you soon!

Star-gazer,
Maddy

***

August 13

Noll,

The second time was the peaches. You remember that? It took me a moment while I read what I'd written, but eventually it came back.

Yes, when the box opened the second time, we were having a sleepover. That kind of thing wasn't normal back then, me being a girl and you being a boy and whatnot, but our parents didn't mind too much. I sometimes thought my mama was unfair and strict for nagging on me for getting messy all the time, but really she loved me and gave me many freedoms the kids around us didn't have.

I think we'd set up a tent in your backyard to do some night sky-watching—something we did more and more as we got older—and were just settling into our sleeping bags when we heard it. A sharp click that rang above the chanting cicadas. We didn't recognize the sound immediately, but before too long our eyes shot over to that treasure box. You know it never left our sight. Sure enough, the latch was undone just as if someone had reached over and popped it open. What would it be this time?

"Can I open it?" you asked, as if it were something that belonged to me. I suppose there was some truth to that though, since I kept the box in my room most nights. I'd say by then I had a sixty percent share of the box and you the rest.

I nodded.

Without getting up, you bear-crawled your way over to the box, hands slapping on the bottom of the tent. It was just as exciting the second time around. Tension constricted my chest as you raised the lid.

Inside were seven of the largest, ripest peaches I had ever seen. They sat heaped in the confines of the chest, dark in the moonlight but still a pale yellow-pink. I think my eyes had grown the size of the peaches, just as round too. The box hadn't given us anything magical, which might've made me twinge a bit, but they were some good-looking fruit.

"Peaches?" you asked. Boy, was that box bewildering.

"I guess so," I said.

"Why do you suppose..." You trailed off and I shrugged in response, but the sight of those peaches made me hungry something awful.

"Maybe it just knew we'd need a snack," I said. I took the first one and sank my teeth in without hesitation.

I think I can still remember that particular peach. It was the sweetest thing I'd ever tasted. My tongue sizzled in euphoria, my eyes closed, head back, trying to keep the juices from overflowing my lips. I didn't want to waste a single drop. Before I'd even had time to register what was happening, I was down to the pit, trying to scrape off every last shred of flesh I could.

"Wow," was all you could manage at my speed.

"They're amazing," I said. "You got to eat one."

So you did. And then we both ate another, and another, until we were ripping the last one in half, each slyly trying to lay claim to the bigger piece.

When it was all gone, the pits lying in a sad group on the bottom of the magic box, I sat back and started licking the stickiness off my fingers one by one, wishing there was just one last bite. The moon shone off my fingers and my bare wrists. I froze.

"Where's my watch?" I asked.

"What?" you responded dumbly, still fixated on your empty palms.

"My wristwatch. The one my mama gave me for my birthday," I said, patting my pockets.

"I don't know," you said. You weren't understanding the urgency of the situation. "I haven't seen you wear it in a while."

"I don't remember having worn it in a while." My hand went to where a breast pocket might be. "Not since—"

I looked out in the direction of the woods. The black figures of trees rising high in the distance danced like dark flames. I hadn't worn it since we were pretending the bandits were after us. You saw this in my face and panicked a little.

"We can't go out there now," you said. I could smell fear in your voice.

I considered this for a few minutes. Truth is, I still kept some fear of the woods myself. Especially after dark. Sure, I was terrified of what would happen if my mother found out I'd lost the wristwatch (and now that I knew I'd lost it, that moment seemed likely any second), but the dark in the woods scared me more. I agreed. We would never find it if we went in there now. Who knew what wandered the woods at night?

At first light though, I shook you awake and off we went. The treasure box was tucked under my arm because I didn't dare go anywhere without it anymore. To my surprise, it had still been unlocked when I woke, the peach pits rattling around inside. We trudged across the field, the grass seeming to pull at my legs now I had this burden. The long shadows cast by the rising sun lost each other quickly in the foliage, and soon we were out of sight again from the edge of the wood.

Retracing our steps was impossible. Once we got far enough inside, nothing looked the same as it had before—like the trees got up in the middle of the night and rearranged themselves. We went this way and that, combing the bushes, eyes on the ground, across a stream, but we could not find a single glint of silver. Finally, we sat back against a large boulder and I struggled to hold back tears. I did not cry. That was not something I let myself do as a child.

"We'll find it," you said, and crossed your arms.

Just then a voice came out behind us. It sounded like a girl singing.

"What is it you seek, young friends?" The voice didn't have a tune per se, but it was melodic and enrapturing. Enough to lessen my anxiety.

We turned to find a young woman sitting back against a tree as if it were lying horizontal on the ground instead of standing upright. She was halfway up the trunk, no gravity pulling at her or nothing. Her dress looked to be made of leaves, or perhaps it was only woven to give the appearance. We might have missed her (and probably already had before) were she not speaking to us.

"You ought to stay away from the woods," she said. Though the words were in warning I felt no urge to heed them. Her voice was too soothing.

"What are you?" you asked, not minding manners because she obviously didn't come from where we did.

She grinned and tilted her head. "Another friend, perhaps."

"I've lost my wristwatch," I said, finding my voice. She looked from you to me, but never moved from her reclined verticality.

"Oh, that does sound important."

"It was silver and shiny and told me what time it was," I said. The words spilled out of me. "I think I lost it a couple weeks ago. I put it in my pocket, see, because the shininess was giving away our hiding spot, but then it must've fallen out because I ain't seen it since then."

"Silver and shiny, you say?" She considered my description while I nodded. "Then it's likely the Fox has it."

"The Fox?" you asked. She described to us a character who had come to the woods at some point in her long lifetime and made it his home. He foraged the land and kept anything unusual for himself (especially things which were shiny). If we wanted it back, though, it would come at a price.

"But we haven't got no money," I said, aggravated. I was mad at myself for losing the watch in the first place, but I was also mad at this Fox for taking things which didn't belong to him and not giving them back to their rightful owner even if they came knocking. That wasn't decency—that sounded more like thieving.

"Oh, he doesn't deal in human currency," our friend said. "He deals in sustenance. A fair trade in food is what he'll make. If you want to tempt him most, sweet fruits are his favorite."

We looked at each other and then down at the box in my hand. I felt my heart sink faster than it ever had before. Why had we eaten all those peaches? Why hadn't we saved a single one? Just one?

"Thank you," you said. Deflated.

"Where can we find the Fox?" I asked. The lady lifted her arm and pointed straight out into the trees to her left.

"That way. He lives in the hollow by the red rocks."

Those directions were vague, but they were plenty for what we needed. We walked in as straight a line as we could, and before long we could hear running water and splashing, like maybe a waterfall was up ahead. Sure enough, mist caught in the air while the stream came crashing down amid rocks jutting out of the earth like teeth. They must've been rich in iron because they were red as an October sunset.

On the other bank was a clearing which sank down slightly into the earth. No grass or underbrush grew there and the dirt was a pale beige. All around the clearing were what looked like jagged stumps from cracked trees, but they were cluttered with so many different items it was hard to tell. Bicycle wheels, glasses, hats, and shoes. A French horn, a cuckoo clock, a model train, a cracked mirror; all these things and more lay in heaps around each of the thin stumps as if somehow sorted. And upon one of the piles, still fresh enough that it bore little tarnish from the extremes, was my glinting silver wristwatch.

I moved toward it, but a shadow crossed my path.

"Well, well. What are we up to?" the Fox asked. His voice was much deeper, much more gravelly than I would've expected from someone with as small a stature as his. He probably stood as tall as my shoulder. And yet, these words coming from him felt threatening and stopped me in my tracks. He stood on two legs but moved on all fours, darting quick as a blink. "You weren't thinking of stealing now, were you?"

"It's not stealing," I said, raising my chin. "That's my wristwatch! It was mine to begin with."

"You left it in the woods," he replied. His jaws barely seemed to move when he spoke, but his voice filled the hollow. "You lost it."

"Yeah, but it was an accident," you chimed in. I'd nearly forgotten you were there, to be honest. But knowing you were still with me eased my nerves a bit.

The Fox *tsked*. "S'too bad, but it doesn't change the facts."

We stared each other down, me feeling my confidence waver but not letting it show. The Fox's face was long, the hairs all groomed in one direction, sleek and shiny like fish scales. It was hard to discern emotion in that face. I had never tried to read expressions in animals before, only humans. It also didn't help that this was the first talking animal I'd yet encountered.

"We'll buy it from you."

At this, the Fox perked up instantly. His ears sprang skyward and his mouth broke into a wide grin. I glanced back at you, seeing the confusion in your face. You knew we had nothing he would want, but I was hoping you'd trust me and follow my lead.

"Yes, I wouldn't say no to a fair purchase," the Fox said. His tone was more pleasant now. Expectant. "What do you have for me?"

"I have the best, most mouth-watering peaches you've ever tasted," I proclaimed.

To my surprise, the Fox seemed puzzled. "What," he asked, "are peaches?"

My smile was genuine. "Why, only the best, sweetest fruit in the whole wide world."

He was licking his lips.

"Peaches can be firm, but your teeth sink right in, like they're butter that's been left on the window sill. Their skin has a light fuzz that's soft on your tongue. And from the first bite, a tangy nectar gushes into your mouth and down your throat." I was doing my best, using all the descriptions we'd learned in Mrs. Alma's class. I could see it was working, which only encouraged me.

"I want them," he said, greed in his eyes. "Where are these peaches?"

"I don't have them with me," I said. At once, he became angry.

"What do you mean, you don't have them? How dare you taunt me like that? Leading me on and getting me all hungry just to tell me you lied to me?" He bared his teeth and hunched on all fours, back curled menacingly.

I lifted the magic box in front of me. "I have something better. I have the seeds." And I opened it, tilting the container forward so he could see the pits.

"What is this?" he asked suspiciously.

"I can see your apple trees were knocked over," I said. I gestured around the circle of snapped stumps. "They look like they've died, but if you plant these in their place, you will have all the peaches you could ever want."

He seemed to mull this over, standing upright again, hand to his chin. He nodded. "Yes, the Palakostos killed my apple trees and they won't grow back. These trees were here even before I came to these woods and now they're gone forever.

Your peaches sound delicious, but how can I make a peach tree from those rocks?" he asked, gesturing at the pits.

I considered this. "I will plant them for you by the stream so they get plenty of water. In a short time, they will grow into peach trees that bear fruit for you."

"How many trees?"

"Seven trees for my wristwatch," I said.

"Deal," the Fox said, and pointed at the chest. "Now make my peach trees."

"Not until you give me back my watch." Now that I knew I could negotiate with this character, I could hold my ground.

The Fox pointed at you. "Your friend can retrieve your watch while you make my trees."

I nodded—these were reasonable terms. While you walked into the clearing, I went down toward the bank and began digging holes with my hands. I remembered seeing my daddy planting a lemon tree in the backyard, and figured I could do just the same. It didn't take too long, and before I knew it, all seven peach pits were buried in the earth. I even ran back and forth to the stream, cupping water in my hands to wet the soil. I had no idea if they were going to grow or not, and I didn't want to cheat the Fox, but I had the feeling the seeds would take just fine. The box had given us a backup plan, knowing we'd eat all the fruit.

You were standing by the Fox when I finished, saying something about fishing. In your hands was my slightly less shiny wristwatch, though I was sure I could polish it back to something like its original self. The Fox was much kinder now that we'd done a deal with him and the sumptuous peaches I'd described were in his future. I told him to pour some water over the mounds where I'd put the seeds daily. He told me my watch was beautiful, and I should take good care of it. Then we nodded at each other in understanding and parted ways.

You climbed a tree and spotted our yellow balloon straightaway. We followed it home and the Fox sank back into the woods. I fastened the watch around my wrist, eager to show it off to my mama, even though it would tip her off that I'd lost it.

I wonder where that watch ended up. I know that for at least a couple years, you would've had to pry it from my lifeless wrist to get it off me, but somewhere along the line it must've fallen out of my favor. I don't remember ever getting rid of it. Wouldn't that have been too much of me, to ask my younger self to keep it? Thinking on it now makes me miss my parents. I have some things of theirs, but that would have been something special to hold on to.

I look forward to hearing from you again.

Melancholy but at peace,
Maddy

***

September 2

Noll,

I was beginning to wonder if I was going to hear from you again. Thought maybe I had said something in that last letter I couldn't remember that might have been insulting. You're doing alright though?

We had everybody over for dinner this past Sunday. Jack

likes to put on old movies (you know, the ones that were new in our day?) after the meal for everybody to watch together while we nibble on whatever fruit tart I've got made up. We got to telling stories though, and Marne and Neil were chomping at the bit trying to get me to say that none of this affair with the box could've really happened. It had to have been our imagination when we were kids. I couldn't help laughing at how hard they were trying to get me to talk, but I told them that what I knew was what I knew. It doesn't matter much if it was *real* or not, does it? Not anymore, at least. We both know what happened, and that's all I can say.

Marne kept this look in her eye the whole time, this "in-the-know" look, if you catch my meaning. Skeptical and all, like I'm putting on a show and couldn't *really* believe any of it. Maybe she's got more of me inside her than I thought.

Anyways, I've had a thought and I really want to get to it. I can't tell you (but I'm being so cruel by mentioning it, aren't I?) until I've gone through with my plan though, so no asking. You'll find out soon, alright?

You said it was Kate's birthday coming up this week, yeah? Well, I hope you have a fantastic time celebrating. Do you think you could give me an idea of what she might like? I want to send her a little something too. Thanks, Noll. Hear from you soon.

On the hunt,
Maddy

***

September 18

Noll,

I thought I'd wait for your response, but I don't know
when I'll get one and I'm a bit excited. I thought you'd be
hounding me looking for answers after my teasing in the last
letter, but no matter.

I'm looking for the box, Noll! I was thinking that for the
life of me, I couldn't remember what had happened to it, but
I didn't think I'd thrown it away. Something like that I would
have remembered the moment I saw it and—although I'm
not the most sentimental person—wouldn't have been able to
bring myself to dispose of it. So it must have moved with me
from my folks' place. I'm sure.

Trouble is, I don't know where. We don't have storage,
meaning it's got to be in either the attic or the basement.
Anyway, I hope you aren't on me for being too tart with that
guessing game and all. I hope to hear from you soon.

Working on patience,
Maddy

***

September 29

Noll,

Look, I'm sorry for whatever it is I've done. Please, don't
be angry with me, Noll. You never gave me the cold shoulder
when we were younger, those few times we bickered. So I
can't imagine why you would now. You got me worried. I
don't like being worried.

I sent Kate a box of bridge mix for her birthday because who doesn't like bridge mix? Hopefully, it will be there soon. I didn't want to get anything else because I don't know much about what she likes.

If you could tell me what I've done, Noll, I can assure you it wasn't intentional. I will gladly apologize. I've been having so much fun reminiscing with you these past couple months. It's helped me bring back things I didn't even know I'd forgotten. The dry wheat smell running around in those fields, the taste of my neighbor's cherries we were always after, the smooth gloss of the paint on the walls of the Corner House. These were things I took for granted, then cherished, then forgot. And I got them back just for a few weeks. I hope you won't leave with them now.

Please, respond, Noll. I'm asking nicely. Please.

Sorry and Anxious,
Maddy

***

October 5

Noll,

I got the letter from Raynor. He let me know what's been happening.

Dossett Hospital? Why didn't you tell me? Why didn't you let me know? All this time I've been writing to you, going on and on about myself and how my life's been and telling all these stories from our childhood, reading out of some little notebook I'd scribbled in as a girl, and you've been in the hospital? You've been suffering? I don't know what to say now, except that I'm terribly sorry. I'm sorry to hear what you've been going through.

Your son is a nice boy. Raynor explained the situation to me. He's very eloquent. You've done right by him, Noll. He sounds like a strong young man, and as good a father as I imagine you were.

I almost feel like I shouldn't say this, but I found the box just like I was hoping I would. Wouldn't you know it, it was in the basement in a larger crate full of all these old things I'd decided to keep—clothes and whatnot. So much for not being overly sentimental. It was sitting there, beside folded T-shirts from summer camp, looking exactly like it did in my mind. Maybe a little more worse for wear, but nonetheless that same box you found at the edge of the woods.

And wouldn't you know, I couldn't get it open. I tried and tried. I pried at it with my fingers, took a screwdriver to it, everything we tried back then. But same as always, it didn't budge. Maybe we didn't make this all up after all. Isn't that right? Maybe we're not a couple of old buffoons.

After a while I just set it down on a shelf and sat back, smiling a little to myself. I wish you could see it, Noll. I wish you could hold it again. The sensation was transportive. Rejuvenating. I really wish you could see it. It makes me think that things are going to get better. Finding the box somehow makes me think you're going to be alright.

Happy, hopeful,
Maddy

***

October 14

Noll,

You don't need to get all uppity, you grandpa. I just wasn't sure if you wanted me to keep babbling on about our adventures. I mean, we both know what happens next and it's not something that's going to lift any spirits. You need spirit-lifting. No amount of you getting on my case is going to change that.

I guess I've got to do what you want though, don't I? Especially if you're going to be pulling that "I'm the one in the hospital" malarkey. So, here it goes.

The day my parents told me we were going to be moving was the worst day of my short life. I was completely unprepared for it, expecting the talk they wanted to have that night to be about school starting back up or about going off to the woods. I was not ready for something much worse.

I didn't even know what to do. Thinking about who I was then, I would think that I would've run off to tell you. It was too late in the evening though, and while I was Miss Independent, I still got the feeling I couldn't leave at that time of night. Instead, I went to my room and I cried. I cried for hours and did nothing else, lying on my bed with my pillow hugged to my chest. How could they do that to me? This was my *world*. This was everything that meant something to me. My school and my friends. This house, this neighborhood, the Corner House, the fields and the woods beyond it. You. I couldn't imagine that anything worth my time was outside those bounds. I may have hated them that night. I may have been so hurt.

But the box opened.

At first, I didn't want to see what was inside. Suspicion clouded my mind; I had to consider the possibility that this box was what was making my parents and me move. What if they knew I'd been going into the woods more frequently? What if they knew I was having grander adventures at its discretion?

But the box knew what was needed, and how could I forgo that? I was the one in such need now. Me. Surely it knew that.

So I opened the box and inside I found a hunting knife. It was wrapped in a worn leather sheath, a dark brown that could've also been green. The handle was wrapped tightly in a leather rope as well, small enough that my nine-year-old hand could just grip it well. The blade, when I pulled it out, was just as long as my hand. Heavy. And though the metal was dull, the edge looked incredibly sharp.

Why had the box given me a knife? For a moment that is frightening to me now, I considered that maybe it wanted me to hurt either myself or my family. Is that how I was going to keep us from moving? Was I supposed to injure someone enough that we didn't follow through? Thankfully, the thought passed as it wasn't logical to me. A cut wasn't going to do more than slow us down. This only made the knife more confusing.

I could see the moon high in the sky, so I knew there was no way I could go tell you about anything that had happened right then. Not the impending move, nor the knife. Instead, after staring at the knife for what I wrote was a couple hours, I set it on my bedside table and fell into restless sleep.

At first light, I was out the door and sprinting to the Corner House. The box was under my arm as usual, but

I'd put the knife in my pocket. Maybe it was going to help me hunt and I would live out in the woods. Hide until my folks had finally moved away and I could stay there in peace. You'd help me, wouldn't you? Of course you would—I knew you weren't going to want me to leave either.

You weren't in your room. Your mama said you were out back, but I didn't find you in the yard either. I was getting angry, unable to let you in on my plan, which I needed to enact as soon as possible. I ran back into your room, wondering if maybe you were hiding in your closet and I hadn't seen. If that were the case, I was going to have to give you a mouthful because this wasn't the time for games.

I found something else. Moss had been splashed over your window sill. When I say splashed, I mean it looked like someone had taken moss and thrown some down over the wooden boards like they were flinging paint from a brush. There was some across your desk. A little on your floor.

That's when I knew you had been kidnapped. Blood rushed to my head. I'd been in deep trouble before, but that was the first time I could remember having my pulse pounding in my ears that loudly. I wanted to throw up. I thought about telling your parents, but I knew they couldn't do anything for you in this case. It wasn't a *who* that had taken you. It was a *what*. And I had a sneaking suspicion the both of you had gone back into the forest.

I ran.

I ran as fast as I could, the tall grass in the field behind your house whipping at my face. There was nobody to chase me. I couldn't look back and see you a few steps behind. The isolation felt devastating. It brought the gravity of the situation more firmly upon me. I crossed the line of trees at a sprint, dodging the underbrush and the upturned tree roots as

I went. I had no bearing but my gut, but I didn't bother
taking a rest to think about a heading. I just ran. In-between
boulders, ducking beneath branches, hopping over a stream.

Then I rounded a patch of trees and there you were, tied
to a trunk by thin, mossy vines. You had those wide eyes,
fearful and innocent. Struggling against your bonds. I dashed
forward and tore out the knife to cut you loose.

"It came to my room last night," you said, out of breath
with fear.

"What did?" I asked.

Your response was only, "We have to hurry." You must've
been out there for hours. How deep in the night had it come?
Was it already morning when it opened your window? Had it
been watching us? You took a good look at what I was
holding while I cut the last of the vines around your
ankles. "Where'd you get that?"

I only needed to look up at you for you to know.

Then arose the slither of dry leaves sliding quickly across
each other. It was sharp, loud, and close. The box! I had set it
down to cut you loose. I turned to see it lassoed and sliding
away into the woods.

Snapping the last bond so you were free, I leapt after it. As
I did so, a rope made of that same mossy vine that had held
you descended around my knees. I fell hard, slamming into
the unforgiving ground, sliding alongside the box into the
tangle of trees and bushes. Working quickly, I rolled onto my
side, grabbed the box, and started sawing at the vine around
it as we were dragged. I couldn't let whatever this was take it.
I just couldn't. Even if my own life was at stake, I was going
to save this box first.

The box came free and I threw it behind me to where you
were coming up at a hustle. "Run!" I shouted. "Don't let it

get it!'"

Then there was a deafening roar. It sounded like a thousand age-old trees cracking as they fell.

I stopped sliding. A hulking figure emerged from the shadows, a man made of the woods. His feet were oozing wet clay, his legs made of twisting, gnarled tree roots. His torso was a mass of solid leaves and his arms were tangles of thick ivy. His head was a rough stone with contorted facial features formed of moss. He had to be as tall as my daddy, but even wider in the shoulders. I was more afraid of him than I'd ever been of anything else.

He started reeling me in again.

Screaming, I clutched the knife in my palm and got to work cutting my own rope. For some reason, it felt like cutting myself free was taking much longer than it had taken to cut the box. I sawed at the vine, the progress not coming as fast as I would've liked, getting pulled closer to that thing. It was clawing at me with one hand while pulling me forward with the other.

Finally, the vine was thin enough that it snapped. I scrambled to undo the knot at my knees, not caring that my stockings were more holes than solid now. The thing was roaring again and I threw myself into a run.

You were standing some ways off, thunderstruck on the spot with the box hugged tight. "Go!" I shouted, waving my arms.

The man—I didn't know what else to call him—was lumbering after me, his heaving footfalls shaking the ground, sending leaves tumbling and dirt falls sliding down into the stream. That woke you up and you turned to run with me. I don't remember what I was shouting but I know I was shouting the whole time. We jumped across the creek.

Then I stopped running and turned on the spot.

"What are you doing, Maddy?" you asked. I could see you debating whether to keep running or stay with me.

"It wants the box," I said firmly. "It wants to take it from us."

"What?" you asked, looking down at the magic box in your arms.

"Hey! Over here!" I shouted, jumping up and down. Good Lord, I was crazy, wasn't I? I did a dance on that bank, making a racket no creature could have missed. You were still debating whether to go, but you didn't. You stayed with me until the end. "Look at what we've got!"

And the man came galumphing out of the trees. He saw us and immediately let out a bellow, one that shook me until I couldn't see straight. I could feel the fear churning my stomach, but still I held my ground, putting my hands on my hips in a defiant pose.

"You looking for this?" I asked, pointing to the chest in your hands. You looked like your knees almost gave out in that moment. Maybe I was using you as bait, just a little bit—I apologize now. "Hold it out," I commanded in a harsh whisper, and you complied with reluctance.

The thing slammed its fist to the ground, another round of leaves tumbling from above and streaks of dirt sliding from the bank. The howl echoed through the forest above. Then it raised its fist and a vine unfurled into the air like a whip.

"Ready?" I asked, and slid behind you. I wrapped my arms around your waist, vowing to never let go.

The vine caught the box. You squeezed and I squeezed. The beast on the other end pulled and we did the same, throwing our nine-year-old bodies back. For a fleeting moment I remember thinking there was no way we were any match, but I got my feet behind some boulders stuck deep in the earth and you dug your feet in and we *made* ourselves a match. We gave all our strength, my arms shaking, holding you tight, sweat dripping from the top of my head. Fought like the nastiest game of tug-o'-war I ever played. I think you were shouting—I was probably squeezing you too hard, but I knew neither of us wanted to let go.

Then the miraculous happened. That thing gave an inch. It gave a foot. Then another.

"Almost there," I grunted. Another surge of strength I didn't know I had came forth. With an almighty tug, the man stepped forward again, only this time his foot came down in the creek. He sank and I knew I was right; the water was grabbing hold of his clay feet. We had him now. The last pull was easy. His other foot came down into the water, and with a roar that shook my insides he was stuck.

With some difficulty, I took out the knife again and managed to cut the vine still roped around the box. We were free. We ran, never looking back. I don't know how we found our way. We didn't stop, didn't think about where we were going. Just ran. I was faster as always, but you were never more than a few steps behind. And when we broke out into the tall grass, I knew you were with me, the long yellow grains rising high into the air, sliding past like a blanket of sun.

When finally we came to a halt at the Corner House, panting and filthy and collapsing to the ground, you asked me, "You think he's stuck there forever?"

"No," I said, staring up from where I lay on the ground. "Only for now."

"How did it find us?"

I had caught my breath. Without another word, I stood. You did too. With steady steps, I walked into the house. You followed. Climbed the stairs, making sure to tread only on the ones that didn't creak. You did the same. Up to your room, where light streamed through the window, not a lick of moss in sight. You behind me. I slid the window open and climbed out onto the awning beneath. You were my shadow. Up the trellis we went, pulling ourselves onto the very peak of the Corner House, nothing but the wind and the sun and the sky around us.

I took out the knife, stepped over to the chimney, and cut the string which tethered the yellow balloon.

It had begun to deflate, but it was buoyant enough that it flew away, shrinking into the sky from out of my fingers. We stood shoulder to shoulder on the roof, watching it soar up… and up… and up…

Then it was gone.

"I'm gonna miss you, Maddy," you said.

"How'd you know I'm leaving?" I asked.

"My daddy told me last night."

They must've planned it. They knew how hard we'd both take the news. I might've felt a flare of anger back then. Now? I think they knew how good of friends we were. I think they were aware of everything that had happened, to some extent at least, and maybe it pained them to pull us apart, but that pain was unavoidable. For reasons unknown to me, sometimes life, inextricably, pulls friends apart.

"You should keep the box," you told me. I protested. After all, you were the one who found it. Even if I had it most of the time, it was rightfully yours. "That might be true," you said, "but that's why I want you to have it. Maybe having something of mine will keep us connected no matter what happens or where you go."

You were right, Noll. It did.

Braver Than I Feel,

Maddy

***

October 23

Noll,

I'm not sending this letter. I know that I'm never going to get a response. Not anymore. Raynor told me what happened. He sent me all the letters back saying I should have them. But what am I going to do with them, Noll? Please, I don't know. It's like holding all I've got left of you when they're in my hands. I don't want that. I want to see my friend again, in the flesh and as lively as we were any of those summer days when we had the comfort of youth.

It broke my heart to see those words.

Jack says we can go down there for the funeral. You know I'm going, but it makes me feel like a hypocrite knowing how I said I couldn't visit before I knew there was anything wrong. I couldn't make the effort to see you when you were alive, but now I can? Isn't that how it always goes?

The worst part is, the box finally opened this morning. I don't know what I did, but I was able to flip the latch easy as if it'd just been greased. I'm a little ashamed admitting this, but I was the tiniest bit hopeful that maybe there'd be one of those yew branches inside waiting for me. Maybe I'd be able to whip something up like Mrs. Akeso did. Maybe I'd add it to some soup and come running down there to save the day. Maybe that would've been enough and you'd have been alright then.

Of course, the box was empty. It was always going to be empty. I knew that, even if it made my heart sink a little bit. It was just a box and, even though we had some pretty fun adventures as kids, it always had been. You know, maybe those stories didn't happen the way we remember, but I'm sure to some degree they're real. And that's all that matters in the end, isn't it? That's all that ever means anything.

So I put our letters in the box and I set it out on my bookshelf. I know they're there and they're safe, should I ever need them. I can always go back and see you whenever I want. Spend some time in the woods and at the Corner House where our families mingled on the warm nights, my daddy playing guitar and your mama and papa singing. My mama couldn't hit a note if it came with a target, but she knew how to get the two of us dancing.

Wouldn't you know, the latch doesn't work anymore. I must have busted it when I was trying to get the thing open. It's a funny old world, isn't it, Noll?

Always Your Friend,
Maddy

BELOW A LOBSTER

The woman walked up to him holding a rather large book in her rather thin arms. She didn't appear to struggle at all, which made him wonder if the book wasn't as heavy as it looked or if she was much stronger than anyone he'd ever met. She dropped an arm to grab a quill from behind her ear and didn't wobble at all, balancing the massive tome on the other hand.

"You were most recently Harold Atwater?" she asked.

Ah, he should have known. She was an attendant. That made sense. She wasn't like him then. Didn't care nothing about physics, did she? He nodded and stood, leaving the rock he'd been resting on.

"That's me, ma'am."

"Good." She made a note in the expansive volume. "You've been here for four Earth years, is that correct?"

"That's right," he said, "and before that, two years of haunting."

Had he really been here for four years? To be honest he'd lost track of time. There weren't exactly *days* in the afterlife, were there? No, the sun didn't shine and the moon never waned, but the clocks moved and so he guessed time still had to exist. Besides which, what did it matter if he questioned her? She wasn't going to be wrong.

"I'm Holly," the attendant said, peering over the top of the book. "Let's get you reassigned."

"Oh, is it my turn?" Harold asked.

Goodness. He hadn't realized there'd be no warning. Well, he'd been told there wouldn't be any warning, but he'd never thought there'd *actually* be no warning. He'd always assumed at some point he'd have an inkling his reassignment was on the approach. Maybe he'd get to be an English chap again. Yeah, that'd be good. He'd never done nothing wrong, after all.

Holly smiled. "That it is." She ran her finger across the page, reading type that must have been very small, for she moved so very little each time she started a new line. Curious, Harold leaned forward, trying to get a peek over the top, but the attendant happened to shift just enough that he couldn't see each time he moved.

"I hope I get something good," Harold mused with a hearty laugh that Holly did not reciprocate. "I heard this Lottie woman I met got reassigned as a lobster. Imagine that? Shells and whatnot. I wouldn't fancy showing up on a hungry bloke's plate, you know?"

Holly gave him a half-hearted grin and continued reading. "Ah, here we go," she said at last.

Harold rubbed his meaty hands together.

"Let's see. You've been assigned as a cabbage."

"A cabbage?" Harold slapped himself on the forehead in disbelief. Of all the things he could have received as reassignment, and he was destined to be a vegetable? "You've got to be joking."

"I don't joke," Holly said. Maybe she had never told a joke in her entire existence.

"But how can I be a cabbage?" he asked. "I was a good person."

"Well…" Holly shrugged. "*Good* might be a strong term. You didn't save anybody, you didn't teach anyone anything—"

"So I was an alright person."

"—you didn't have any hobbies, you didn't make any trips anywhere—"

"Yeah, but I didn't *murder* nobody. I didn't *steal* things!"

"That is true," she said, then put a finger back on the page, tracing a line. "It seems a large part of what's against you is how you died."

"How I died?"

"It was kind of a useless death. 'Preventable' is the term used here."

"I choked on my mouth guard!"

"Yes, but you could have woken up your wife for help or called an ambulance. Instead, you tried to drive yourself to the hospital and crashed along the way."

"Ah… well, it seemed like an alright idea at the time, but I could see why that's bad. Yeah," Harold mumbled, crossing his arms. Then he shook his head. "A cabbage, though? That's what the exchange is?"

Holly's eyes scanned the page until she raised a hand and shrugged as if to say there was nothing she could do.

"A human's completely out of the question?"

Holly laughed. She actually laughed. Then, as if realizing he hadn't cracked a smile, struggled to regain her composure. She shook her head. "Sorry, no."

"You can't make an exception?"

"We had four hundred thousand births yesterday from bumping people up a class. That was a bit over the average. We can't possibly afford two sequential days of the sort. Plus, you just haven't got it in your charts."

"What about, like, a giraffe or something? You know, the tall ones?" He raised his hand as high as it could go. "They're rather nice."

"Mmm." Holly shook her head again. "No, see, to get a giraffe, you'd have to have taken care of someone elderly for at least eighteen months. Then you might've also been a thief and still qualified."

"Well, what about a bird? They've got little brains, not much pleasure there."

"Yeah, but they fly. That's a bonus."

"Alright, what about, like—like a toad or something?"

She consulted the book, mouth moving quickly as she read. "It says you could murder one person and still get toad, but… ah, you had to have positively impacted fourteen lives."

"*Fourteen?* Damn." He scratched his chin. "What about trees?"

She smiled again. "I'm getting the hang of your jokes, Harold. The best souls are trees. They live hundreds of years, closest thing you lot can get to immortality."

"Who makes up these bloody rules?"

"Not me."

"Lobster?"

Holly shut the book and put a comforting hand on Harold's shoulder. Her touch was like ice through his clothes. He wanted to squirm away, but felt the gesture wouldn't better his chances any. "Look, Harold. I can see you're a nice soul, but it's not in the cards for you this time. Being a cabbage… it's not all bad."

"That's easy for you to say—you're a timeless, immortal being perceived by the beholder as their idealized form of beauty."

"Yes, yes, but besides all that, I really do understand," she said. "Just be the best cabbage you can be, and before you know it your soul will end up right back here and we'll have something new ready."

"The best cabbage…" Harold huffed, dropping his head in his hands. He stayed this way for a few moments while the attendant waited patiently. "I suppose it'll only be, like, four months or so."

"That's the spirit, Harold."

"You think I can be a good cabbage?"

"Oh, you'll be a great cabbage."

"People like cabbages."

"That's right. You'll be full of nutrients. Kids need their greens. And all the best family recipes have got cabbage in them, haven't they?" She nodded.

"I suppose they have. Mine always did."

Holly beamed. Her brilliant, shining teeth and wide clear eyes were quite persuasive.

Harold smiled, Holly's encouragement catching. "All I've got to do is grow, right?"

"That's it."

"And I'll be on a better page."

"You'll always be on the same page of the book— it's *your* page."

"What was that?"

"I said, 'Best damn page we've got.'"

"Alright." Harold placed his hands on his hips. "Alright, I

can be a cabbage."

"That's great," Holly said. She opened the massive tome back to the same page as before, where the quill still rested against the fold. "All you've got to do is sign here."

When she tipped the book forward, there was nothing but blank sheets with a line and an "X" for his signature. Harold took the quill and scribbled his name, wondering if this was the last time he'd use it. He was about to become a cabbage, after all, and cabbages didn't have names like Harold, did they?

With a snap, Holly closed the book again.

"Thank you very much, sir," she said, and gave him a sort of salute. "You have a nice life."

"That I will," Harold said. "That I will."

MOMENTS OF CLARITY

Clouds covered the sun, confusing the dusk with the dawn. The lone car turned off the road and onto the barely paved lane winding into the trees. Renee watched the fork disappearing in her rearview mirror and thought to herself how odd it was that even though she'd lived here once, she didn't know where the other road went. She'd be staying for a while now, though. She could take time to check.

Then the lane curved and she lost sight of the fork completely.

Aspens dominated the landscape on either side of the road, their shimmering leaves like fishing lures in the faded light. As she drove, the leaves caught memories from her mind and pulled them out of the fog. She'd never have guessed she'd miss this place, but here she was watching herself play capture the flag in the forest with Alberto, Jean, and Lucinda. A small smile curled the corner of her mouth—just a small one. Good memories could lead to bad ones as well.

She blinked the thought away. Now was not the time to let

insecurities about her sister get in the way. Jealousy, her therapist had recently pronounced. Jealousy had driven her hatred for Claudia. Being in someone's shadow could make anyone feel that about a person. Even the nicest could be the subject of jealousy—not that Claudia was the nicest; she had her petty moments. Still, it was time for Renee to leave that behind and perform her duties as a daughter. She had been neglectful until this point, discouraged by Claudia's presence in their mother's house. That had to end. She could not let her mother die a stranger.

The lane ended at the foot of a brown-and-gold house. Two floors stacked neatly one on top of the other like a double-layer cake. A disheveled hedgerow and garden path wrapped around the ground level, once the perfect arena for tag. Most of the brown shutters were closed, though a few windows had one or both swung wide. At the very least, Claudia had kept the siding as pristine as it had been the last time Renee had been here, a decade prior.

Stepping out of the car, Renee stretched. She pulled out her phone and saw that she had one voicemail. Claudia's voice spoke in her ear.

"Hi, Renee. Glad you're coming, I can't wait to see you. Mum is excited too—when I told her she positively lit up. So thanks for coming. I had to go into town to post some things to my clients, but the nurse should still be there when you arrive. I asked her to stick around since, well, you know… since Mum can't be alone. It shouldn't take me too long though. Your old room is still open if you want it"— Claudia laughed to herself— "Anyway, I'll see you in a bit. Bye."

Renee snapped the phone shut and opened the boot. Had Mum really been excited to see her? Renee was skeptical. Those sorts of reactions didn't exist for their mother anymore. Renee would never truly know, though, whether that statement was accurate. And at least in its mythical validity, she could smile at feeling potentially welcome. That was better than being unwanted for sure.

The slam of the boot was absorbed by the trees. Renee struggled to hold her suitcase up at her side. One hand on its handle, the other wrapped around that of her duffel. She mounted the front steps, then set the suitcase down while she rummaged for her key. It fit smoothly into the lock, the same as it had ten years ago. The door opened with a scrape and then she was inside her childhood home.

Renee stood in the doorway, a breeze at her back. Everything was exactly as she remembered. A mélange of seventies furniture: the box television with bug antennae on top, vinyl armchairs of mustard yellow, hexagonal hanging lights with floral plastic casings that threw an amber glow over the room, the pressed-wood coffee and end tables. She might've choked up a bit, but instead she cleared her throat. She was home.

Renee closed the door and the quiet grew. Ticking reached her ears and she immediately turned to the grandfather clock sitting in the corner by the fireplace.

"Mum," she called. "Mum, I'm here. Nurse Aoife, it's Renee, Andrea's other daughter."

No response came.

Renee pulled her things up the stairs, having to take multiple breaks to keep from dropping the suitcase. If only she hadn't packed so heavily—but if she were going to be living here for as many months as she expected, she had to be comfortable. Renee left her luggage on the landing. She could come back for it later; she was overcome with the urge to see her mother first. Down the hall parallel to the stairs she went. Her mum's room was the closed door at the end. The click of her shoes was foreign on the hard wood; they had always been sock-footed indoors.

"Nurse Aoife?" Renee gripped the door handle; the knob was cold. She turned it and pushed. "Nurse Aoife?"

Andrea stood in her pale blue linen nighty. Her frail and wrinkled hands gripped the window sill as she stared out into the cloudy sky. Behind her, the bed was messy, sheets strewn onto the floor, the duvet bundled at the foot. Renee entered the room. No nurse in sight. She picked up a newspaper from the floor, folded it and placed it on the chest of drawers. Then she shut a box on the writing desk and slid the latch into place. Her mother watched her do this with quiet reproach on her face.

"Be careful with that," she said. "Liam Whitcomb gave that to me when I was a tot. Don't go breaking it."

Renee stood straight, a careful distance from the box with its sleek surfaces painted to look like a forest of birch trees. Her mother's statement was true, which was promising. Then Andrea continued.

"This is my house, you know. I don't know why there are so many strangers fussing about, but they'd better leave before Charles gets back. He won't take any of their nonsense. Not any of it." Her voice shook so much when she talked her words were hard to understand. "Do you hear me?"

Renee found herself frozen to the spot. She didn't know what she'd expected; she'd been told about her mother's condition, of course, but facing the reality stole her breath from her. Again, she might've felt a lump in her throat, but she cleared it with a cough.

"Did you hear me?" Andrea repeated. "I don't know who you think you are, bursting in here, but Charles will not be happy. He will *not*."

Renee blinked furiously, then put on a forced smile. "It's me, Mum," she said. "It's your daughter, Renee."

"Renee." Andrea huffed. "Well, I suppose. My daughter Renee went off to university, you know. She's a lawyer."

"I'm a painter," Renee muttered. "Let's get you back into bed, Mum."

***

Renee walked back down the hallway. Every once in a while she shook her head, partially in disbelief and partially in an attempt to clear the swirling thoughts. She had not expected to greet her mother for the first time alone. Claudia was supposed to be here, as was the nurse. The house was definitely empty, though. Had the nurse left without waiting for Renee like she was supposed to? Renee hadn't arrived any later than she'd estimated. If that was the case, it was very irresponsible on the nurse's part.

Renee traipsed back into the living room, her steps taking her where she hadn't consciously decided to go. Muscle memory still held, then; she still knew this place as if she'd left yesterday. She walked right up to the grandfather clock and gazed into its face, tracing the elegant strokes of the numbers. Above the hands, a moving dial tracked the lunar cycle. Renee had always loved this because an old ship was painted above the dial as if it were sailing over the moon.

Hurried steps.

Renee's heart lurched and she turned just in time to see a man heading toward her. Screaming, she ducked beneath his

135

arms, which clutched at the spot where she'd been standing.

Renee ran from the room, her heart pounding in her ears. She fled back to the stairs. "Mum!" she called, taking the steps two at a time. On the top step, her heel missed the edge and she came down on her knee with a bang.

Renee moaned. Stillness ensued. There were no signs that the man pursued her. She looked down the flight of stairs. There was nobody there. Who the hell was he? Why had he lunged for her?

Struggling to slow her pulse, Renee stood. Her knee pained her but it didn't seem to be injured. She stood on the landing, one hand on the rail, and listened with intent. The faint ticks of the clock found their way to her, but nothing else. No one else's footsteps. No moving furniture. Nothing.

Had she imagined him? No, that wasn't possible. He had definitely been real. He had been so solid. And the air had moved around him when he darted for her. She'd felt his presence just as she could have anyone else's. He couldn't have been in her imagination.

Then where had he gone? He wasn't just standing down there waiting for her. Renee reached into her bag, which still sat beside her old bedroom door, and pulled out her umbrella. It wouldn't provide much defense, but it was better than nothing. Slowly, so as not to make any noise, she crept back to the stairs.

First step, then another, then another. She moved down, slightly crouched, umbrella poised at the ready. The silence persisted, but as far as she knew, he could be doing the same as she: creeping along the other side of the wall. Waiting for her to turn the corner. Renee reached the bottom and spun around the divide.

The living room was empty.

How could that be?

Running water.

Dropping the umbrella on the couch, Renee moved quickly to the fireplace and snatched up one of the pokers. With the weight of the iron tool, she felt more empowered. See him try to lunge at her now. The running water was coming from the ground-floor bathroom, and unless she was mistaken, it was the tap filling the bathtub. Was the man trying to distract her? Make it so that she couldn't hear him walking about? What was he doing here?

As she drew closer to the bathroom, Renee heard a voice. Only, it wasn't a man's voice but a woman's. She was muttering to herself, quick quips that were abnormally punctuated and which Renee couldn't understand over the din. Even so, she could tell the woman was aggravated. Nurse Aoife? Renee drew closer and the words became clearer.

"... looking like that. What do you think they'll say about us? Eh? You think they'll look *kindly* on our family with a daughter all made up running around looking like a hussy? But of course, you don't care about any of that. You don't care how we feel, do you? Well, you don't get a choice this time. I'm washing all of that off you now. I'm going to clean your filthy body..."

Renee stepped into the doorway. A woman with wiry blonde hair sat on the edge of the tub. Her black skirt fanned over her legs and toward the tiled floor. As Renee stood there, the woman turned to look at her. She dragged on a cigarette, eyes red and tears spilling down her face. This was definitely not the nurse.

Dread seized Renee's heart as she and the woman locked eyes. For a moment, they only stared, the woman puffing heavily on her vice.

"I don't know why you put us through so much turmoil. My hair is turning gray. Just look at it," the woman said. She stood, her skirt flowing like shadows around her. Her sensible maroon heels knocked on the floor tiles. Hurt and anger furrowed her brow. "Come here. *Come here now and take off those clothes.*"

Seized by fear, Renee reached forward and grabbed the bathroom door. She slammed it closed and held tight to the handle. It rattled violently and several times the woman on the other side slammed her palm against it, shrieking at Renee.

"You come in here right now and let me wash the filth off you!"

The door shuddered, the handle shaking against Renee's hold. And then it all went still.

Renee realized she was breathing heavily, gasping from constricted lungs. She could still smell the cigarette fumes but they were fading quickly. How could that be? Had the woman extinguished it?

Was she still in there?

After a full minute of nothing, Renee released the knob and backed away from the door. Nobody tried to get out. Silence.

First the lunging man and now the blonde woman. Who were these people? Were they ghosts? What were they doing in her mother's house? Renee's head spun and she clutched it with both her hands. These were real apparitions. She wasn't going crazy—*couldn't* be going crazy. And if she wasn't crazy, then her mother was in real danger.

Still clutching the poker, Renee headed back toward the stairs. She would gather her mother's most important things and convince her that they had to go. Maybe she could tell

138

her Charles was waiting in the car if Andrea didn't want to move. It didn't matter that Renee's father had died twelve years before; if her mother had been saying his name not even an hour ago she'd believe the excuse. Then they'd wait outside for Claudia's return. Did Claudia know about the apparitions? Had any of this been happening when Claudia was here? And what about Nurse Aoife?

As Renee crossed the doorway of the kitchen, a shrill scream sounded. A body tumbled into view. It hit the kitchen floor with a sick thud, a hand falling out through the doorway into the hall. Renee jumped, screaming and flattening herself against the opposite wall. A woman, this one with short, curly gray hair, sprawled on the linoleum. She wheezed and turned her head up to look at Renee.

"Help me," she croaked, and grasped for Renee's ankle.

Renee bolted. The woman's voice wheezed after her, but she didn't register what she said. Her heart was pounding for the third time that hour. What the hell was happening? No. It didn't matter. She had to get her mother out of there.

"*Andrea!*" A boy with puffy eyes, holding out a broken doll. In an effort to get out of his way, Renee flung herself into a display table and pain ricocheted through her body from her ribcage.

"Shit!" she cried out, swinging the poker wide as she tried to steady herself. It stuck into the wall, tearing a hole in the plasterboard. The boy stood watching her, pieces of the disfigured doll clutched in his hands. Behind him, the gray-haired woman was dragging her body through the kitchen doorway, still gasping for help.

Water running.

Sputtering incoherently, Renee righted herself and continued down the hall. She clutched her side with her free hand, hoping the ribs were only bruised.

"Mum!" she called. "Mum, hold on, I'm coming."

The living room.

The man from before was standing by the grandfather clock, his mouth split wide in a grin. Renee turned the corner and started up the stairs, keeping her eye on him as she went. When she reached the second step, he moved.

Renee let out another yell and fled. His running steps filled her ears and she knew any second he was going to grab her and pull her back. She could already feel his fingers wrapping around her ponytail. He was so close.

Renee dove for the first room: the one that used to be hers. She twisted the knob and opened the door just enough to slip through. She slammed it shut and twisted the lock with a satisfying click. "What do you want?" she screamed. The room blurred, swimming.

Nobody tried to open the door. The handle didn't rattle, no fists pounded against the wood. In fact, the house was perfectly quiet again. And this time she couldn't even hear the ticking clock. Her pulse pounded so loudly in her head it drowned out her thoughts. Words flew through her mind at alarming speed. None of them made sense on their own, but all pointed toward leaving as soon as possible. Renee stood, hands pressed against the door, letting her breathing calm. What was happening?

"I drew it."

Renee's heart sank. She was not the only one in the room.

"It's you, and Daddy, and Claudia, and me."

That voice. She recognized it. But it couldn't be. She couldn't...

Very slowly, Renee turned. A strange fluttering filled her. It was not fear, not any longer, but something else.

Something she hadn't expected. With her arm, she wiped away the blurriness, trying to clear her vision for a sight that she was entirely certain could not be. Yet it was.

By the bed with the flowery pink duvet stood a small girl. She had a white headband and a yellow dress that went perfectly well with her chestnut hair. On her feet were clean white socks. She couldn't have been more than six. Yes, Renee knew—she was exactly five years and four months old. She smiled with dimples in both her cheeks.

In one hand, the girl held a thin paintbrush. In the other, she clutched a sheet of paper with four figures drawn in front of a large yellow-and-brown house. Above the figure on the left was written *Mummy*, above the one next to it was *Daddy*, and beside them were two little girls labeled *Claudia* and *Renee*.

Renee watched her younger self beam, extraordinarily proud of her accomplishment. Again a lump formed in her throat, but this time she was helpless to stem the flow of tears.

"What?" she sighed.

Then the girl disappeared.

It happened in a blink. One moment, a young Renee stood before her, and the next the room was empty. Renee couldn't move, crying in spite of herself. It wasn't until she noticed a small slip of paper lying on the bed that she found the ability to walk again. She picked up the scrap, torn from a newspaper, and flipped it over.

Black, shaky handwriting scrawled across it. Renee recognized it as her mother's.

When Renee was five, she painted a picture of all of us in front of the house, it said. Renee clutched the note as if it meant keeping herself alive. Struck by understanding, she fled back to the door and unlocked it. She flew down the stairs into the living room.

The man was there, standing in the corner. He smiled, but it felt less intrusive now. Renee knew he couldn't touch her, and though she continued to be wary, she was not as afraid as she had been before. Still, when he moved forward she took a step back, though he vanished like smoke before reaching her.

It didn't take long to find a second ripped note sitting on the mantlepiece.

James Lancer finally kissed me by the grandfather clock. He was so nervous it looked more like an attack. We laughed about it later.

Renee moved to the hallway. On the decorative table was another note.

Randall broke my doll, but he didn't lie about it. I forgave him because he didn't lie.

Renee looked up into the boy's eyes. They were puffy from crying. He held out the pieces of the doll apologetically, ashamed of what he'd done. Renee moved on.

The woman was still lying on the floor. Her curls moved as she looked up at Renee, feeble and pleading. "Help," she said, though there was nothing Renee could do for her now.

Renee slid past the woman, looking around the kitchen. Gray light shone through the window above the sink. An assortment of pots and pans hung from hooks set in the ceiling. She found the note on the counter by the stove top.

Aunt Greta fell while trying to get a saucepan down. Everyone else was in the yard but me. We got her to the hospital. A broken hip and a broken leg. Always meant to move where we kept the pots and pans after that.

Renee went on to the bathroom, where water was running into the tub again. She could hear the woman muttering and paused. Of all the apparitions, this was perhaps the one she feared the most. Maybe it was how aggressive the blonde woman had been, maybe because she had shouted so loudly.

But the woman wasn't where she'd been before. Instead of sitting on the tub's edge, she was slumped against its side. The water was nearly to the brim, but she hadn't turned it off. Instead, she sobbed, collapsed in an inconsolable heap. The note sat by the sink.

Mum broke down when she was told Father died in the war. She took it out on me, but I know now why she was so upset.

Renee collected the note and headed back upstairs. She stared down at the memories in her hand as she walked. Her mother had lived her entire life in this house. Renee had known that but hadn't comprehended it. What must that mean to her mother now? Now when most of the time she couldn't even remember her own children?

On the landing, Renee turned toward her mother's door in time to see it close. A man had stepped out of the room. He was tall, broad-shouldered, with dark hair and eyes. He walked slowly, his presence powerful yet gentle. She could smell his spiced cologne. Knew how it felt when his arms held her up.

Renee watched her father until he disappeared. Then she hurried into her mother's room.

Andrea was standing at the chest of drawers, pen poised above a torn slip of newspaper. Though she had obviously been writing, she looked up, lost now. She startled when she saw Renee, then looked down at the note under her fingers. Disgust came over her face and she pushed it away. She walked off in a fluster.

Renee glanced at the note.

Charles left when he was called into service. He was the second man I

143

lost to war.

"The moments come in flashes," Andrea said. Her voice was surprisingly lucid. She sat on the edge of her bed. How frail her body looked, how shaky her limbs were.

Renee didn't know what to say, but her mother continued. "Everything. I'm losing everything, Renee." Her voice was stern, angry at her lot in life. "I hate that I'm forgetting it all."

"Sometimes you remember," Renee replied unhelpfully. She clutched the notes tighter.

Andrea didn't answer for a while, staring down at the floor. Her hands wrung together in her lap. Outside, through the open window, Renee could hear a car pulling up. Claudia must be back.

"What are you doing in my room?"

Renee let her eyes close.

"Who are you? Get out before Charles comes back. He won't like that you're in here."

Renee forced a smile. "I'm here to help you, Mum."

"Help me? Well, good then. If you're here to help me, make yourself useful and clean something. This room is a mess."

"Just putting away these notes," Renee said, holding up the collection. She grabbed the most recent one from the chest of drawers and took them all over to the writing table.

"Careful!" her mother exclaimed. "Liam Whitcomb gave me that box when I was a lass."

"I know," Renee said patiently. "I'm just going to put them inside it. Keep them safe." She closed the lid, latching it. "We don't want to lose any of them, so I'm keeping them together."

"Did you know, I've lived my whole life here?" her mother said, patting the bed post. "I could never forget this place. It's filled with memories."

Renee nodded. She stood up and left the room, heading down the stairs to greet her sister.

MEMOIR OF A RIGHT FIELDER

Right field is a dump.

I know what I'm talking about. See, my dad has this green pickup truck that we keep in the backyard unless we need to use it. I think we're the only ones in the entire family who have a truck because relatives are always asking him to move stuff for them. Of course, because I'm the only son still around, I get lassoed into helping out. We've had to take things to the dump loads of times. Mattresses and old mirrors, things like that. I've seen how smelly and disgusting the place is. As soon as you cross that car-weighing thing they have at the entrance, you pretty much have to hold your nose or you gag on the fumes. Everything there is broken and cast aside and rotting.

But don't be fooled. The true wasteland of the American spirit is in right field.

No one hits anything to right field.

The fact that we're all kids doesn't help. I've seen guys in the major leagues get some action every once in a while. They get lefties who come up to bat and they can get the ball soaring into the grass.

But in Pinole Hercules Little League Baseball there's no such luck. Pop-ups *never* make it over the head of the first baseman. Maybe some of the line drives have enough steam to get off the dirt, but Wallace is pretty good, and he catches everything before it gets to me.

The 'roided guys are all right-handers. So Johnny Wong over in left field gets plenty of balls hit his way. Even when the batters swing late, it only goes to center. I'm not center. That's McMartin. Don't ever try to catch any of the balls in his area. He'll slug you.

So me? I get *nothing*. I mean literally, big, fat, nothing. I'm like a spectator who gets to watch from the field instead of the stands. Only the people in the stands get more action than I do because of foul balls. They're closer to the game too. I guess I've got it even worse than them.

It all has to do with the fact that I suck badly. No, no, don't try to deny it. I know because Randal Williams' mom told me after that game we lost 5–4 last year to the Athletics (league team name, not big shots in the MLB) because I struck out when we had a guy on second and third. Don't feel bad about it though, like, she laughed and everyone else laughed, and I laughed too. I don't like getting the little trophy at the end of baseball season, because I know I don't deserve them. That's not why I'm here. Mom still put last year's on the bookshelf with the others though.

Anyways, I know I suck and that's why I'm out in right field, but I tell myself that someone's got to do it, so it might as well be me. At least I still get to play. Some kids' parents make them do other things, like basketball. I can't imagine having to play basketball.

A new batter comes up to the plate. I've seen him before.

He's not one of the well-known guys or one of the coaches' sons, so I don't know his name, but he's pretty wimpy. I don't need to pay attention.

Handfuls of bees are plopping from weed to weed on the ground. The little white flowers—the ones that are everywhere in any grassy field if you look hard enough—don't even move when the bees land, they're so light. I used to try to step on the bees while they were landed, but one flew up and stung me once so I don't do that anymore. I still find them really cool to watch. Dad said if you don't bother them they won't bother you.

The kid swings and misses. Parents in the stands clap, either telling him he's doing alright or telling the pitcher to "keep 'em coming."

Our pitcher is Davie Goldberg. Mom sometimes jokes that he's really a twenty-year-old dude who got held back in school or something to qualify for the league. I know she's joking, but secretly I think she's right. He's got hair on his chin and everyone in the league knows he has a really deep voice and wears an extra-large cup.

The kid batting strikes out. I knew he would.

Some clovers and dirt fly into the air when I kick the ground. We've got one more out to go this inning. I'll be fourth in line when we head for the dugout, so I'll probably be up to bat. My batting's better than my catching; I've gotten on base a few times this season.

The first time this year, I actually got to second base. I hit a line drive in-between short-stop and second. I ran right away because when I practice with my dad he's always telling me not to look at the ball when I hit it. If someone catches it before it hits the ground, the umps will let me know. The most important thing is that I get to first base.

I was doing just that when the base coach started whirling his arm in a big circle. That meant I had to go to second. I couldn't believe he was telling me to go to second! I wanted to shout at him and ask him if that's what he meant or not, but I didn't want to be a punk. So I kept running.

Everyone was shouting. I mean everyone. I could hear people yelling at the center fielder to get the ball in. I could hear people yelling my name, telling me to run faster. And all the infielders were yelling at each other, trying to get me out.

I'm no good at sliding, so in the end I jumped up and landed with both feet on the base. Luckily, I hopped right over the second baseman, who was expecting me to slide, and landed perfectly. Safe. That was a really cool moment and I eventually scored a run when Marshawn Johnson hit me to third and then McMartin hit a grounder and I got to go home. Everyone was patting me on the back after that.

A crack shakes me out of my daydream. The crowd gasps. What's going on? I missed it.

Oh shit! They're all looking at me!

I look up to see a little white speck flying high in the air, soaring far above the first baseman. Someone hit the ball into right field! It's coming straight toward me. Crap!

Seeing where it's going, I turn and run, sprinting deeper into the outfield. That thing is hurtling, gaining altitude like a jet fighter. Any moment now I'm sure it's going to break atmosphere and I'm going to lose the ball simply because it takes off into space. See you later, alien collector's item.

Still, I've got to try. I keep running, my cleats digging into the grass. That ball's going to go straight over my head if I don't leg it. McMartin's trying to get over to me but there's no way in hell he'll make it in time to help. This is squarely my ball, but that's alright because I don't want him stealing any of my play.

The ball is coming down now. Maybe I can catch it, maybe it's not going to take off like a rocket. It's definitely headed toward earth. My legs are screaming and so are my lungs—baseball doesn't prepare you for a lot of running. The sun is trying to blind me, but I can still see the ball careening through the air. A missile now. Is it whistling, or am I just hearing things? Closer now, I can see the threads. I reach my glove hand up over my head, reaching up to catch that damn ball. This is going to be mine. I can feel it. I can already feel what it'll be like squeezed inside my mitt.

WHAM.

Stars erupt in front of my eyes. All the wind is knocked clean out of me and the world is up-ended. Only when I hit the ground do I realize I've fallen. Everything is spinning. What the hell? What just happened? I can't see straight, my chest hurts. Am I in shock? Have I broken anything? Is anyone going to call an ambulance?

I look down and see the fence at my feet. I ran into the fence! We're only eleven years old and that dumbass kid hit the ball to the fence. I mean, it's only 220 feet, but Jesus Christ. Then I look down at my hand.

I've still got the ball.

The white baseball is peeking out between the clenched sides of my glove. Somehow, even though I ran full speed into the fence and knocked the living daylights out of me, I held on!

I hop up onto my knees and hold my glove up for the world to see.

Everyone cheers. For me. I caught it!

McMartin runs up to me and grabs my arm, helping me off the ground.

"Nice catch, Lopez," he says, and slaps me on the shoulder. I can't stop smiling as we hustle in toward the dugout. I still have the ball in my glove. McMartin laughs and has to take it from me to toss it back to the pitching mound. I caught the ball! And with only minimum damage to my ribcage!

I hope I get to bat this inning.

PUMPKINS AND PINCUSHIONS

[Recorded by Bea O'Leary on 14 August 2016 in her home on Gillman Street in El Cerrito, CA. The following is a direct transcription.]

So, why don't you begin by telling me a bit about yourselves?

Well, I'm Fabian. I'm a pin cushion collector originally from Arkansas. Been in El Cerrito for about seven years now—

Eight, dear.

Eight? Is it eight? Really that long?

Yes, remember the Obamas—

Right, Malia was ten. Yes, yes, you're correct, my love. So, I've been here for eight years. Then I met this little turtle dove.

Sorry, pin cushion collector? You glossed over that.

Ah, I thought she might want to know more about that. Didn't I say, Gem? Don't worry, Bea, happens all the time. Everyone always wants to know. To put it in layman's—I find rare and antique pin cushions all over and acquire them for my collection.

Fabby really has such a keen eye for exquisite pieces—

It's the culmination of years of research—

decades, really—since I first discovered my obsession.

There's money in that?

Well, pin cushions are—they're really an under-mined resource in our nation's history. Think of all we could learn that we haven't yet learned from pushpin cushions.

Right.

I get a steady stream of support from like-minded archivists and historians who wish to preserve and expand my collection. I always carry a few pieces in my vehicle. We can have a look after.

We'll see if we've got time. How about that? And you, miss?

Hi, I'm Gemini. I'm a registered International Marshal of Botanical Substantialities, or IMBS, as you might know them.

That means you judge—

I'm called all over the world to judge Largest Crop competitions. So, Largest Pumpkin, Largest Cucumber. I've done them all.

Really?

Yes.

Turtle Dove has quite the reputation in the field of BS.

All over the world, you say?

Yes, we went to Laos in 2014.

And we went to South Africar the year after.

Dear, that was for vacation though.

I'm sorry, did you say Africar?

Did I? [laughs]

You'll have to excuse him. Fabby's of English descent. Sometimes it slips out.

That's—that's alright. You were saying?

Well, Laos is the only one so far, but I'm sure more will come along. Her profession is always in demand.

I always get questions about my registry. Like how difficult it is to get registered. The road to becoming an IMBS is difficult. I had to dedicate lots of time to study. People think it's just simple weight, but you have to think beyond just the weight of the crop. The whole plant itself, you know? If they're tomatoes, are they firm or saggy? If it's a cucumber, there's length and girth to take in. So there's a lot more than people understand. I'd say in terms of difficulty, like...

Like an engineer.

Yeah, engineering at least. Or lawyer. Somewhere in there. I can—

I don't want us to get too offtrack, just looking at the time. Sorry, Gemini.

S'alright.

So, when people ask me to officiate their weddings, they really like for me to personalize the ceremony, you know? Incorporate some of the things that make them special as a couple.

Well, we like going to Whole Foods together after Sunday-morning pilates.

I've found that Lululemons are really an all-around pant—

What about how you first met?

June twenty-second, 2008—

My twenty-fourth birthday. My friends and I were having a girls' night, so naturally we went to get henna tattoos and bindis to celebrate our inner peace.

I was working at the parlor at the time as an artist. Gemini was so adorable. She was afraid of getting the tattoos, you see—

Well, I'm allergic to calligraphy!

But her friends convinced her to come into my room.

They knew I was smitten by him.

I was developing quite the reputation for being a bad boy. What can I say? I'd just moved here a few months before. New digs, new rules. Am I right? [laughs]

I don't…

My youth really could've taken a turn for the worst. I had such a thing for bad boys back then. You were wearing that shirt—you remember?

That's right, unprofessionally cheeky—sorry, my English again. "Cheeky" means "silly"!

But you're—

[laughs] The front said, "What do you call an astromech droid who does traffic duty?"

And the back said, "R2-Detour."

Witty.

So witty.

Wittiest shirt. Oh, the bad boys did it for me back then.

Well, "bad boy" has lost all meaning.

What was that?

Nothing.

Anyway, we agreed that I'd tell her friends she'd gotten her tattoo in a naughty place—

Then I wouldn't have to show them I hadn't got one, which made it more risqué. But really he hadn't seen me naked at all.

Yet.

Oh, Fabby, you're making me blush. Bea doesn't want to hear that.

I really don't.

We had to watch out for loose pins—

Jesus, Mary, and Joseph. I think I have enough to go on here.

You sure?

Yeah, it doesn't take much. I can just weave in some

of the details you've given me and that'll be enough so that everyone—

It's just us.

What?

The ceremony is going to be just us.

Oh, so why aren't you just—

You see, several of our friends are homosexuals, so we didn't want to have them there and make it seem like we were parading our heterosexual privilege in front of them.

But we couldn't not invite them.

So instead we're just having a private ceremony.

How very kind.

But I let them shop with me for my dress.

And there is it. Well, I suppose I'll see you both on your wedding day. If you have any further questions, please send me an email and I'll get back to you as soon as I can.

You haven't yet seen my collection.

The cushion collection is something to see.

I don't think I need to, I can sense their energy. Maybe next time.

THE BUTTON MAKER

I can't feel the wind.

I can see it breaking the surface of the water below. I can see it moving the branches on trees that cling to the hillsides. I can see it terrorizing the hair of the woman who's snatching her towels off the railing of her balcony. But I can't *feel* it.

I hear it. When the trees shake, their leaves rattle. The powerlines bounce up and down, making the wooden poles creak. Howls fill my ears each time a strong gust kicks up, knocking the collar of my coat askew.

But I can't feel it.

I don't. And that only makes everything worse.

Only five cars have passed by tonight. Their headlights grow blinding against the side of my face, tires grumbling on the asphalt. I imagine what would happen if one lost control and mounted the curb, but none of them have so far. This is such a straight bridge, I don't think any of them will. Their lights only glare so bright until they're past me. Then there's nothing again but the soft buzz of the nearest lamp and the wind whispers. Drivers are more careful when they see people. Or maybe they don't see me at all. Maybe it doesn't make a difference that there's someone standing at the exact midpoint of the span, hair tossing like long grass.

Would they stop if I did *it* while they were watching?

I imagine the squeal of tires as they come to a halt. Snowflakes continue to stream through the yellow cones of light while they rush to the side of the bridge, hurling themselves at the railing. They take out their cell phones, wondering why their fingers can't find the correct numbers when it's most important. By then, I would be out of sight. Lost to the water marbled black and white by night and wind.

No. I won't do it while someone's watching for the same reason I won't step out into the middle of the road when they least expect me to. I do not want to become someone else's problem. To go quietly would be to fight the rising entropy of the universe. That will be my token contribution to this good night.

That would make me feel something.

I miss my chance. Footsteps approach on my right side. Boots alternating between hollow knocks on the wooden planks and crunching on the inch-thick layer of snow. I don't look, waiting for them to pass me. If I can read the signs correctly, our shared corner of the world is terribly cold, even if I can't feel it. Anyone out tonight will not linger for too long. They have warmer places to be.

But the boot-steps stop just as they reach me. A woman with curly dark hair bursting from beneath her knit cap. She draws her peacoat tighter, her breath crystallizing in the frigid darkness. Mine, I notice, does the same. Without looking at me, she leans against the railing, staring out at the lake.

"It's cold tonight," she says.

I know that I'm the only soul around, but I can't be

certain she's speaking to me. Her tone is so casual while she clicks her toes against the ground to knock the snow from her boots. I watch her but don't respond. We've never met before—I'm sure of it—so she will move on if I ignore her. She doesn't know why I'm here.

"I've never run into you," she says, almost as if reading my thoughts. "When I go walking, I mean."

I continue to watch the back of her head. She rubs her gloved hands together.

She speaks again. "You know, if this was your first time here, and you just happened to stop and look out at the lake, you'd think this place was dark and terrifying. You'd never know that when the sun rises over those mountains over there and the light hits the water, this whole basin comes to life. Even when it snows—I swear. Every paper-white bank shimmers like it's covered in diamonds. And you have to wonder then why we don't treasure those sunrises like we do them stones."

"I live here," I say. I know what she's talking about. I don't need her to describe this place to me. I've seen enough of it in daylight for a lifetime. I've seen plenty of sunsets too—probably more of those than sunrises, come to think of it.

"So do I," she says, and points off the bridge. Down close to the water is a small house I hadn't noticed before. Through the window, I can see a living room complete with a shag rug, a corduroy couch, and a cherry-wood coffee table.

"This is what you do then?" I ask.

Now she looks back at me. Her skin is dark, but she's close enough that I can see freckles splashed across her face under the streetlamp.

She shrugs. "I like to go for walks."

"On winter nights?"

"Sometimes on winter nights," she says. "Especially when I see someone I'd like to meet."

"And I am..."

"Someone I wanted to meet. Yes."

"Why?" *Why? If you don't want to see me fall, close the blinds at night. Look the other way like everyone else.* It's easy to do. I know. I've done it before to people just like me. I've even done it to people I loved who had looked me straight in the eye.

"Because you're a person," she says. When I don't respond, "Isn't that reason enough?"

"What makes you think I want to meet you?"

"Nothing at all. In fact, you probably want me to leave you alone. Don't you?"

Again, I don't say anything. She hit the nail on the head, but I have enough decorum left in me to know it's impolite to say so. And maybe I don't want her here, but it's been five minutes and I haven't asked her to leave so maybe I don't *not* want her here. Even just a little bit. I'm not one of those cases though. I know she can't help me. I'm not going to start sobbing and fall apart in her arms. If I talk to her now and tell her everything she wants me to tell her, I'm still going to feel the same shitty way come dawn when all her pretty diamonds come shining through the snow banks.

"What do you do?" I ask. "When you're not stopping people from jumping off bridges, I mean."

"I'm a button maker," she says. She doesn't address the second part of my statement.

"A button maker? That can be a profession?"

She smirks. "Almost everything can become a profession, I think. Someone's got to do it. My buttons are unique— higher quality than what usually comes on shirts and things. I use wood and stone, all kinds of materials."

"Do you just make buttons, or…"

"Mostly buttons," she says, "but sometimes I make clothes or trinkets to go along with them. Most of the time, people bring me their blouses or pants because a button went missing or broke. I sew on a new one. Maybe change them all out if they like."

"You're able to make a living that way?"

She laughs. It's the first I've heard in days. "Word of mouth is a powerful resource. Etsy helps too."

A button maker. How about that? I didn't think anyone still did trades of that sort. I thought we'd all agreed to leave it up to the factories. She's young too. If I could have placed anyone as a button maker, I would've selected someone in their fifties at least. An old, graying woman, perhaps, with too many cats to keep track of.

The wind gusts again and we shiver.

I shove my hands into my coat pockets, wondering if she's willing to wait here with me all night. I'd bet that if I'm unresponsive enough, eventually she'll turn around and hightail it back to her lakeside cottage where the warmth of her bed and her four sturdy walls await. Everyone has their limits. There are no exceptions.

"I used to think the moon was a button," she says.

"A button for what?"

"To hold a blanket over the sky at night. You know, to block out the sun." She says this as if she might still believe it. "That's what gave me the idea to start collecting and making my own buttons. Then I guess I just never stopped."

I shake my head. "How? There can't be that many different kinds of buttons to make."

"You'd be surprised," she says. Then she waddles back

and forth in a two-foot line in front of
me. *Actually waddles*, like a penguin. I don't know if this is
some poor attempt at warming herself up or the start of a
moon-button ritual, but before I can decide she stops and
turns to look at me again. "Why don't I show you?" she asks.

I stare back at her, unsure whether she can be serious. I
didn't come here tonight to talk to her. I came here with the
intent that I would never talk to anyone else again. She has
good intentions, but she's finding me too late. I know that
she can't help me, and only a person who has no experience
feeling what I feel inside me every day could think otherwise.
I've been hanging at the end of my rope for too long, friend.

Another gust blows cold down my neck and makes my
shoulders scrunch.

"Please?" she asks. "I'd like to show you."

I nod. I don't even realize I have until I'm following her
along the bridge, seeking out that orange window in the dark.
Maybe I'll be back on the bridge tomorrow, and if not then
maybe the night after, but for now I've stepped on solid
ground again. For now, I'll follow her home. I don't even
know why. I have little interest in buttons. I've never paid
much attention to them before, but I'm chasing a promise
now to see more buttons than I ever knew existed. I hope she
has one that looks like the moon.

PICKING UP GRANNY

They weren't knocking on the door. They were threatening to break it down.

Alberto was shocked out of his slumber, still groggy though adrenaline coursed painfully through his veins. He sat upright. Half-immersed in his dream, Alberto spent a frenzied moment believing the room was collapsing around him before he heard the voices from the hallway.

"Open now, boys!"

"We know you're in there!"

"No use hiding."

They were going to wake up the entire dormitory, if they hadn't already. Alberto scampered out of his bed, kicking the sheets onto the floor in the process. His bunkmate, Jamie, was similarly baffled, all bleary-eyed and disheveled blonde hair. He was rubbing his face with both hands.

"Whattimeissit?" Jamie asked.

Alberto snatched a pair of flannel pajama bottoms and pulled them up over striped boxer shorts. On second glance, he shoved on a cardigan as well. "Dunno."

"Move it, kiddies!"

"We will break the hinges!"

"Jack and Lyle from the frat?" Jamie said.

"Damnit," Alberto muttered. He stumbled over to the door and grabbed the deadbolt.

"Wait!" Jamie cried, but it was too late. Alberto had turned the lock.

The moment the deadbolt cleared, the door flew open. Jack and Lyle weren't alone. They'd brought two other beefy members of the fraternity along with them: brothers Alberto vaguely recognized but couldn't remember the names of. The four men entered the small room, smirks plastered on their faces while they surveyed their surroundings.

"Nice place you got here," Jack said.

"It's late," Jamie muttered.

"Well, we couldn't have you ready for us," Lyle said. The other three laughed.

"Ready for what?" Alberto asked.

"For what? For initiation, of course." Jack placed a hand on Alberto's shoulder and gave a firm squeeze.

"Ini—initiation?"

"Yeah, you boys didn't think you were just gonna waltz into the club, did you?" Lyle came up on his other side. "Did you, now?"

Alberto was staring back and forth between the two of them, his mouth slightly open. All he could do to answer was shake his head. He and Jamie had been sworn in earlier that day, back when it wasn't—holy hell, did that clock say half past two in the morning? Honestly, he *had* thought the ceremony was the end of it, and so, it seemed, had Jamie.

"Enough talk," Jack said with a jerk of his head. "We're leaving."

He and Lyle took Alberto by the arms. The other two

beefy guys reached up into Jamie's upper bunk and pulled him down unceremoniously. Jamie fell with a clatter and a cry. The poor boy wasn't even allowed to grab any clothes before he was dragged from the room in nothing but his boxers and undershirt. Both Alberto and Jamie protested, convinced they should at least be allowed the courtesy of appropriate outerwear. After all, the night was chilly. Their protests carried no weight, however, as none of their brothers relinquished their hold.

The boys were dragged out of the dormitory building to the pavement in front, where a car sat dark and empty. Alberto thought it miraculous that not a single soul had come to see what all the commotion was about. Either the Resident Assistants were all heavier sleepers than Alberto had bargained, or they'd decided they couldn't care less about what happened to their residents. Did the fraternity brothers have the resources to buy off the RAs?

He was shoved headfirst into the back of the car and Jamie came in after him, determined to keep the hem of his boxer shorts pulled down as low as possible. One of the nameless guys squeezed in after Jamie while the other walked around to Alberto's side and pushed himself in so that the roommates were sandwiched between them. Jack and Lyle sat up front.

"Everyone settled in? Good." Jack didn't leave time for a response. The engine ignited and the car sped away across the brick road.

Streetlights slid by, momentarily bathing the interior of the vehicle in yellow light. Alberto and Jamie nearly sat atop one another in order to fit between the two monstrosities who would've already been cramped in the back seat on their own. Jack and Lyle, who were undoubtedly the heads of this operation, kept talking to each other in low tones that Alberto couldn't understand, but every once in a while, Lyle turned back to him and Jamie with a wicked grin on his sharp features. Alberto didn't have a very good feeling about tonight's agenda.

"Wh—where exactly are we headed?" Jamie cleared his throat, trying to mask the nervousness in his voice.

"We're not going to tell you," said the bulky boy on the left, his arms—which were thicker than Alberto's thighs—crossed over his chest.

"That's not true, Elmer," Lyle snapped. "Don't answer for me."

The one called Elmer's face fell, the cocky sneer faltering for the first time that evening.

"Where are we going then?" Alberto asked.

"There's no need to worry," Lyle said, his tone suddenly kind—well, kinder than before. "Your face is so tense, Alberto. We wouldn't do anything bad to you, so please just relax."

Despite Lyle's words, Alberto didn't feel any of the tension in his body loosen the slightest degree. If anything, his heart began thumping faster.

"Yeah," Alberto said, trying a smile. The expression felt foreign and forced. "I just thought it might be helpful to know where we were going."

"We're picking up Granny," Lyle said, all teeth. His three comrades let out low chuckles. Neither Alberto nor Jamie said anything in response.

The rest of the ride took about ten minutes, during which Alberto willed his body to calm down. His breath kept catching in his throat, his stomach was in knots, and his side was already aching from sitting perched in such an awkward position. He didn't drive much, having no need of a car at school, so he'd no inclination of which roads they were taking. At night, it was impossible to tell where they were headed. Recognizing that he didn't have much of a chance of escape while the car was in motion, Alberto let his mind wander.

Less than twelve hours after being inducted, he already regretted joining this stupid frat. He used to make fun of frat boys in films—their haughty behavior, their problematic sense of brotherhood over decency. Yet somehow he'd found himself swept up in rush week when he'd followed Jamie—the only person he knew on campus—to the events. His inability to say no had taken over.

He'd need to work on that.

Alberto kept trying to steal glances at Jamie, but the other boy was staring firmly out the window, his pale face reflected in the glass.

The car pulled over to the side of the road and came to a stop.

"Here we are," Jack said.

Alberto couldn't see anything through the glass except darkness, but Jamie squealed. The sound made the four frat brothers laugh with delight.

"The fuck was that?" Lyle grinned. "There's a piggy in the car?"

They continued laughing.

All four doors opened and the brothers exited. A moment later, Alberto was pulled from his seat. He stumbled out into the night air, feeling the cold sting his cheeks. Elmer was digging around in the trunk. He emerged carrying a large canvas bag in which was wrapped a long, pole-like object.

"What's that?" Alberto asked. "I thought we were picking

up Granny."

"We are, dummy," Jack said, slamming the trunk shut. "But you'll be needing these."

He took the bag from Elmer and reached in. That was when Alberto realized there were two long objects inside. The pole shapes were handles. At one end of each was a black, rusty spade. Jack was carrying a pair of shovels.

He hadn't thought it possible, but Alberto felt his insides tighten further. Eyes wide, he scanned the field beyond the car and saw to his horror the rows and rows of neatly gridded granite tombstones.

"You don't mean…" he said, unable to finish the question.

A roar of mirth was his reply. One of the shovels was thrown into his hands and he barely managed not to drop it. Jamie didn't react quite as quickly and his shovel clattered to the floor. The boy dove to the ground in fear, shivering violently against the cold and his terror. While he was down, the fourth brother, whose name Alberto still did not know, nudged Jamie hard enough with his shin to knock him over.

"Squeal, little piggy," the bulky boy said.

Jamie scrambled to his feet, whimpering softly.

"We're running out of time," Jack snapped, cutting through the *fun*. "Get going, maggots."

He walked over to the edge of the sidewalk, waving his arm for them to follow. The chain-link fence only came to waist height. Apparently, nobody had ever thought more security was needed at this graveyard. Climbing over was easy. Before long they were standing amid a misty field of wet grass. Old headstones peered out of the fog, names obscured by weathering and darkness. Alberto clutched to the shovel for support, though in the end, he knew it might betray him.

Beside him, Jamie was audibly shaking now, his teeth chattering loudly enough to wake the dead.

"Here it is, boys," Lyle said, gesturing to a grave. The stone looked new, untouched by nature, as did the mound of earth before it, which had yet to blend into the surrounding grass. The grave read FELICITY ALBA. "Granny hasn't gotten up yet, can you believe that? She doesn't even care that we're going to be late for the party!"

Alberto and Jamie were both shoved forward until they were standing on the grave. Alberto's stomach was squirming, but Jamie looked like he was about to be physically ill. Under his thin white shirt, he had diminished, his stature turned skeletal.

"Don't worry, though," Lyle said. "If you get her up, we should still have enough time."

Then the four brothers stepped back so that they made a square around the gravesite. Alberto looked around at his captors, who stared down at him expectantly. Each had their arms crossed, daring him to object in any way. He could see the sneers lurking just below the surface of their stoic expressions. But how could they watch him like that? What were they waiting for? They didn't really mean for him to... to do this?

"We're waiting, guys," Jack said. "You don't want us to make this harder than it needs to be."

Neither Alberto nor Jamie moved, still stunned. None of the brothers were laughing anymore; they meant business.

"We could take away your clothes and make you do this nude," Lyle said. "Or we could take away your shovels and make you dig with your hands."

"Yeah," the nameless meathead interjected. "Then *we* could use the shovels to make you real uncomfortable."

"Richard," Lyle chided.

The one called Richard stepped forward, hands outstretched, and this was all the motivation Jamie needed to lurch into action. With another squeal, he turned and buried the head of his shovel in the dirt. Soft and wet as the ground was, the blade sank easily beneath the surface. Alberto did the same, his heart continuing to race. His mind flashed images of all the terrible things that could go wrong. Grave robbing, he was sure, was illegal. A police officer might come by and catch them at it. Alberto couldn't stop, though. He wasn't sure how many of the threats his newly made frat "brothers" were willing to carry out. The idea was only slight worse than the sickening outcome should nothing go wrong at all.

He and Jamie dug, hoisting dirt out of the hole, which grew deeper at a painstakingly slow rate. He felt like they had been at it for hours. His arms grew sorer by the minute; he didn't visit the gym very often. Jamie was panting, his face flushed and sweaty despite his lack of substantial clothing. And all the while, Jack, Richard, Elmer, and Lyle remained stony-faced and silent.

When the ground was finally near the level of his head, Alberto's shovel connected with something hard. A great *thump* sounded through the graveyard. He and Jamie made eye contact, and Alberto could see just how terrified his roommate was. Then they made to uncover the coffin, sinking their shovels into the soil more carefully than before. The cherry-wood lid emerged out of the black dirt, the once-polished surface just beginning to show signs of deterioration. How long ago had this grave been filled? A week? It couldn't be more than that.

Alberto looked up to see that the four were standing at the lip of the hole, staring down at him and Jamie.

"Open her up," Jack said.

Alberto had no idea how to open a coffin once it had been shut. He scrabbled over the surface and eventually found a way with his shovel. The coffin groaned in protest at his meddling. Jamie had to press himself against the wall of the hole in order to get out of the way.

The coffin was open. A horrendous odor wafted out of the cushioned interior. The stench of decaying flesh, fully underway, punctured the mild evening air. Alberto had to cover his mouth to keep from vomiting and Jamie did the same. When he could open his eyes, he looked down at the poor Miss Alba, who had no idea her corpse was about to be disturbed. Insects had already found their way into the coffin, perhaps through the floor beneath the body or perhaps through a crack Alberto hadn't seen. He remembered reading somewhere that coffins didn't take long to pop once they'd been buried.

The woman's overall appearance had visibly degraded, but most of her skin remained intact—gray and lifeless, but intact. Flies fled into the night, a cloud bursting from the enclosed space. Maggots gyrated along her white dress and the pillowing beneath her. Other beetles and worms wriggled here and there. Alberto thought he might never eat again. His bowels had a strong urge to evacuate themselves.

Something dark and limp flew past him. Someone had thrown the canvas bag at his feet.

"Bag her," Jack said.

"What?" Alberto asked, looking up in bewilderment. Surely, that was too much. Surely, the joke had gone far enough. But Jack's serious expression never wavered. In fact, if Alberto wasn't mistaken, a certain lust flickered across his eyes. The boy was hungry to see more, for the demonstration to continue. "I can't," Alberto protested.

"You can," Elmer said, and Alberto saw that he now held the shovels he and Jamie had propped against the side of the hole. He grasped one at his side like a club, the other leaning against his hip. "Are you in or out?"

Alberto had a fleeting vision of the overly muscled boy swinging the shovel and knocking him and Jamie down. He'd stir as the brothers scooped dirt back into the grave, the piles growing heavier and heavier on top of his body.

Instead, he grabbed the bag and opened it.

"Help me get her in," he hissed to Jamie.

"What?"

"Help me get her in," he said again, giving his bunkmate a look that stated, *We're in this together, you have to do your part too.*

Thus unfolded the least enjoyable task he had ever committed. Alberto didn't think he'd soon forget the feeling of the corpse's rotting flesh on his skin. Nor could he shake the image of her sunken cheeks and withering lips mere inches from his face while he bent low to maneuver the bag around her head. He had a sneaking suspicion she might open her eyes at any moment and grab him. He was very glad this vision never came true.

Then he was hoisting her out of the grave and kicking the coffin shut beneath him. His fingers groped the grass as he prepared to scramble back onto the surface. None of his "brothers" made any moves to help, but he managed on his own. Jamie nearly slipped and fell back in, but Alberto was quick enough to grab his arm before he could. They pushed the displaced piles of dirt back over the open hole, then were on their way out with Alberto and Jamie carrying the body between them.

"That wasn't so bad," Lyle said with a sinister grin as he shut the trunkon their newly acquired cargo.

"What are you going to do with her?" Alberto asked.

"Me?" Lyle seemed surprised. "Your night isn't over yet. Haven't you been listening? We've got a party to go to."

So back into the vehicle they went, Alberto making silent, desperate appeals to any higher power listening that if he made it through this night unscathed—or no further scathed than he already was—he would strive to be the best person he could imagine. He would study hard. He would devote himself to charity work. He would help others and never, ever allow himself to consider another questionable organization again.

Where had Jamie even heard of this fraternity? How could hazing practices like this remain covert?

To no surprise, the car arrived at what looked like an abandoned parking garage in an industrial district. The streetlamps here had almost all gone out and no effort had been made to replace them. The car's headlights led the way, panning over graffitied concrete walls and bouts of trash and mold.

They rounded a corner and the scene changed.

Red light flooded the enclosed space, fanning out from floodlights along the base of the walls. Enshrouded by shadows stood groups of men talking to each other in low but light tones. The clarity in their words was muffled by the size of the room. Some laughed, though the sound was insidious given the choice of scenery.

Nearer the center stood a circle of dazed and/or terrified young men. They were perfectly spaced as if given a spot to

173

stand and told not to move. Yet they looked around constantly at each other or at the people behind them, whom they couldn't see properly. Alberto recognized a few, and then realized these were the boys who had been inducted into the fraternity alongside him. Every single pledge had been brought here tonight, and from the look of things, they'd all been required to commit the same act. In the very center of the room, canvas bags similar to the one in the trunk behind Alberto were arranged in a neat pattern: one end of each touching in the middle, fanning outward so they made a star-like shape.

Only one leg of the star was missing.

Two spots in the circle of boys were empty.

Alberto swallowed hard.

The car came to a stop and he was yanked out once more. Jack held him with his hands behind his back while Richard and Elmer grabbed the body from the trunk. Swinging it carelessly, they brought it over to the center of the space and lined it up same as the others. Every voice in the room fell silent. The star was complete.

A sobbing Jamie was led by Lyle toward the circle. Jack made to do the same with Alberto, who fought against him. Alberto didn't know what was going on, but he sure as hell didn't want any part of it. If he was going to get away, his chances weren't going to get any better, now that he was out of the moving car.

"Stop it," Jack said through gritted teeth. He was strong, his grip tightening until he was hurting Alberto's arms. Alberto couldn't overcome him, but he was successfully making himself a nuisance. "It's too late for you."

"No," Alberto said, jerking himself left and right, trying to break Jack's hold.

"Someone help me!"

After finishing whatever he was mumbling into Jamie's ear, Lyle came running over. He punched Alberto in the stomach without saying a word. Alberto grunted in pain and doubled over, giving Jack the chance to drag him quickly into the ring.

"If you move, we will hurt you," Jack muttered. "If you run, we will tie you up."

Then he backed away.

Still struggling to catch his breath, Alberto looked up at the faces around him. Like Jamie, a few others looked as if they wished they'd never had anything to do with the brotherhood. To Alberto's surprise, some of the guys looked excited, ready for whatever was going to happen next.

They didn't have to wait long.

The brothers around the periphery of the room, enshrouded by a dense fog of darkness, began chanting in unison. Alberto couldn't understand anything they were saying, even as their voices grew louder. Perhaps it was another language. Even this he could not tell. One thing was for certain, though: he couldn't just stand here; he had to run. This was getting stranger with every passing moment and he didn't like where it was going. He kept looking over at the canvas-bagged bodies, wary of their role in this event. If he made a break for the exit, he could hide before they had a chance to catch him. Maybe he could find the police. He didn't have money for a payphone. If he just—

He couldn't move.

Alberto realized with mounting horror that his feet had become planted. He tugged on his legs as hard as he could, but neither his shoes nor his feet inside them budged one bit. It was like they'd become trapped in resin.

The chanting grew louder.

"I'm sorry," Jamie was saying, his words barely audible over the chorus of voices. "I should never have convinced you to join. *I* should've never joined or sought them out! They promised they had the ability to change my life, to seek my full potential. They promised they could show me how to explore parts of myself I didn't know were there."

Alberto stared back at him, wanting to say that he forgave him and it wasn't his fault, but he didn't know if the sentiment was true. He couldn't put much blame on Jamie; the promises sounded like the typical fare self-help groups pedaled at individuals with weak confidence. Alberto looked back into Jamie's eyes, seeing the panic and the desperation there. He was at a loss. There was no way out of this. Their future did not look bright.

"It's alright, Jamie," Alberto said. "You didn't know."

That seemed to be what Jamie was looking for. His face relaxed some—not much, but some—and he silently turned to look at the arrangement of bodies in the center of the ring. Alberto did the same. The chanting was so loud now that it was all he could hear. It filled every part of his mind, seeking out the dark corners and filling them as well. There was nothing but the chant. No silence but the chant. No peace but the chant.

And then the bag containing Felicity Alba lurched.

DESIGN OF DARKNESS

He sat diagonal to her, on the other side of the booth across the aisle.

"Do you believe everything happens for a reason?" he asked. Big, beautiful brown eyes crinkled from his smile— half good-natured, ironic in another sense. She was afraid to admit she was falling victim to them.

"I hope not," she said. She picked up another piece of bread from the basket on her table. Twenty minutes had gone by now and not a single call. She was quickly losing what little hope she had left.

He smirked. Two fingers traced his cheek, feeling the clean-shaven features. He wore a blazer and button-up. Product kept his hair neat. She could smell the faint, musky aroma of his cologne. This was supposed to be a date night, yet he was alone. That made two of them.

"What's your story?" she asked. Her finger traced the rim of her margarita. She'd only had half, but didn't know if she felt like having the rest.

"Well, I made the mistake of thinking I was celebrating my

anniversary tonight. I guess I was also under the impression that I'd be eating dinner," he said. As he spoke, he took the napkin draped over his lap, folded it diagonally, and dropped it on the table over his clean salad plate. "About ten minutes ago, I was left at the door to this fine establishment. She said she couldn't do *it* anymore."

"Oh, I'm so sorry."

"It's alright. Although, I wish she'd told me before we got here. Or maybe before I made reservations, even."

"That's tough."

"Yeah, that's life for you." He shrugged, though his stare betrayed the fresh hurt inside him. "What about you?"

She sighed. "It's inconclusive, but statistics would probably say that I've been stood up on date two."

He frowned sympathetically. "That's terrible."

"I'm going to have to tell *my* friend that she needs to stop setting me up with *her* friends."

"I guess we're both having rockin' Fridays," he said. "I'm Gordon, by the way. Gordon Larkin."

"Macy Rhodes." She waved. He waved back.

"This guy sounds like a prick for standing you up. He could've at least called to cancel," Gordon said.

"Ah, well that would be considerate, wouldn't it? It's much easier to just disappear." Macy looked back down at the basket of bread, at her barely touched margarita, at Gordon. "May I join you?"

Gordon looked startled by the idea, though he was trying to hide it. The tiniest flicker of a raised eyebrow interrupted his ironic smile. Macy wondered if she shouldn't have asked, but she already had and she couldn't take it back now.

"Why not," he said.

Collecting her purse, Macy slid out of her booth and into his. She couldn't help but laugh a little at the circumstance. She was date-hopping. Although, to be fair, neither of them was having much of a date to interrupt.

So they ate their meal together. Gordon ordered mushroom ravioli and Macy the shrimp scampi. She found him surprisingly easy to talk to for a stranger, but perhaps the initial vulnerability under which they'd met had helped. More than that, he seemed to be an adequate conversationalist. For someone who was supposed to be having his anniversary dinner tonight instead of finding out he was single, he steered clear of the subject of his ex. Macy even began to wonder if perhaps some part of him had been expecting the breakup, or he was just very clever at hiding his emotions. That could be dangerous.

As they cleaned the last morsels of food off their plates, he paused for the first time, looking almost embarrassed. Macy did him the courtesy of pretending not to notice until he had recollected his thoughts.

"Here's the thing," he began. "Ashleigh and I were supposed to be seeing a concert tonight—the violinist Leah Miyamizu."

"God, that must've been expensive."

He laughed, swirling the remainders of sauce on his plate. "It was. And now I don't know what to do with the tickets." He looked up and—whether he meant to or not—hit her with those eyes again.

"That's a real shame," she said, not wanting to assume.

"It is, but see, I really wanted to go. I guess it was more for me than for her, if I'm being honest. Have you ever seen Leah Miyamizu in concert before?"

"I haven't, but I bet she's brilliant."

He smiled and nodded, raising his eyebrows as if to say, *You could find out.*

And what else did she have to do tonight? She had been expecting to be on a date that would have lasted at least into the evening. She was already out and had on a lavender dress she'd specifically bought for tonight's dinner, hoping it would go well—she hadn't had a date go well in years though, so maybe she should have expected the sour turn.

Gordon reached into the pocket of his blazer and brought out two tickets.

He was a stranger though. She couldn't agree to just go somewhere with a stranger, much less to an expensive concert. But then again, he wasn't a *complete* stranger. She knew more about him than she did the man who'd abandoned her. If she was honest with herself, the first date with *him* hadn't gone nearly as smoothly as this.

"Why not," she said.

She paid for the meal, since he'd paid for the tickets, and they left the restaurant under the silver moon, amid the cool summer night air.

"I'm afraid I can't drive us," Gordon admitted sheepishly. "I had too much to drink plucking up the courage to ask you to join me. So I'm going to call us a cab."

"That's alright," she said. "I'll drive."

"Are you sure? Driving in the city is a pain."

"Yeah, it's fine." They found her car, a shiny emerald Toyota Corolla parked beneath an aspen. She appreciated having the foresight to get it washed two days ago. The sight of a bombardment of bird shit was less than romantic. He was careful with the doors, as if he knew someone who was sensitive to slamming.

She drove.

"Who's this?" he asked, pointing at the wallet-sized photo taped to her dash.

Macy hesitated. She hadn't had anyone new in her car in a long time. She'd forgotten that people liked to ask questions about photographs. Not that she didn't want to tell Gordon; it was just that the topic was sensitive to her. "That's my brother."

"Older or younger?"

"Younger by two years."

"Nice. What does he do?"

"He was a machinist."

"Was?"

"He's died. He was hit by a drunk driver."

Gordon was silent for a moment, one hand lingering on the corner of the photo. "I'm sorry to hear that."

"Me too," she said. "It happened two years ago. That picture was taken about a month before he passed." Macy didn't much feel like going to the concert anymore, but she knew it was too late to say anything about it now. The buildings had grown tall when they entered the downtown district. Lights flashed at her from every direction. San Francisco had materialized about them.

"Were you and your brother close?"

"Ollie and I had our differences, but we were alike in many ways."

"Such as?"

"We both loved reading. We could talk all day about the books we'd read, and we were constantly loaning them back and forth to each other." She still had a few of his volumes. The last one he'd sent her was David Mitchell's *Ghostwritten*. "His favorite was *Beloved* by Toni Morrison."

They were close to The Masonic now. Heavier traffic ensued. Driving in the city was shit.

"I've never seen a concert here," Macy said, tactlessly changing the subject of conversation. Death was a heavy topic for a first date. "I'm excited."

Gordon had reserved a spot in the attached underground garage, making parking immeasurably easier. They found their seats without issue: far to the left of the stage, halfway up the balcony. From here, certain members of the orchestra accompanying the violinist had their backs to them, but Miss Miyamizu herself was in clear profile. Macy hadn't much experience with classical music, though she listened every once in a while when she needed something to help her concentrate. This concert was something else, however. She watched the musicians' fingers flying across their instruments, making complex shapes as if speaking to the instruments in code. The instruments responded with song, telling the audience the story the musicians wove. Leah stood tall in the center, adorned in a deep red taffeta dress. The same red that apples are colored in animated films to make them look so appealing. Looking at Leah, you wouldn't know that anyone else was in the room. She and the violin were so knowledgeable of one another—so able to guess and finish the other's story—that they shared a bond more intimate than romance. When the lights came on for intermission, Macy was startled.

"No! That's not it, is it?" she asked.

"Just intermission," Gordon explained. They walked out to the second-floor lobby with the throng of people, loitering outside the auditorium. Neither of them needed the restroom, so they stood beside the wall.

"Isn't she great?" Gordon asked.

"She's incredible," Macy said. "It doesn't look like she even needs to think, she just *exudes* the music. You know what I mean?"

"That's exactly how I feel," Gordon said. The both of them were practically bouncing up and down with excitement. Macy had forgotten all about how the conversation in the car had made her feel. Music had that effect.

"I'd never thought about classical music much. I mean, I knew her name, that was all—watching her is different."

"I've been waiting for Leah Miyamizu to come to this area for so long. I can't thank you enough for coming."

"Excuse me." A man walked up to them. Immediately, Macy and Gordon fell silent. He was dressed like a member of the security staff, blue blazer and pants with a shaved head and a coiled earpiece. Even though Macy was certain she and Gordon hadn't done anything wrong, she still felt like she was in trouble. The man had such stoic features.

"Yes?" she asked.

"I couldn't help overhearing your conversation," he said. Macy and Gordon exchanged a glance and broke into smiles.

"Sorry if we were being too loud," Macy said.

"Not at all," he said, clasping his hands into a single fist at his waistline. "Leah appreciates fans who are enthusiastic about her work. How would you two like to meet her after the show?" He said this all without any trace of emotion. Macy and Gordon's mouths fell open.

"Are you serious?" Gordon asked.

"I am."

Macy laughed. She looked to Gordon, but knew without a doubt that his answer would be the same as hers. "Yes, we'd love to."

At the start of intermission, Macy would have assumed she couldn't enjoy the second half of the concert any more than the first. By the end of the show, the first half of the concert seemed a distant memory. She watched the rest of the performance enamored and in disbelief that she would meet this brilliant musician in a few minutes' time, wondering what she might say. How did you speak to someone who was not among the average crowd?

When the music ended, she and Gordon both stood and applauded, then found the guard from before and waited in the lobby until most of the guests had filtered out. When the place was starting to quiet, he led them through a door Macy hadn't noticed and down a series of hallways before coming to a stop at a room marked MIYAMIZU.

He knocked.

"Come in," came the reply.

They entered.

"Winston!" Miss Miyamizu was standing by a mirror, still in the elegant red dress, her pearl earrings catching the oversized lights above the vanity. Even in heels, she was a very petite woman, coming up to no more than Gordon's shoulder. She seemed so frail, thin enough that she might fall down should they close the door too quickly. Perhaps it was because she lacked her violin. Onstage, she had seemed so strong holding it. Onstage, she had seemed to take up the entire room with her presence. Macy had felt dwarfed by her. In here, Leah was human.

Winston the bodyguard greeted Leah, then stood by the door.

"I'm Leah," the violinist said unnecessarily.

"Gordon."

"Macy." They shook hands. Leah's grip was firm.

"Have a seat," she said, gesturing to a couch against the wall. Gordon and Macy sat, while Leah spun the chair at the vanity around to face them. "First of all, thank you so much for coming to my show. What did you think?"

Gordon seemed to have been waiting for this specific question. "Oh, it was beautiful! Every song was so, so good."

"Thank you." Leah's smile radiated. Her teeth were stark white. Her skin looked soft and clear. "We had a show last week in Seattle—it was terrible. Marceline, the conductor, had a bad cold and kept sneezing during the production. We had some interesting tempo hiccups that night." Her laugh was as wispy as her voice.

"Well, a terrible night for you is still probably better than my best days," Gordon said.

"You play?" Leah asked.

"I did. It's been a few years though."

"Why did you stop?"

"I never had the time for it. Toward the end, when I did play, it came out forced."

Leah nodded. "Music cannot be forced—it must be felt. How's that for a postcard slogan?" She winked, then stood and reached into a mini fridge positioned by the door, pulling out a bottle of pinot gris. "Would you like any?" she asked. They both refused, so she poured a single glass. "I am lucky. Music gets to be my life and I have nothing else. What do you do?"

"I sell furniture," Gordon said. "So if you need an overstuffed armchair for your next concert, let me know."

Leah laughed again. "Your home must be very comfortable."

"I try," Gordon said. "Mostly, it's my family members who have the comfortable homes. They all use my discount."

"Families are good for that," Leah said with another wink. She turned to Macy, who hadn't spoken since providing her name. "And what about you?"

"I work in digital design."

Their hostess nodded. "Ah, design. A form of art I am hopeless at." She raised her glass. "Kudos to you. Design often goes unnoticed, though it is so integral to everything."

They talked. Macy was shocked by how open and lively Leah was. If Macy had been the one to perform earlier in the evening, she wouldn't have wanted to expend so much energy talking to strangers after such an exhausting show. She would have wanted rest. But the show didn't seem to have taken much from Miss Miyamizu. It was easy. In the moment it was critical, but afterward she was unaffected. Whether or not this intimation was true, the violinist certainly didn't given any evidence to the contrary. She sipped her wine and asked them about the things they liked to do and whether or not they were a couple ("This is our first date, but I'm hoping she'll agree to a second!"). Leah lived in Vancouver and had been to California once, though she didn't remember it. Every night of the tour, Winston would find some fan who wanted to meet her because Leah liked to keep personal with the people who connected with her music.

"What do you do in your spare time?" Gordon asked.

"Spare time." Leah smiled. "I obsess over the violin."

"You have to take a break from it sometimes."

Leah's posture never broke even while she thought. Macy wondered if she knew how to slouch. "I suppose you are correct," she admitted. "I sometimes read."

She nodded at the end table to Macy's left. A small pile of novels sat in a neat stack. A red cover stood out, bright and bold amongst the others. *Beloved* by Toni Morrison. Macy felt her breath catch.

After about another hour, Leah bade them farewell, thanking them again for coming to her concert and agreeing to meet with her. Winston escorted them from the building, which was empty of guests, who had been replaced by cleaning and maintenance staff. Gordon took her hand and she did not refuse, swimming in the surreal texture of the night.

"Thanks for that. I cannot imagine how different my life would be had I not gone," Gordon said.

Macy nodded. She drove him back to the restaurant, where his car waited patiently for his return. When they embraced, she thought he might kiss her, but he only drew close enough for her to see his startling eyes again, clear in the moonlight. She thought of a particular song Leah Miyamizu had played during the show, where the quick flutter of high notes had made Macy's heart leap.

"Good night," Gordon said. His number was written on the concert ticket in her purse.

She drove the rest of the way home in silence, preferring not to turn on the radio. She needed time before returning to the rest of the world of music.

The glow from her house number greeted her. Macy parked in the garage, the engine dying while the door slid down behind her. For a moment, she did not leave the vehicle, stroking the picture taped to her dashboard with her thumb.

Then she grabbed her purse and hoisted herself out of the car.

Night did not exist inside the house. It was only dark, the windows like hung portraits of a town bathed in the glow of streetlamps and a backdrop of stars. Inside, she heard the hum of the refrigerator instead of the drone of traffic. She switched on the light in the living room, the standing lamp coming to life in the corner. She wanted to take off her dress and her shoes and her makeup and her jewelry. Instead, she walked over to the bookcases against the wall.

Five of his books were still stacked there, separated from her own as if she still meant to return them.

She flipped through the first four, the ones she had read. Lines of prose jumped out at her, but she wasn't searching for anything in particular, just feeling the pages. The last she picked up and turned over and over in her hands. The cover was pleasing: stripes of overlapping blue and black like patterns of moonlight through slanted blinds. The one-word title was printed in all lowercase letters: *ghostwritten.*

Then something fell to the floor, sliding from between the pages.

Macy stared down at the folded slip of paper at her feet. For a moment, she could not move, confused. The book was in near-perfect condition; the paper could not have fallen from the binding. She noticed then the bulging protrusions running across the sheet from words on the inside. It was a handwritten note.

She set the book down and bent to retrieve the paper, eyes burning already.

As she had dared to suspect, her brother's scrawl greeted her. Macy had to sit, unable to read the note until she had let herself cry for a minute. When her vision cleared, she read.

Macy,

I know. What am I doing handwriting a letter? It's the big 2k after all—weren't we supposed to have flying cars by now?

Anyway, I just finished reading this one and it made me think of you—not because of the overarching story, it's good but not related to my connection—but because you're always talking about how little things affect other people's lives. At least in this book, I think our debate about whether everything happens for a reason is settled. Isn't it nice that an author can decide these questions for their universe? Maybe that's why Brooklyn preferred his worlds to our own. My partner, the writer. I miss him always. We have our problems, but we'll sort them out. I'll go back to him soon.

Which brings me to my next point. Thanks so much for being my support system through this. Coming back to California was a hard choice, but you made the transition as easy as possible. You can keep this book as my payment. Or I guess I can take you out to a fancy dinner sometime if you prefer.

Alright, enough being mushy. I'll probably see you this weekend. Mom and Dad say they want to see your new place!

Love,
Ollie-ollie-oxen-free

Macy read the note several times, searching for any pieces of her brother she might have missed. She read the note until she could almost repeat the first paragraph without hearing him recite the words in her mind. When she realized this, she stopped, wanting to preserve his voice. Wanting to preserve some of the spontaneity of a first read. How had she never found this note? Why had he not said anything when he gave it to her? They had come up to her house that weekend as Ollie had predicted, he and their parents. They had come to visit and he'd handed her the book without mentioning that he'd written her a note inside. Without mentioning that he'd recommended this one next because it reminded him however tangentially of her. Without mentioning that within months he'd be gone and they would all have to contend with nothing more than his memory.

Macy set the note on the coffee table and kneaded her forehead with her knuckles.

Did everything affect everything? And did everything happen for a reason? If so, what was the reason for his death and why was she being reminded now? What were the events that brought about his passing? What events had led her to meeting Gordon Larkin tonight? He was a sweet man, and they'd had such a surreal and unexpected experience together. She had been so happy at one point this evening. Now look at her.

Life was nothing like literature, with its neat systems created by authors playing God. Perhaps she would have to contend with never having answers. That was the most frustrating aspect of living. Macy picked the book up again, running her hand across the cover. The design was flawless. A perfect composition of the abstract. She flipped to the first page.

MIXTAPE MANIA

In the background, crowds of people chatter loudly. La Guardia Airport must be packed, which is understandable given that it's about…5 pm there right now. Everybody's heading somewhere at the same time my baby's trying to get home.

"Marshall?" she asks, because I've been silent. "You still there?"

"Yes, ma'am," I say and she laughs.

"I thought maybe you'd hung up."

"I wouldn't dream of it," I say, "Not 'til we said 'I love you'."

She laughs again. "You are so ridiculous." It sounds like a complaint, but make no mistake, if I ever stopped being ridiculous she'd be pouting.

"How was the wedding?" I ask.

"Interesting," she says.

I laugh. "Describing a wedding as 'interesting' usually means it didn't go so hot."

"No, I didn't mean that," she says, backpedaling. "The wedding itself was great, the rest of the night just got weird.

I'll tell you later."

My interest is piqued, but she obviously doesn't want to say over the phone, so I don't push the topic.

"Listen," she says, "this morning I was shopping with the girls and we found this old record store."

I don't know if I like where this is going, but I play along because you should never react until you know all the details. When Larissa tells a story, she builds it dramatically so that she holds all the important things until the end. I thought I was supposed to react to each trickle of info when we first started dating, but that was a mistake. You don't want to be acting all happy when she drops the bomb, because then you have to backtrack and that gets messy.

"They had all these old records, like Marving Gaye and The Commodores and Earth, Wind, and Fire. Classic R&B, you know? Stuff my mama used to listen to," she continues. I hear a waitress approach, but Larissa assures her she's got everything she needs. She must be sitting in a restaurant. "We were dancing in the store, it was so much fun."

She pauses for a reaction, so I give an encouraging *mmhmm*.

"Anyways, I found they had this section of music systems in the back and there was a used cassette boombox!" The excitement in her voice peaks. This was the climax. "It made me think of that mixtape I gave you on our first anniversary."

A test.

"Yea!" I say. I didn't have to lie about remembering the tape. It was a sweet gesture, the type Larissa liked to make that I loved getting. "It had *The Greatest Love of All* on it."

Bonus points for naming one of the songs.

Larissa laughs. "Yes, baby!"

"Man, I ain't listened to that since the tape player on our stereo broke," I say, running a hand over my head.

"You still got it though?"

"Yea, of course I still got it."

"Good! I was hoping you'd say that. I bought the boombox, I thought maybe we could listen to the tape when I get back."

I don't still got it. Shit.

"I love you, baby. See you soon." Larissa hangs up and my heart leaps from my chest all the way to my throat. My brain rings like an alarm clock. Why, Marshall? Why in the *hell* did you say you still had that tape when you knew damn well you didn't?

Simple, because she would have been hurt if you said you got rid of it.

But you did get rid of it! So she's gonna be hurt either way.

I bury my head in my hands, rubbing my temples like I've seen them do on TV. Like it'll help or something if I massage the stress. I was talking out of my ass, and she's gonna know soon as she comes home and there's no tape.

Or will she? Do I know for a fact that I threw that tape out? I mean, it was really special to me. Sure, I didn't know she was gonna ask me to play it seven years later when tapes ain't even a thing no more, but I liked it back then. Maybe I didn't throw it away.

I run to my dresser. If I hide anything special, it's in here. I know that's an obvious spot, but she doesn't look in my drawers. I clean them out one at a time but it's only my clothes inside. Socks and underwear and shirts all going everywhere, but no tape. That's alright, where next.

The hallway closet! We keep all the VHS tapes she records

her daytime shows on in there! Maybe I stashed it long ago.

I run out of the room and to the hallway closet, throwing open the door. Underneath the hanging jackets and behind the vacuum is a banker's box sitting on the ground. I pull it out and tear off the lid. VHS tapes, just like I said. Damn. And not a single cassette tape inside. Shoving the lid back on, I push it into the closet again.

I see another box.

Dear God, I pray, *if you give me this one thing I promise I'll never ask for nothing more again.*

I pull out this box and rip off the lid.

It's mostly empty, but under an assortment of instruction manuals, I hit the mother lode. The entire bottom is covered in a layer of cassettes.

I point a finger up at the Big Man. *You the best.*

Then I start going through them all.

As I search, I realize one thing: you can fit a ton of tapes into one layer of a banker's box. We've got mixes of Stevie Wonder, Jimi Hendrix, The Pointer Sisters, Boys II Men, and something called "High Energy Baby-Making," but not the tape I'm looking for. My heart begins to sink as I'm nearing the end. This can't be happening. There are so many tapes in here. How can the one I want be missing?

In the very last row, I pull out a case and flip it over.

"Happy First Anniversary" is scrawled on the paper insert in Larissa's neat handwriting. Just my luck though, because the case is dead empty. Dammit.

I open it up anyway to get a look at the insert. Usually, people write the track-list on these slips of paper. I could recreate the tape easy as that, but the insert has got *nothing* but the title on it. Instead, there's a folded piece of paper inside with more of Larissa's handwriting in red ink.

Probably something that was a cute little note at the time, but is now a cute little pain in my ass.

Yep. As I thought, the note is numbered 1-11, but instead of track names, I've got annotations about the songs.

Can you believe this was the first song we danced to? I know it's not romantic, but we can't change history, and it's not like this is a bad song! At least we've got rhythm!

That could be enough though. I still can put the tape back together. As long as I can tell what songs she was referring to, then it's as good as having the actually list, right? Larissa's going to be at the airport in 6 hours, not banking on any delays. That means I've got the rest of the day before she's back. I can do this. I can put together the mixtape just like it was before and she'll never know the difference. I can solve these riddles. I ain't like one of those men who don't remember anything about their relationship.

I psych myself up for the challenge. *You can't do this, Marshall. This is the ultimate test. Ready? And...GO!*

I sprint to the kitchen, snatching the list pad off the fridge. Tiny puppies stare back at me with over-large eyes. I use the cuteness, imagining they're cheering me on. No puppy has ever wanted someone to fail.

Alright, the first one is easy as they come. We danced on our second date at TJ's twenty-fifth birthday party, that took place in...1998, but it was eighties themed event. Larissa had come up to me and said Janet was her favorite and if I didn't dance with her she wasn't going on a third date. I went with her to the floor and found out soon enough she didn't need no help. She'd studied all the moves from the video.

"Rhythm Nation!" I shout, despite being the only one home. I write the name down under the puppy at the top of the paper, then run back to the living room to our CD rack.

Janet's on the top shelf because, just like then, she's still Larissa's favorite. I grab the album and lay it by the stereo.

Next.

I love this song because I can picture you singing it to me. He sounds exactly like you when we're waking up on a Saturday morning.

This one's a little more challenging. Baby says I sound exactly like Barry White. So, I know he's got to be the singer. But Barry's got more songs than a church hymnal and I can only choose one.

Well, if it's a song I know the words to, that narrows it down. And the song has to be romantic—but that's at least seventy percent of Barry's repertoire.

What would she imagine me singing to her on a Saturday? I comb our shelf for Barry White albums. She's got *Greatest Hits vol. 2, Barry White Sings for Someone You Love,* and *Can't Get Enough.*

If I had to pick a song to sing, it'd be from that last one. *Can't Get Enough of Your Love, Babe* comes to mind and I know it has to be right. I don't think she could say I'd pick anything else. So, I write it down and pull the jewel case out.

My brother's going to want to sing this on our wedding day. I can't listen to it without crying, but if you don't learn that this song is one of my favorites, then you don't know me.

Another easy one because it actually came true. On our wedding day, Jerome got up after dinner to sing this song alongside a slideshow. Every single damn person in the room cried their eyes out. I may have even shed a tear, I don't know. Afterward, Larissa's mama and Jerome came over to our table and the three of them hugged. It was Luther Vandross, *Dance with My Father.*

I scribble it next on the list. I know we don't have the album for this track, but Jerome made us a mixed CD of

Luther Vandross songs. Larissa keeps that one in her car. I can grab it later.

So far, so good.

When I hear this song, I think about the part where they mention how close their lover is, like they're one of their family members who love and support them. All my family loves you already! They talk about you as if you're one of them.

Ah, shit. This one's more difficult. To stop myself pacing, I go over to the couch and sink down onto the cushions. They mention 'how close their lover is, like they're one of their family members.' So, family members are mentioned in the song? And Larissa says *they*, so it's got to be a group singing. What groups are singing about family members?

I don't know what the hell she's talking about. I'm sure plenty of songs talk about family members…or at least mention their mamas. Hell, this could've come from a lot of artists. R&B groups are almost more common than R&B soloists.

Close like a family member. Close to them, I churn the words over in my head, sitting back on the couch. I've had it too easy up 'til now. I've been checking them off but it was bound to get harder at some point. I rub my eyes with my hand, trying to think.

A group singing about their lover being close like family.

Unless it isn't a group. Then why would she have called them 'they.'

It could be a duo.

Close to me you're like my mother, close to me you're like my father. The lyrics come to me in a rush and I jump off the couch. "All My Life" by KC and Jojo! That's it! It's got to be. That song was everywhere the year she made this. It has to be right. She listened to it nonstop!

I don't think we own this one, but Cassie does!

I sprint out of the house, puppy papers in hand, down the drive to the home next door to ours. As I'm running up the steps, our neighbor opens the door, her purse slung on her shoulder. She looks startled to see me, concerned that I'm barreling toward her.

"Cassie!" I shout, knowing I must look crazy. "Cassie, you got the KC and Jojo album?"

She backs away a step. "What are you talking about?"

I come to a stop, waving the paper at her. She snatches it from me, her eye brows raising.

"I've got to make our mixtape—Larissa—the anniversary—don't know where it is."

"Marshall," she spots the puppies. "Have you hit your head?"

"No!" I take the paper back. "I can't find the mixtape Larissa gave me for our first anniversary. She's coming back today, so I gotta re-make it before she finds out."

"Mmmhmm," Cassie gives me a shady look. "You lost the mixtape?"

"We don't even have a working tape player anymore!"

"Okay, Marshall. I believe you," she says in a voice that clearly says she still thinks this is my fault. "What'd'you need?"

"KC and Jojo. All My Life. I don't have it on CD."

"Ooh, she's got good taste." Cassie makes to start singing the chorus, but I cut her off.

"So, you got it?" I ask, trying to plead with my eyes.

She holds up her left hand, in which she's got her car keys hanging on her finger. "I was about to go to the store." I groan. "But, you can get it yourself, just don't mess up my things."

I leap a little with joy. "Thanks, Cassie, you the real MVP."

She rolls her eyes. "You're lucky Larissa's my friend. Lock up when you leave."

And with that she walks out to her car sitting at the curb. I waste no time going in. Larissa and I have been over here thousands of times, so I head straight for the living room where I know Cassie keeps the music. She alphabetizes everything and Lord help anyone who screws up her system, but bless her. She's got KC and Jojo right where I need it. I pull the album out.

The next two are easy. They're even by the same artist.

You told me you loved me at the bowling alley while this song was on. Yea, you needed bumpers to play, but your moves were bumpin on their own.

That's definitely "I Will" by Usher.

We said "I love you" for the first time to the last song, and we made love for the first time to this one. Guess we got a thing for your boy, Usher.

"Nice & Slow."

We've got both of those back home. I'm never getting rid of that album until the day I die. And maybe I'm going to have my family bury it with me. Who knows.

This is another one that's maybe a little sad, but it was the one I sang after you convinced me to join in the Karaoke at Naomi's party. I never would have gone up there, because I don't do well with crowds, but you kept talking about how much you loved my voice and well, I had so much fun after I did it.

Karaoke at Naomi's party. We aren't even friends with Naomi anymore. She turned out to be a stuck-up homewrecker who ruined another one of Larissa's friend's relationships. That was a whole thing. But what did Larissa sing at her party? I remember convincing her. She kept refusing, but I knew if I got her up there she'd have a blast. Baby just needs a little push. I can even see her on the stage, but what was the song?

The way she was moving…it had to be slow and jazzy. And she says in the note that it's a little sad too, but what was it? Something about falling for someone I think. One of those jazz standards that doesn't have a real chorus, just like a line that gets repeated at the end of each verse. She was falling…or she fell? She fell I think. "I Fell For You," that sounds about right!

That one will be difficult. It's probably by Etta James or something. I'll have to go to a store to find a copy of that. I move on to the next.

Another one of my favorites. Although I never went to a camp in my life, this one makes me think of summer. And especially summer with you. Plus, I hear you singing this one in the shower all the time.

I've only got one shower classic. That's "Always Be My Baby," by Mariah Carey. Yea, I sing other songs while getting clean too, but they come and go. That bop is always on rotation.

No tape is complete without Whitney—

I don't even need to finish that one. It's definitely "The Greatest Love of All." She even confirmed it when we were on the phone.

This one'll make you laugh, but that movie was great and I have to admit, white girl's got lungs.

This one's not too hard either. Larissa doesn't listen to too many white girl singers. And if the song is tied to a movie, there's only one tune I can think of: "My Heart Will Go On" by Celine Dion. I'll even admit that I might know all the words to that one. We don't have it though, and neither does

Cassie, so that'll be another CD I've got to find at the store. Great. I write it down below the other's.

Finally, there's just one more song to go.

I've put a lot of slow songs on this tape, but we like gettin down as much as we like romancing. I decided to close it out with this one just because we love dancing to it so much and it's always on the radio! So get educated!

Alright, so this one had to be popular right when she was making this. We liked dancing to it? That hardly helps. We always had the radio on back then, we were always grooving. But if this was popular right next to our anniversary, that had to be on the charts in January of '99. What was bumpin at the start of '99? Brandy was all over the radio, I think, but I don't remember dancing a lot to Brandy. R. Kelly too, but baby was never as wild for R. Kelly as everybody else was. Will Smith was a rapper back then and he had a lot of hits. "Get Jiggy wit it" was a favorite of ours. Could that be it? If so, we have his albums, I'm sure I could figure out which it was. That has to be it, that has to.

I take a few steps toward the door, but hesitate. It doesn't seem right. There's still that last part of the note: *So get educated!* What does Will have to do with education? I guess he was the Fresh Prince...and the Fresh Prince was in school all the time.

Wait a minute. *Get educated.* There's only one album that can refer to. A classic. "The Miseducation of Lauryn Hill."

I laugh because I'd almost been duped. Now that I'm thinking about it, I do remember something by Lauryn Hill being on the tape. A sure-fire jam in our book. "Doo Wop (That Thing)" was playing all the time. And who's gonna get rid of a classic album like that? We've got that one for sure.

Elation hits me. I've done it! I've figured out all the songs on the mixtape. She didn't write anything more, so it must've been only one side! That means I'm in the clear, all I've got to do now is get the songs on a tape before Larissa gets back. She'll never know the difference.

I stop doing my victory dance when I remember I'm not finished yet. A) I've got to buy some blank tapes and B) I have two songs to get on CD first.

I run back to my house and grab the keys to my car. There's a Best Buy in the plaza a few freeway exits down. That's probably going to be the safest bet. I speed the whole way, thankful that no policemen are around. I've got about four and a half hours before Larissa gets back, but that time will be gone before I know it.

The store is super packed this weekend and I have to practically fight my way through the aisles.

Finding a copy of Celine Dion's "Greatest Hits" is no problem, but none of the Etta James albums have a song named anything like "I Fell For You." Although it makes my skin crawl, I know I've only got one option if I want this problem fixed quick. I need to ask an employee for help.

I tap one of the fellas in a blue polo.

"Excuse me, I'm trying to find a song," I say. The kid is all smiles. He's one of those people who's actually enthusiastic about customer service. I feel kinda bad, because I probably would've made fun of him in high school due to his braces. He doesn't look too bothered by anything though.

"Certainly, sir," he says. "Do you know who it's by."

"Not really, no," I admit. "I think it's Etta James, but I'm not sure."

He thinks for a second. "Well, if you don't know, we can always check the computer."

He leads me over to the nearest employee station and

inputs his passcode. I swear, the dude's practically humming while he helps me.

"Do you know the name of the song?"

"I think it's called 'I Fell For You'. Something like that."

He types that in and presses ENTER. The computer brings up a link asking if we meant "*Since* I Fell For You." A memory clicks into place.

"Yes!" I exclaim, pointing at the screen. "That's the one. That's what it's called."

He clicks the link and a page of entries comes up.

"It seems like the song has been covered numerous times," the kid says, scrolling quickly up and down the page. "Which artist are you looking for?"

I scan the list. There's no Etta James entry. Dammit. Which one would Larissa have put on the tape? Let's see…I'm pretty sure it would have been a woman. I don't know why, I've just got a feeling. Why did I think it was by Etta James? Was that only because I knew it was an old jazzy song? Or maybe it was someone else who was similar?

"Sir?" the kid asks because I've been silent.

"I don't know which artist," I say, rubbing my hand on my face.

"Well, there're plenty to choose from," he starts reading the list, "Louis Armstrong"—no, I'm sticking with female—"Eartha Kitt"—could be, but she had a bias against Eartha since her grandmother wasn't a fan—"Earl Grant"—again, not a woman—"Nina Simone—"

"Nina Simone!" I say. Her grandma loved Nina Simone! That's where Larissa would've gotten the song from. I'm sure when she upgraded to Compact Disc, her grandmother would've asked for all the Nina Simone albums. "Do you have that one?"

He clicks. "You're in luck, sir. It looks like we have one copy of *Nina Simone Sings the Blues* in-store."

I could kiss him. He leads me to the album while I'm buzzing with excitement. I nearly leave the store before remembering I needed to get blank tapes as well. Cursing myself quietly, I go back and purchase the tapes, the same check-out girl laughing at me as she rings me up for the second time. Then I blast my way home. I've still got three hours! No problem at all.

Because our tape deck is broken, I take all the CDs over to Cassie's place. She's still not home, so I'm sure she won't mind if I go in again. I set up in the living room, ten discs stacked neatly beside the stereo (both Usher songs are on one album! Lucky me). Then I get to work.

The first try, I'm halfway through when I realize I've put the Usher songs backward because I'm not paying attention to what I'm doing. Grumbling under my breath, I take the tape out and toss it aside to throw away at the end. I start another tape.

This time, I get too eager and press the STOP button before "Can't Get Enough of Your Love" is over. I know Larissa will notice if the song gets cut off. And it'll be really obvious if I try to start it up again in the same place or if I tape over it and the old recording plays when the new one stops or something, so I tear the tape out to get started again, letting a cry of frustration fill my neighbor's house.

It turns out, the third time's the charm.

Song after song plays, and I end up leaning back against a wall in the living room listening to each as the stereo sends me almost a decade into the past. Knowing Baby's reasons for including the songs helps me place the feelings they recall. I can remember being nervous to dance with her the first time, or watching her eyes fill with tears when her brother says he's going to dedicate a song to their deceased father at our wedding. I can see her in my first apartment, acting a fool to "Doo Wop." How could I ever have gotten rid of the real tape?

At last, the songs are all recorded and I breathe a sigh of relief. I've still got about an hour and a half before she's at the airport. Feeling somehow exhausted, I grab my CDs and wander back home, the tape cradled in my palm. I fold the list of clues and slide it back into the proper case, then put the tape inside. Hopefully, she won't be able to tell the difference.

When the time comes, I get my ass to the airport and pick Baby up, giving her an extra kiss and a hug for getting home safely. Soon as we walk back through our door, she's got the tape player out to show me. I hand her the phony tape, hoping to God she can't tell I made it.

We listen together, laughing and reminiscing, even crying (she cries, but I only come close). My breath is held the entire time, not wanting to believe I've pulled it off. Then, the last bit of Lauryn Hill ends and she still doesn't look suspicious. If anything, she looks like she's about to cry again.

Larissa comes over to sit on my lap.

"You're the best, you know that?" she says.

"I know," I say, winking.

She flicks the tip of my nose affectionately. "I knew you'd keep it."

I laugh. "You must be psychic," I say, really wishing we could change the subject.

Then the phone rings and I sigh in relief when she offers to answer, hurrying out of the room to the kitchen. I can't believe she didn't notice anything. If she'd written something on the tape itself, I would have been screwed because I can't copy her writing for nothing. But she didn't look twice at the tape. If she'd recorded herself saying something, I would've also been screwed for obvious reasons. But when the music stopped, she didn't wait around for any other messages. Everything is good.

Until she comes back into the living room with an attitude and a half, jabbing her thumb into the END button on the phone as if the *beep* will be louder that way. She doesn't say anything, just stares at me, but I know something's wrong.

"Uh, who was that, Baby?" I ask, hoping this has nothing to do with me.

"That was Cassie." Larissa puts her hands on her hips. "She says you left her front door open."

Words fail me. I was so close. *So close.* And yet I know now it will all come crumbling down. At least she isn't furious, more annoyed than anything. I can salvage this. Maybe.

"She didn't want to tell me, but I managed to get her to confess that you'd left two tapes on the floor. Asked if you wanted them back."

I search Larissa's eyes, trying to find glimmers of mercy in them. If they exist, they're being stubbornly hard to find.

"She also said you put KC and Jojo behind KC and the Sunshine Band even though 'S' comes after 'J'."

They were on the phone for one minute. How could she have possibly gotten all this information? My mind races, flashing through options like flipping through a rolodex. I could deny the whole thing, just say that I'd thought maybe I'd leant it to Cassie at some point and thought she might still have it. I could give the whole thing up, grovel on the floor for forgiveness. I could use something else as leverage, try to get a 'we're even now' thing going; that always backfires, though.

"I lost it," I say, before I can make a conscious decision. Her eye brows raise, surprised that I've gone with the truth. "I...admit that I lost it. I only found the case with your note inside." She's about to interrupt me, but I speak up again, thinking quick. "But you shouldn't be mad because I remembered each and every song just by using your note! I didn't forget nothing about our relationship, because I got them right. All I needed was your clue."

My heart hasn't beat this fast before. If she doesn't kill me, maybe a heart attack will. For a second, we're both motionless. I'm not fooled by Larissa's stance. She may look relaxed, but she could probably pounce at any moment. My hands are clutching the edge of the couch so tightly, I've probably gotten as close to 'white-knuckled' as I can get. If something don't happen soon, the air between us might just split in half.

Then a miracle occurs. She smiles.

"You know what," she says, shrugging. "You're right."

I can't believe the words I'm hearing. My mouth is agape.

"I'm not going to be one of those people who makes a bigger deal than they need to. You are right," she says. "I could be mad that you lost the tape, but you still had the case and the note, so it was obviously an accident. And the most important part is that you still knew every song that I talked about. And you got them all back together in less than six hours. That's kind of impressive."

She laughs that warm-as-honey laugh that still gives me goosebumps. I love my Baby. She comes back over to the couch, sets the phone down on the coffee table, and sits in my lap again.

"I love you," I say.

"I love you too," she sings. She presses REWIND on the tape player and the device whirs to life, sending the cassette of all our songs back to the beginning.

I can't wait to listen again.

SHADOWS AND SHAPES

James McGowan knew his voice was gruff and unapologetic. That was how he usually got his way. "Tell us what happened."

The boy continued to stare at his own hands; he couldn't seem to see anything else. McGowan couldn't even tell whether he'd heard the question. The boy just kept staring at his damn hands. The officer rolled his eyes. One of *these*— and he swore the sons of bitches got younger every year. But maybe that was a sign of him getting old.

"Alberto?" asked his partner, Jean O'Hair. "Did you hear Officer McGowan?"

The distracted Alberto looked up, lost. His face was pale and McGowan didn't think his eyes had been any less than the size of golf balls since they'd picked him up. Jesus, that scene was a mess. Evidence would be there for weeks.

"You called *us*, kid. I assume that means you want to cooperate. So you can do that by telling us what happened," McGowan growled.

Alberto nodded faintly. He cleared his throat with the

tiniest sound possible.

"They—they were hazing us. Made us dig up a corpse, threatened to hurt us if we didn't."

"Who are 'they'?" O'Hair asked.

"The fraternity brothers. The—the ones who weren't initiates," Alberto stammered.

"They made you dig up a corpse?" Jean asked incredulously. "That's morbid. How many bodies?"

"One per pair of pledges."

McGowan slid a sheet of paper across the table and slapped down a pen next to it. "Do you know the names of the corpses?"

Alberto shook his head. "No. Only mine. Her name was—it was Felicity Alba."

"Felicity Alba." McGowan stood up, turned, and marched out the door. In the observation room, three other officers were standing at the window, their arms crossed solemnly. "Did you get that?" he asked.

"Yeah," a slim woman replied. She turned to leave. "I'll look into it. Identify her body on scene."

McGowan nodded, then plowed back into the interview room. He needed a coffee. This was too much for eight in the morning on no sleep. Problem was, no way in hell was this a quick wrap. Not with the scene they'd found. They were going to be at this for a while.

"… some sort of ritual?" Jean finished asking.

Alberto nodded.

"Please answer aloud for the camera," McGowan said. He tried to sound polite, but that never came off correctly when he did it.

"Yes," the kid responded. "They took me and my roommate Jamie to the graveyard, had us dig her up, and then brought us to… to…"

"The abandoned Mills factory," O'Hair finished when it was clear the boy couldn't remember where they'd been.

"Yes," he said. "They put all the bodies in the center of the room—"

"They being the Omega Alpha Lambda brothers?" McGowan asked. When they'd picked the boy up five blocks from the crime scene, those were the first three words he'd said to them. Lupe was looking into the organization as they spoke.

Alberto nodded.

"Please, answer aloud—"

"Yes, the brothers," Alberto said. "Then they had the pledges stand in a circle around the bodies while the brothers stood in the shadows by the walls. I thought it would be my chance to get away, but I was stuck. I couldn't move."

"By 'couldn't move,' do you mean they had restrained you in some way?" O'Hair asked. She crossed one leg over the other.

"Yes," Alberto replied.

"What did they use? Chains? Rope?"

"It was…" The boy's brow furrowed as if he couldn't quite conjure the correct words. He stared at his hands. "They didn't… use physical restraints, but I couldn't move. I tried, but my feet were stuck."

"An adhesive on your shoes then?"

"No, they didn't have anything on the floor. The guy who positioned me walked away just fine."

"Were you maybe paralyzed with fear?" O'Hair tried.

"No, I was trying pretty hard to lift my feet. I tugged this way and that—they just wouldn't move." Alberto's response was the typical fare of a normal victim emerging from extreme circumstances. Details always garbled themselves in the victim's mind. They'd remember rope when it was chains. That sort of thing. If Alberto really hadn't been chained, though, then it must have been fear. Perhaps the boy was embarrassed to admit this.

"Sometimes, in times of great stress, our body doesn't seem to listen to what our mind is telling it to do. It can seem like you're stuck—"

"I'm telling you, that's not it!" Alberto was getting frustrated, color rising in his cheeks. McGowan resisted the urge to roll his eyes. If the kid couldn't admit this simple fact, then he was going to make things more difficult for all of them. "I... I think..." He was almost trembling, his fingers twitching under his own gaze. "I think it was something paranormal."

McGowan could have groaned. Not one of these crazies. The more this kid talked, the worse it got. That was all they needed to make the investigation even longer than it already would be.

Officer O'Hair showed no signs of judgment; she even nodded a bit. God love her. If anyone could coax the kid into realizing that the only thing extraordinary about that night was the cruelty of the fraternity brothers, it would be her. McGowan knew he didn't have the patience for that sort of emotional guidance, so he did his best to stay silent.

"Tell us what happened then," she prompted.

Alberto swallowed hard. "They, um... they all started chanting. Real loud like, and unintelligible. I think they were speaking another language. Latin, maybe"—it was *always* Latin; the poor language had garnered such a bad reputation—"and some of the other boys and I, we were screaming. The chanting got so loud we couldn't hear ourselves. It made my skin crawl. I felt like the chant was making my heart race.

"The bodies in the canvas bags began to move. I don't know, they were trying to break out or something. And eventually they did rip through the bags. I thought I might die just from shock. I couldn't breathe. It was all so terrifying." Alberto stopped as if the memory were enough to send him back into that horrified state. McGowan could see moisture gathering at the corners of his eyes. Alberto flexed his fingers and continued. "Felicity Alba walked over to us. She looked nothing like she had when we took her out of the grave. Her eyes were swollen and red, her skin looked like it had been burned in places. She kind of limped her way to us, an awful rasp coming out of her.

"Jamie... Jamie screamed, and I think that's why she went to him first. I—I didn't want to watch, but I couldn't look away. The brothers had all gone silent, so there was nothing but the howls from the pledges. That and the awful rasping sounds from the corpses. She kept moving toward Jamie, limping. And when she got to him, she fell on top of him and knocked him over. He was screaming so much, but he couldn't get away, he couldn't push her off him. She was strong, so much stronger than she looked. I thought she couldn't be much more than a skeleton but he wasn't able to get her off him.

"She placed her hands against his chest and started pressing down hard. His screams had turned to sobbing by then, but she kept pressing more and more forcefully. She wasn't giving up, until finally..." He heaved a sigh, struggling to hold back tears. "Her fingers sank into his chest. I couldn't believe it—I think I almost vomited—but that wasn't the worst part. Before I could look away, she yanked open his ribs. *Literally* yanked open his bloody ribs. The crack was the worst thing I've ever heard."

Alberto collapsed into heaps of sobbing, his face buried in his hands. His shoulders shook uncontrollably, all the strength gone from him.

But McGowan had had enough of the theatrics. He tried to catch Jean's eye, but she wasn't looking at him. She was still stuck on the kid's last words, her mouth hanging open. She didn't believe any of it. No, there was no possible way—she was too logical. Sure, they had found the bodies in... the prescribed state, which corroborated that part of the story, but that didn't mean a corpse had come along to rip them open. She was just surprised by the accusation.

"And he kept screaming," Alberto whispered. McGowan glanced back up at him. His skin crawled. He couldn't help it. The boy believed every word he was saying. That or he was the best actor McGowan had ever encountered.

O'Hair asked, "But how could he—"

"I don't know, but he was still screaming bloody murder when Felicity Alba turned on me," Alberto said. McGowan searched his face for signs of lunacy. He didn't see anything obvious, but no matter. The face was not where one usually diagnosed insanity. "I couldn't see straight—I think I was crying too much at that point. I wanted to get away from her, but I couldn't stop looking back at my friend. I mean, his *heart* was beating out in the open. His ribs were sticking into the air like fingers. And she was coming for me. She was coming for me and I couldn't move.

"I felt her hands touch my legs. I felt how powerful she was. She knocked me over. My ankles nearly broke with my feet sticking to the ground, but the spell or whatever held me released at the last moment. Instead, I got stuck on my back, splayed like the Vitruvian Man. Nothing but my arms worked and I tried to fight her off like Jamie, but it was no good. She was hissing at me and had her hands against my chest and God she was pushing hard, I'd never felt so much pressure. Everything was in pain and I couldn't see and I couldn't hear anything but my own wails and I thought, *All I want is for the pain to stop. Nothing else, I just need the pain to stop.*"

The boy fell silent. In the absence of his words, the overhead lights buzzed. McGowan was sitting on the edge of his seat—*actually* poised on the forwardmost inches of the chair. The boy was good, he had to give him that. If his story was ludicrous, at least he was convincing.

"How did you stop her?" O'Hair asked, breathless.

"I didn't," Alberto whispered. "She ripped open my chest. I heard more than felt my ribs crack, screamed because I saw what was happening as if I were a person standing beside us watching. I expected death to come quickly, but it didn't, just as it had ignored Jamie and all the other pledges.

"I was the last. After me, the room was silent. The other pledges stopped screaming, nobody was chanting, the corpses stopped their godawful rasping. I should've still been wailing, but again, I didn't feel much pain. That was… the strangest part, I think. I felt apprehension, tension, and fear. I looked around but couldn't move much. Everybody was waiting, staring at the center of the room. That's when the shadow came."

"The shadow?"

"Yes. I could see my lungs hitch, my stomach clenched, and my heart started beating faster. It's hard to explain. The shadow was there, but I couldn't look straight at it. It was

215

more like an area that the light seemed to miss. But it was immense. I could feel it bearing down on us. I know it wasn't fear that trapped me before, Officers, because that was the moment it paralyzed me.

"One of the brothers standing around the edge of the room came forward. I could tell he was afraid of the monster too by the look in his eye, but he had a duty to fulfill. He went to the boy next to me, knelt next to him and lifted his hand. I couldn't see very clearly, but it looked like he had a tattoo on his palm. An upside-down triangle. He pressed it to the boy's heart and he began crying out in agony. Then the shadow got him."

"What do you mean, the shadow got him?"

"It attacked. The whole room kind of moved when it moved, shuddering under the immense weight—almost like an earthquake. One moment the boy was screaming and the next he was silent, staring blankly up at the air. Dead. Then the brother moved on to the next pledge.

"I started panicking. I didn't want him to get to me. I didn't want to find out what death was like under that shadow. I had a feeling it wasn't the same as normal death. I had a feeling it dragged you down into darkness. I started doing all I could to move, slamming my fists into the ground, trying to roll myself over. Meanwhile, the brother made his way around the circle, boy after boy meeting the same fate, their lives swallowed by the monster. Every part of me willed me to run, but that wasn't enough. He was only five pledges away when I did the only thing I could think of—I grabbed my ribs and started pushing them closed."

O'Hair gasped in disgust, her hand going to her mouth. McGowan fidgeted.

"At first they didn't budge, but I felt them give a little and then a little more. I'm not strong at all, but I pushed with everything I had, watching the bones bend themselves back into place while my time ran out. I got blood all over my hands—my own blood. And there was so much of it, I don't know how I didn't pass out. Wanting to survive makes you strong, I guess. Thinking now, I would've expected someone to come stop me, but nobody did. God, I've never tried so hard at something. And he was at Jamie when I was closing myself the last few inches. I had it all the way as he was kneeling over me, hand outstretched with that tattoo coming toward my chest, and I reached up and gripped his hand in mine to stop him. And the spell binding me broke—"

"Enough," McGowan said. He was standing before he realized it, breathing heavily. Both Alberto and O'Hair were looking at him, startled. Alberto seemed to have forgotten the two officers existed during his retelling, while the look on O'Hair's face was one of incredulity. Did she really want—no, *need* the boy to continue? He was spouting nonsense. Rambling on about shadow monsters and spells binding him to the floor, not to mention reanimated corpses. The boy had obviously watched too many movies and if he wasn't the murderer of all those bodies they'd found splayed in that abandoned factory, he sure as hell wasn't going to help them capture the culprits. If O'Hair wanted to hear more of the gory tall tale, she could, but he had no interest. He said again, "Enough."

"I can show you," Alberto said, and stood. McGowan's first instinct was to leap forward and wrestle the boy to the ground before he could attack them, but the kid only reached up and started undoing the buttons of his cardigan.

"What are you..." McGowan fell silent. The boy was quick and the last button was undone before he could get in another word. Alberto pulled the jacket wide. The T-shirt he had on underneath was ripped and more scarlet than white. Down the center of his chest, all the way from his collar bone to his stomach, was a long, mottled scar, fresh, pink, and inflamed. The ribs were bruised where they had been bent—*allegedly* been bent. Blood stains painted the boy's skin.

Neither officer said anything for a while, not to the boy and not to each other. They stared at the wound, grasping for its meaning.

But again, this was ridiculous. The wound didn't have to mean anything. They didn't know this kid's medical history. He could've had a recent surgery, or it could've just been a bad injury from coming out on the wrong end in a fight. Nothing so far supported the cock-and-bull story of supernaturalism.

"O'Hair," McGowan said gruffly. "A word."

Officer O'Hair stood. "We'll be back." She led the way out of the room.

The general feeling in the observation room was that of stunned silence. McGowan searched all their faces, but was met with nothing but an aura of the disturbed. He could admit the boy's story was effective, but hopefully none of them believed it. Was he the only sane person?

Another officer entered the room in a rush, holding a clipboard in her hands. It was one of the floaters, Lupe. The one who'd gone to talk to the school representatives. She seemed oblivious to the stunned atmosphere, talking loudly and out of breath.

"We have positive identification on five of the eleven disfigured bodies, all freshmen and sophomores at the university. Four of them lived in the dorms, one was a commuter."

"Thanks," O'Hair said. She turned to McGowan. "Aubrey took the six unmutilated bodies—I suppose those'd be the dug-up corpses. She said she'd get back to me soon as she could about time of death. But you know they had all been deceased long before the disfigured bodies at the scene. You could see they were already in various stages of decay."

"They looked older," McGowan agreed, "but I don't *know* anything."

"Don't withdraw your guesses just because they corroborate his story," O'Hair said.

"What story? You mean that freakshow shit he just spouted in there? You don't mean to tell me you believed it?"

"I don't. Or at least, I don't think I do, but we have to hear everything. At the very least, it's what he thinks happened."

"Yeah, and that's partly what I'm worried about."

"You don't think he could've done all that, do you?"

"I think people are capable of incredible things." McGowan looked back up at the boy behind the glass. All this time and Alberto had looked away from his damn hands only once. Once. The rest of the time he'd been so focused on them, like an infant discovering his own body. He couldn't possibly find them *that* interesting.

"There's something else," Lupe continued. "I asked about the fraternity, Omega Alpha Lambda, but the university has no record of them. They deny such a fraternity exists, never heard of them even. Obviously, they couldn't give us the names of any members, but they offered to send us a list of the registered fraternities on campus."

McGowan didn't respond. Instead he drifted over to the

one-way glass, contemplating the boy. Alberto was flexing and unflexing his hand, running the fingers of his left hand over the palm of his right. His shirt was still open, the gruesome wound plainly visible in the harsh light, grotesquely twisted. And yet, he was so focused on his hands—his right palm in particular.

Show me, McGowan thought. He could've easily marched back into the room and demanded the boy open his palm to him, but he didn't want to. He wanted the reveal to come of its own accord. He had a feeling, a good feeling that if he stood there watching, eventually Alberto's palm would come to face him. Then he too could know what had so keenly captured the boy's attention.

"Sir?" Lupe asked.

Alberto rolled his right hand over and over, massaging the wrist. Looking at the palm, worried and confused. He moved the fingers as if surprised to see the muscles still obeyed him. Did the palm hurt? Was the hand prickling? In pain? Numb?

Then he rolled the hand again, open this time.

Yes.

And McGowan saw it. He saw the markings. An upside-down triangle tattooed across the palm.

McGowan didn't believe anything. And yet, maybe he believed all of Alberto's story. He couldn't place why, but seeing the tattoo made his heart leap in his chest. He wanted to know if O'Hair had seen it too. The first thought that occurred to him was, *The boy is one of them now.*

This would be a long case, and McGowan wanted no part of it.

REESE REYNOLDS AND THE DAY I ALMOST DIED

Let me tell you about the day I almost died.

At the time, I was a Lyft driver based in Sacramento, CA. Things weren't too bad, and they definitely could've been worse. In fact, recent times had been looking up for me. I'd decided to go back to Sac City College to work on that degree I'd never got, I'd taken up this new driving job, and I'd finally lain my on-again/off-again stalled relationship of three years to rest. I mean, I guess *I* hadn't really been the one to lay it to rest; *she'd* been the one cheating. But I caught her, and that means I deserve some credit for ending things, right?

Anyway, I was feeling pretty chipper that morning. The dash of my silver Ford Fiesta told me it was a breezy sixty-five degrees outside—meaning it was going to be one of those perfect mid-May days. I was crossing the Tower Bridge, crumpled Starbucks bag with vanilla scone remains in the passenger seat, Tycho radio thumping just under the conscious noise level, when I saw a nearby customer pop up on my app. She was a new user by the name Kit Katrina. According to my phone, she was in Old Town and needed to get to Elk Grove. Easy enough.

I accepted.

The pedestrian entrance to the Old Town parking garage is in an alley between the Laughs Unlimited Comedy Club and the brick garage itself. I pulled up, the roads as empty as expected on a Tuesday mid-morning, and came to a halt while looking for my passenger. This was where she'd pinged me, but there wasn't a soul in sight expect for an old man changing the bags in the trash bins. I doubted he was Kit.

Just when I was about to call my missing customer, a woman emerged from the garage. She was of athletic build, probably a few years older than me, but not much past thirty if that. Her stride was powerful, though she kept her head down and her hands shoved into the pockets of her black leather jacket. I couldn't take my eyes off her hair. It was lime-colored.

I unlocked the doors and she pulled a hand out of her pocket long enough to get inside.

"Good morning!" I said, putting on my best cheerful voice.

She nodded. Her brown eyes pierced through me in the rearview mirror.

"To Elk Grove, then?" I said.

"Please. Hurry," she said.

"I'll see what I can do." I'm not going to lie, I get miffed when customers tell me to hurry. That's my biggest pet peeve. I'm no Sunday-stroll driver, but I obey the traffic laws. I'm not going to get a ticket for some chump who couldn't call for their ride a few minutes earlier if they wanted to be on time. I had half a mind to take it slow, but I'm not a fan of driving slow regardless, so I pulled out of Old Town at normal speed. The cobblestone road turned to asphalt. I could tell I still wasn't driving to her liking though, because she kept glancing around the windows all antsy-like. My blood was beginning to go hot.

Just then, two black SUVs came careening onto the road behind us, tires screeching on the pavement. Typical obnoxious California drivers. They think the road is their raceway and the rest of us are just obstacles to dodge.

Ms. Katrina's eyes widened and she flung herself around to look at them out of the back window. They were barreling down the avenue, mirrored windshields reflecting the sun in our eyes.

Her demeaner changed in an instant.

"Go now!" she commanded.

"What?" I asked. Didn't she know they were just idiot drivers? I'd seen people like them before, drifting across all lanes of the freeway without regard to anyone else on the road. Of course, they were usually in beat-up sedans, not pristine GMs, but I figured there wasn't much difference.

"You need to step on it!" she shouted, facing me now.

I was shocked by her transformation more than anything. "What's going on?"

She pulled her hands out of her pockets. She was holding pistols.

"Go! *Now!*" she roared.

Out of instinct, I floored it. The Fiesta did nothing for a second before the old four-cylinder roared into action. My body pushed slightly against the seat as we accelerated. The guns clicked as she cocked them, ready for use. Perspiration broke over my brow.

"What the hell is going on?" I asked, glancing in the mirror as often as I dared to watch the approaching pursuit vehicles.

"Don't let them catch you," she said. This was no explanation, but it's hard to argue with someone holding two firearms. Granted, she hadn't pointed them at me yet, but I wasn't waiting for that moment. "Turn right," she said, "once we pass this—*Turn off your indicator!*"

"Sorry!" I shouted, flipping the lever back to neutral.

"Right! Here!"

I yanked the wheel and the car maneuvered around the corner, tires skidding over the asphalt. My mind reeled, as did my stomach. What the hell had happened to my calm, chipper morning? One minute I'd been thinking about how good life was becoming, the next I could taste my vanilla scones again.

Behind us, the black SUVs drifted around the turn and continued bearing down on us. Their grilles glinted like plastered sneers. Who were these people? What did they want from my customer? And who exactly was this Kit Katrina in my car?

"Can't this thing go any faster?" she yelled.

"We're riding on a hundred and eighty horsepower. This is the best I can do!"

"Left!"

I swerved again as we drew parallel to the freeway, riding in its shadow. I kept having to dart around other cars on the road, some of whom slammed on their brakes when I passed, others sliding quickly out of the way, horns blaring. The true miracle was that no cops had shown up yet. I was going fifty-five on surface streets!

Kit leaned forward. I could tell she'd taken off her seatbelt, but after I opened my mouth to point this out, I thought better of it. She jammed her finger into the control panel on the ceiling and the sunroof started to open. Wind whipped over the top of the vehicle, filling the interior with a howl.

"What are you doing?" I asked over the din, but she didn't answer me. Instead, she raised her torso out of the car and turned back to face our pursuers. Then I heard it.

BANG. BANG. BANG.

"Oh my God!" I screamed, my throat dry. At each gunshot, I jumped, struggling to keep the wheel steady.

"Will you keep straight?" Kit screamed down at me.

"You just fired gunshots!"

"I know! I'm trying to stop us from getting killed!"

BANG.

One of the vehicles careened as its tire blew out. For a second, the SUV did nothing more than lose speed. Then it jerked and spun out. Amazingly, none of the cars behind it—which had been cautiously providing a wide berth—crashed into the sideways vehicle.

Now we were down to one pursuant.

"Who are you?" I called.

"No time." Kit pulled herself back into the vehicle and closed the sunroof. Her green hair was windswept, covering half her face. "Put the car in cruise control."

"What?"

"I said, put the damn thing in cruise control."

I did as I was told, still afraid of her guns and not quite sure if I was helping out the right side or not. Were there sides? Who exactly was everyone in this scenario? I mumbled, "Cruise control. Don't even know what's going on... probably going to die..."

Then I screamed.

Kit had undone my buckle. In a swifter move than I'd have thought possible, she had hoisted me out of the driver's seat and into the back with her, one hand on the wheel the entire time. She used her foot to help kick me into place, then slid into the spot I'd just vacated.

"This's my car!" I screamed. "What are you doing? You can't just take my—"

"I'm getting us out of here," she said. Then yanked the wheel over.

I was thrown from my seat, my head bashing against the door. The world swam in my view, pain ricocheting through my body. I didn't have the breath to scream anymore. In fact, I just lay there, half on the back seat and half stuffed into the fiesta's limited leg room. The center console was uncomfortably jammed against my pelvis, but I didn't think I could move. Not yet, at any rate—we were still swerving here and there at random. The wheels screeched loudly in protest.

Great, I was probably going to need new tires after this.

"Hold on," Kit said. Although to what she intended me to hold on, I couldn't imagine.

The car turned, the centripetal force bringing me upright. We were drifting through a helical interchange, moving from Highway 50 to Interstate 5. The crumpled bag from my breakfast flew up and tapped me on the chest before spinning away into oblivion. The car couldn't stand drifting at this speed; no way would we make it through the turn. We were going to flip.

And yet, we didn't.

My Fiesta straightened out just as we merged onto I-5. I was holding my breath, clutching the upholstery with a strength I didn't know I had.

Then I realized the other black SUV was gone. I kept watching the onramp behind us, but the intimidating vehicle never appeared. Had we lost them? I didn't dare say anything.

I didn't need to.

"They'll circle back around onto Five another way," Kit said. "We haven't lost them yet."

"Haven't… we haven't…" My mind was still largely blank. "We haven't lost who? Who are they? Why are they after you, Kit?"

To my surprise, she sighed. We were going seventy now— a normal, inconspicuous speed for a freeway. She changed lanes, using the blinker and the sideview mirror and everything. Then she ran a hand through her green hair. I knew I shouldn't ask again, so I just sat back and put on the middle seatbelt.

"My name's not Kit," she said.

"What?"

"It's an alias. I'm really Reese Reynolds."

"Reese Reynolds," I repeated. "Why do you have an alias?"

"I can't tell you that."

"I suppose then you also can't tell me why they were trying to get you?" I asked, pointing a thumb behind us at the city we'd left behind. If my mother watched the news tonight, she'd probably see something about this. I made a vow not to let her know of my involvement, but then I thought about the fact that my passenger—well, driver—had an alias. Secret stuff was going on. If spies were involved, maybe my mother wouldn't see anything about this after all.

"I can't tell you why," she said. "They work for a man called Hishe. I'm sorry you got caught up in all this."

"Did you not have a car of your own?" I asked.

"I did. My partner was supposed to rendezvous with me this morning. They got her." She sighed again. "Poor Mems."

"I'm sorry," I said. Thinking about her partner, I could see the sadness on her face. I was getting the full gambit of emotions this morning. I felt like I was in a televised spy drama.

"Emon and I went way back. We went to the academy together. Helped each other through training." She drove in silence for a while, her jaw set. Her sadness burned like anger, and I wondered if she often confused the two. I said nothing as we continued south away from Sacramento. For a time, I wondered where she intended to take me, if I would be allowed to go home at some point. Then I realized we were headed for Elk Grove. Perhaps she still hoped to stop there. If she had backup or something waiting, maybe I could leave then.

The car's Bluetooth rang. I was getting a call. I leaned forward to answer, but Kit—I mean Reese—cut me off.

"It's for me," she said, then pressed ANSWER.

"Reese," a man's voice said.

"Director Muskataro."

"What are you doing in this unidentified vehicle?"

"Please, Director. Agent Mems was apprehended. I had to find another escape."

"Agent Mems was taken?"

"Killed, actually, sir."

A long pause. "I'm sorry to hear that, Reese. Emon Mems was a brave woman."

I wondered if I was supposed to be hearing any of this, but I figured Reese knew what she was doing. If I wasn't supposed to hear, she wouldn't be letting me hear. I didn't want to consider any other possibilities.

"Unfortunately, I had to involve a civilian, sir," Reese reported, glancing backward at me.

"I see," Director Muskataro said. "You know where to take them."

"Yes, sir."

"Are you almost at the contact point?"

"I am, sir."

"Good. Report when you have wheels up."

"Will do, sir."

"And Reese?"

"Yes, sir?"

"I told you, you don't need to call me 'sir.' We've known each other for two decades now. You can call me Trey." The line went dead.

We exited in Elk Grove. My heart had finally stopped racing, but when we boarded the offramp, my pulse kicked up a notch again. I still had no idea where I was headed—where, exactly, Reese *knew* to take me. Did this mean my old life was over? If she was taking me somewhere, did that mean things were going to change? I thought about my apartment in West Sacramento. Visits to my mom on Thursdays—God, my mom! What was she going to think if I didn't show up in a couple days? Was I ever going to see her again?

"I'm sorry to have involved you," Reese said as we came to a halt at a stop sign. "I thought if I took an anonymous ride in an innocuous vehicle... after all, I never made contact with them. But I dragged you into this. I'm sorry."

"It's alright," I said, though I didn't know if that was true.

"I'll be leaving you with Jolene Rancher—she's head of witness protection."

I nodded, though I don't know that I was understanding what she'd said. The last hour was beginning to take hold of me. What was about to become of my life? If I was going into witness protection, that definitely meant I couldn't see my mother. Would they tell her what had happened? Was communication strictly forbidden?

"Are you listening to me?" she asked as we pulled into a parking spot in front of what looked like a candy shop.

I nodded again, and for the third time, Reese sighed. "Go in there. A woman behind the counter will ask you what you want. Ask for a pound of rocky road and a half pound of white chocolate fudge. Then they'll bring you to Agent Rancher."

"Alright," I said. Numb. I had no other options but to listen. I could run, but I had a feeling they'd be able to catch me before I got too far. And if I didn't agree to their terms about staying silent, I wouldn't be in their good graces for much longer.

"Good luck," Reese Reynolds said. In her eyes, I saw she meant it. "You'll never see me again."

I stepped out of the vehicle, trying not to shake as I walked up to the glass door and entered the shop. A bell announced my entry into the stark white interior. When I turned around, my Fiesta was already gone.

A voice came from behind me. "Welcome! Can I get you something?"

"A pound of rocky road," I whispered, "and a half pound of white chocolate fudge."

THE MOON, THE LITTLE BLACK CLOUD, AND SHE

The music in my mind crescendos: Beethoven's *Mondscheinsonate*. My back arches, opening my chest skyward until my spine creaks in protest. I may have thought my contortion would appear grotesque, but I had seen another male dancer perform the movement earlier in the week and knew what sort of austere beauty the lines of the body evoked with this posture. I hold it until the crescendo dies and exit the movement through a roll.

Midway to the floor, I notice the shadows trickling.

The raked seating in the empty auditorium is poorly lit, but even so I cannot pretend that what I see isn't real. Amorphous clouds of darkness slide along the balcony, the closest rows directly in front of where I lie on the stage, and through the scarlet drapery cascading down the walls. They're converging.

I stand, feeling my breath hitch in my chest as I struggle to wrestle it into a normal cadence. My heart hammers away. The expressive euphoria which had been carrying me for the last five or six minutes ebbs and I am returned to the real world. A cynical world. A world that doesn't flow from one choreographed movement to another.

The shadows converge stage right, lingering behind the first row of hanging curtains. I have sometimes imagined hidden figures watching from behind the folds like ghosts. I would revel in their voyeuristic gazes, imagining them admiring my fluid movements. This doesn't feel the same way. Skin crawling, I move away from center stage toward the gathered shadows. My wrapped feet make no noise on the black vinyl flooring. Now that I'm not dancing, the cavernous theater feels cold. I wish I were wearing more than this thin clothing. I'm not yet shivering, but if I stay this way, I may start.

I draw near the curtains and the shadows move. They slip off-stage and though there are no lights on back there, I can still feel them present in the black. Maybe this is why I'm so cold now.

At least two weeks have passed since I last saw the darkness. I had begun to hope, as I always end up doing, that I might never see it again. I never fully believed this hope, but it was nice to entertain the idea that I might continue to exist without having any more encounters. I would be able to convince myself that I was like everyone else. Wouldn't that be something extraordinary?

But this idealized future is something that will never come to be. Not for me. Never again.

I just hadn't expected anything tonight. Where would they lead me? I am not headed for an exit. At least, none of the exits they usually lead me through. I am being drawn farther into the backstage area, past half-erected sets and stored props. Black cloths are draped like regal gowns over plastic statues and fake foliage. Wooden pillars carved to look like

Roman columns stand in my way and I follow the shadows around them. There is nobody back here. I was alone; I'd made sure of it before I began my practice.

Then I see the light beneath the door of one of the stage managers' offices. My heart sinks as we draw nearer. It's Ms. Foster's.

I dilute. My body sinks out of the visible spectrum. Though there is no sensation associated with this transformation, I imagine the sight of my body collapsing like water without a container. I know that I have gone from a solid figure standing in the darkness in black pants and a black shirt to nothing at all. Nobody will be able to see me now.

Nobody but the person I'm supposed to meet.

The darkness lingers above Ms. Foster's door, but I know I've found where I'm supposed to go. Though the welcoming Tabitha Foster keeps her door open during regular rehearsal and class hours, she locks it afterward. A locked door will be no obstacle for me, though. Death waits for no woman.

I turn the knob and enter the small square space.

I've been in this room several times before. The walls are covered in posters of successful dancers, many of whom were once Ms. Foster's pupils. Interspersed between these posters are groupings of photographs displaying her travels. Because she's had so many students go on to find success around the world, she's managed several trips to beautiful locales in many countries. In the center of the room is a simple rectangular desk. The tabletop is piled high with errant stacks of forms and printed emails and rough sketches of the choreographies she has planned. Two green polyester chairs sit on one side of the desk and Ms. Foster sits opposite them.

She looks up at me as I enter, surprised. There's no mistaking now. If she can see me while I'm diluted, then she is the one I've come for.

"Silas," she says. She has a book in her hands, but it's closed on her finger. Was she staring off at nothing?

"Hello, Ms. Foster." I walk right up to the other side of the desk, between the green chairs. She looks up at me, dazed almost, like she still has one foot in another world. Her eyebrows furrow.

"What are you doing here? How—how did you get in?"

"It's going to be okay," I say. I don't bother answering her questions. It won't make a difference. "How are you feeling?"

"How am I feeling? I—I don't..." she stutters. I hate it when fear is what they feel upon seeing me. Acceptance or understanding is preferable. I sleep easier at night that way. I don't toss and turn hearing their questioning voices, wondering if there wasn't something I could have done to make their last conversation more peaceful. To make them understand that I don't mean to hurt them.

I pull out one of the chairs and sit down, trying to keep eye contact with her even though it pains me. I also don't like *knowing* the people I visit.

"What are you doing here?" she repeats.

"How are you feeling?" I say again. She looks from me to the door behind me, which is closed and locked now as if I'd never opened it at all. Is she going to cry? I can't tell. Her eyes are still so dazed and watery.

She sighs. "I don't know, Silas. I haven't felt like myself lately. Not at all. I have this pain in my chest." She kneads her knuckles into the area above her left breast. The area over her heart.

"A pain?" I ask.

"Yes," she says. "It's been there since Wednesday. Very distracting—I haven't been able to get any of my work done. I thought it might go away on its own, but I think I'm going to have to phone the doctor tomorrow."

Tomorrow.

A deep sadness weighs heavily inside me. Without looking, I know the shadows are creeping into the room, spreading along the walls like trickling paint. They cover everything indiscriminately: the posters, the photographs, the drywall. She can't see it yet. She keeps looking down at her book. Then she chuckles. "I was still getting distracted, so I thought maybe if I took a short reading break…"

She looks up at me, a lingering smile on her lips still.

"What are you reading?" I ask.

"*The Ocean at the End of the Lane*," she says. "Neil Gaiman."

"That was a fantastic one."

She nods, places a hand on one of the forms stacked in front of her as if to read it, then sighs. "May I ask one more time? What are you here for, Silas?"

"To help you move on," I say, trying to choose the right words. No matter how many times I've done this, I've never been able to decide. Anything I say always feels wrong.

"To move on?" she asks, confused.

"Yes."

"Move on from…" She looks from me to the door and back to me again. The fear seeps into her eyes. I wonder if she can see the darkness yet. "What do you want from me? How did you get in here?"

"Please, don't be afraid," I say, placing my hands flat on the desktop to show her that I have nothing to harm her with. "I'm not here to hurt you. I'm here to sit with you, to listen to you, to keep you company until it's all over. You won't be alone. I'll be here with you."

She fights for a minute, shaking her head and gasping syllables that never quite transform into words. She looks like she might try to get up and run to the door, but she doesn't, maybe because she's too afraid to or maybe because she hasn't the will. She knows something is wrong beyond what she'd previously understood—I can see it in her hesitation. As she works herself up, her eyes gloss over again and she begins to cry.

"I can't... This isn't... What do you mean? I just—I'm only." Then she devolves into tears, great droplets dripping onto the back of her paperback. I've heard she never had a family of her own. She has her adoring students who will carry on her legacy. Most of the pictures hung around the room are either with them or her alone.

After a few minutes, she calms herself. Her sobs lessen into quiet sniffing. I stare down at my hands, letting her have her time to grieve. There is no easy way to realize you are dying.

"It's this pain, isn't it?" she asks, hand over her heart again. "I should've called sooner. Would it have made a difference?"

I shrug. "I don't know."

"How quick will it be?"

"I don't know that either. Though I'm only ever called in the final minutes."

"What are you?" she asks. "An angel?"

I shake my head.

"Will you hold my hand?" she asks. I'm used to this request. Even when I do not know the person the darkness

brings me to, they often ask for this simple form
of comfort. I reach out across the desk and she takes my
hand in hers.

"I thought I would be older," she says. "When I was still a
girl I would comb through the library, through the travel and
reference sections. I would look at all the pictures in the
books and plan all the things I would learn and the places I
would see."

"It looks like you managed to check quite a few things
off," I say, tilting my head toward the collections of pictures
around us. She smiles and laughs, her face red through the
mixture of emotions.

"I did, didn't I? There's so much more to learn, though. I
thought I had more time. I thought—" She cringes as a wave
of pain floods her. She's still clutching the book with her
other hand, holding her place with her finger.

"Oh God," she whispers, eyes shut. "Can you tell me if
there's anything more? After this, I mean."

"I'm sorry," I say, feeling useless. "I don't know that
answer myself."

"Can you take the pain away?"

"I can do that if you like."

My tone makes her open her eyes again to look straight at
me. I know she can see the darkness now; it's reflected in her
pupils. "Do you mean...?"

I nod.

She looks around at the walls, which are slowly
disappearing beneath shadow, portraits fading into black, the
memories absorbed. She and I will soon be the only things
left in the room, holding hands while the world disappears.

"I suppose so," she says. Her voice is so soft, she might
not have spoken at all. A few more tears escape. "I'm ready."

"Alright," I say.

We make eye contact again. She is so worried about where she is going and what she will find there—or even if *there* exists at all—but I can see too that she's reliving all the greatest moments inside her mind. She's seeing every place she's ever visited. Embracing every student who ever told her that she was their inspiration. She watches these memories like a film, one that only she can see, while her eyes slowly close and her head sinks forward. In the end, she sits in her chair, slumped with a book in her hand. Her finger marks her spot as if maybe she's just resting her eyes and will be back to reading any moment now. The darkness recedes and the office is normal once again.

I sit there, lingering by her side until the sadness is manageable. Then I relinquish my hold on her hand and stand up, sliding the chair out behind me. I look around at her posters and collected memorabilia, knowing that I needn't worry. Her death will be grieved by plenty. She has not died unloved.

So I turn and go, hoping for a longer reprieve before the shadows find me again.

IN ME ALL THAT FIRE

We were given years, but had only moments. Our brief flashes of togetherness flared like the strike of a match. I was unprepared for them when they came—and more unprepared when they left—but even so, I am grateful to have had those moments at all. Light, after all, is still light no matter how long it burns.

Sometimes I am surprised by my own boldness. I could have blamed my exposure on you, but I do not. My mind and heart were bound to come spilling out of me sooner or later. And when I look upon the troubled awakening of many of my peers—who did not have a You or even the idea of a You until much later—I am glad that I was exposed so early on. If only to myself, of course. It took me longer to tell friends, much less my family. I was loquacious as a boy, didn't you know? Somewhere in my early adolescence that disappeared. Somewhere in those years it was quashed by reminders of my condition, an affliction I knew nothing but shame for.

And then there was you.

My friend Nicole warned me about you. Before we met, she pulled me aside and said, "Aidan is bisexual," her tone at once accepting of your condition and aware of its obtrusive affront to normalcy. She said it as you might say, "He's got anger management issues—you've been warned. Don't be alarmed."

This was long before my stages of denial had concluded. Long before I ever considered myself one of the afflicted. In fact, I had, in recent years, defended those who fought the disease, much to the chagrin of people who knew more about me at that point than I knew of myself. Perhaps my opposition to what I am stemmed from my discomfort at the thought of these free-minded individuals whose willingness to self-celebrate I envied. Is this where all opposition stems from? I was not very vocal with my oppositions per se, but they had been voiced once or twice. I used the same words my elders taught me to use. I doubt if Nicole had ever heard me say as much, but she was born into the same ideology as I. Likewise, she expressed the same concerns when it came to your affliction.

You were nothing to worry about, though. Or perhaps everything to worry about. You laughed and smiled with crinkling eyes. Your voice, though post-pubescent, still carried a strand of higher femininity than some boys our age. You were thin, gangly. Styled your blonde hair so that it curled up in the front like a straw-colored ocean wave. And you had thin glasses that neither magnified nor shrank your eyes but framed them. Pale blue, like faded jeans.

***

I did not like you then. I *craved* you. If anyone had asked me how I felt after that day, I would have given them no indication that I understood my affliction more than I did before the encounter. But I would have expressed how drawn to you I was. This irresistible attraction carried no ulterior motives I could detect. I simply wanted to be the best of all your friends and you the best of mine. I wanted to dress like you, with your black commando vest and plastic, monochrome bracelets. I wanted to enjoy manga and young adult supernatural romance novels like you did. I wanted the faint sexual allure you exuded in your confidence, an allure which perhaps I was the only one in the room to feel. I cannot be certain.

As with many great events, the time surrounding ours blurs when years have passed. Were we immediate friends after the Great Hang Out? I don't remember. Did we see each other often? I don't recall, though I would have said not often enough. Did I remain hidden? Of course. I will not say that everyone our age hid their affliction, but I was not as strong as some, nor as confident, nor as freed from denial. A scant few boys I knew wore their sexuality on their lapel. I abhorred them. I buried mine in the cemetery behind my school and snapped at anyone who called it into question.

I wonder sometimes if the only thing which drew you to me was our sharing of the rare condition—the "slim pickings," as it were. I wonder if you felt the same attraction as I did, or if your attention to me was similar to that of animals which in the case of a drought will eat plants they wouldn't normally. That analogy is cruel. I don't let myself believe it often. There were boys in your school who were the same as us; you could've pursued them much more easily. You could've had someone less blind than I.

Even after the second big event we shared, I could not place my feelings—though the inklings did begin to take root.

Another friend's house, a party this time with many of our mutual acquaintances and friends. I could've spent the entire evening with the people I knew, cavorting and bantering the way teenagers do to flagrantly demonstrate the resilience of their youth. I'm not so old now, but without a doubt I've lost the stamina to uphold such interactions. As I've said before, I've lost the ability to banter. Instead, I absorb words like carpets absorb sounds, muffling the echoes.

We found each other and I was helpless. Maybe I spoke with other people in short batches of words, but the focus of my attention was on you. You didn't command the room, but you commanded my mind. Gillian, our host, had erected a tent in the backyard and at some point in the evening I sat myself on the floor inside it. I remember people drifting in and out. Then you entered.

I don't remember what was said, but you got to the ground between my legs and leaned back against my chest. In the boldest move I had ever made, I let you. I let you sit against me. We didn't say anything about it. We talked about other things. We laughed. We flirted as any of the other teenagers did with members of the opposite sex. One of our friends even said to us, "That's disgusting." Somehow your apathetic response convinced me to stay and he left the tent instead. If I could have reached up and pinned the moon to the night sky, I would have done so and never let go.

Your mother knew about you, but not your father. I told no one. Keeping you a secret was not difficult for me. I was well versed in keeping secrets. I dwelt in secrets as others dwell in homes. I would arrange them in my bed at night and sleep soundly surrounded by the things I didn't tell others. Under overwhelming stress others will wash their friends in great tides of words. My instinct was to pull my experiences deeper within me. And as with anyone who considers themselves an artist, I don't just feel things, I obsess.

***

I confessed to you shortly after the party in the most coquettish of ways: with a discarded phrase that could not be misconstrued and was lacquered in nonchalance. My confession must've been obvious to you. How could I be anything but? Only nights ago, I had let you lie against me. You had floated on the cadence of my breath. I had never been so close to anyone, and maybe the same was true for you. The effect of my confession was immediate. We decided to try a relationship, ignoring the difficulties that would unavoidably plague us. But what adolescents *do* consider such difficulties? We are strong as teenagers, aware of struggles but invincible to them. We blunder through emotions, unlearned in what is truly meant by having your heart broken. Until that point our heart is whole and new. Our heart has no seams or stitches; it beats proudly and unafraid. I cannot blame adolescents. My heart is wiser—I will not claim it is wise—stitched together in several places but whole still and beating steadily. Yet if I had an unblemished heart again, I would do no differently. I would run headlong into danger, feel the passion, the sweltering, fearless heat, that flaring strike of a match. I would welcome that adolescent ignorance of imminent pain, let the match burn for too long until it singed my fingers. If my heart were fresh again, I would do all these things as I did before, regret all these things as I did before, and know passion.

You may think I am sad. I am not sad for my worn heart.

I have love now. Love that I earned beat for beat, which is whole and sturdy. I found what I have been looking for and I hope you would never begrudge me this, just as I would not for you. We cannot say all the terrible anger and pain we feel does not help to shape us. I needed you. From you, I learned how to approach another so that I could go out on a date and have some idea what to do with the placement of my hands or what I should say. I learned so that future dates would not be as awkward as ours were, though I find them funny if still embarrassing now. Our first date alone stands as a testament to the true nature of first high school romances. Never mind the quirky-but-clever banter of the precocious teenagers in films, the ones who speak using long words and understand the perfect use of irony. We were nothing like them.

Our mothers dropped us off at the movie theater, mine a bit earlier than yours since I was nervous that she would see just us together. I stood against the wall beside the box office, staring at my phone, pretending to be busy doing who-knew-what. You came along soon after and joined me outside, waving your mother away. We didn't hold hands, stumbling instead through nervous laughter. You talked more than I did, but that was exactly how I preferred things. I wanted to listen to you and soak up your voice. I was there to catch the light which radiated from you always.

I can't recall what we saw, only that I spent the film wondering if my leg was too close to yours. Sweat drenched our clasped hands and probably still stains the armrest of that theater seat, but I was too paralyzed by my foray into moral deviancy to care. Going to a theater for our first alone-date was the perfect choice. Hidden by the darkness and safe among a crowd whose collective attention was drawn to the film we'd all agreed to pay twelve dollars to see, I could explore some new shred of myself with minimal fear of exposure.

In the time following our end, I would beg my past self to be bolder on that date. To take not only your hand in mine but your arm. To keep you not just close, but pressed against me. I would beg the me in the theater to make our first kiss then and there instead of months later. Now, of course, I know that could not have been. My timidity was part of the experience. I could not ask more of myself.

You were picked up shortly after the movie ended. I wandered around the mall on my own, drifting in and out of shops, staring at clothing items without seeing any of them. I thought about what it meant to be the person I was, what it would mean to my family. I thought about what a person like me could hope for in life and compared it to that of normal boys. I contemplated my timid nature and wondered if this would always hinder my experiences. A version of myself between then and now berated myself for not being bolder. But telling that boy wandering the mall alone to be something he is not could never be the answer. Today, if I had that opportunity to speak to that boy wandering the mall, I wouldn't say a single word. Perhaps, in the confidence of speaking to an older version of himself, he would tell me everything. He would say all the words it would take him years to say to anyone else. Perhaps then he wouldn't be so sad.

***

I think boldness may not be the correct term for you after all. You didn't commit acts for the sake of making statements. You did them just because you wanted to. That may be the essence of what drew me to you: your flavor did not taste of arrogance, it tasted of vitality.

I did eventually out myself to my closest friends and, upon reflection, I owe some of them a greater debt than I understood at the time. One friend in particular, Anthony—who was the closest person I had to an emotional outlet and who I miss now whenever I reminisce about the friends who have come and gone in my life—showed exceptional willingness to help me. He had a car and agreed to drive to your town so that we could double-date with him and his girlfriend.

In typical Anthony fashion, he corralled us into one of those hormonally induced teenage games. Whenever we passed beneath a yellow light at an intersection, everyone had to hit the roof of the car. The slowest had to take off a piece of clothing. When the idea was introduced, I laughed along with the rest of you while secretly mortified by the idea of removing any clothing in front of anyone, even while the darkness in the vehicle was nearly complete. I nodded my compliance, but knew I would never participate.

You, on the other hand, surpassed my expectations. We went through only one yellow light before the game ended and you—whether by chance or design—were last to hit the car roof. We all laughed, I think driven by the suggestion of what the rules entailed. Unperturbed, you removed not only one item of clothing, but all your clothing. In a manner of minutes, I was sitting in the backseat of a beat-up sedan with a boy who had completely undressed.

Shadow hid the details of your nakedness, leaving only the barest contours of your design illuminated. And do you know, in that moment I was most thankful that you could not see me blush? Of course, I wanted to see you in your entirety.

I wanted to lean over to see better what was hidden in darkness. I wanted to experience you fully. At sixteen, I could have seen in person the figure I had only briefly imagined when my guilt and my conscience would allow, but I didn't. I locked eyes with you instead.

You wore a daring smile that took my breath away. My face burned hotter and I found myself unable to hold your gaze. In the end, you put your clothes back on and my view remained tantalizingly restricted. I saw the strength of your thighs with hair much darker than on your blonde head. I saw the way you slimmed at your narrow waist, the curve at the small of your back, the shallow valley beneath your navel and between your hips, the slope to your pubic bone, and then nothing else. You tortured me, or rather I tortured myself by not seizing the chance you'd presented me for a better look. I was at fault for that.

I think I mustered the courage to tease you a little, before you left the car, about the show you'd put on. We kissed that evening. I had many doubts about myself before and even after that night, doubts about who I could allow myself to be without ruining the things I held dear: my family, my bland reputation at my small school. My attraction to you, however, could not be denied. It could not take any other shape now that I had laid it out there for myself to see. I had crossed a threshold and the door had closed behind me. You had locked it.

***

Things have an uncanny habit of ending just when we admit we wish for them to last. People mock the love of adolescents, saying it is not a real love. I reject this small-mindedness, this constriction of love's definition. Teenagers, just as adults, can love and fall in love. Just as they are juvenile, so is their love, but just as they are a real person so too is their love real. It may stand on shaky legs and stumble forth in short bursts, losing its balance often and toppling over. But how else can it learn to walk, or, for that matter, to run?

I loved you. And even now that I have a love which is stronger and better accustomed to the needs of two individuals, I do not dismiss the love I once had for you as false. I know it was real because when you told me our relationship was over, I felt my heart break. I hung up the phone and could have traced the very crack down which my heart was splitting. Many thoughts ran through my head, but the one which came to the forefront time and again was *What do I do now?* I had opened myself in an unimaginable way. I had changed the way my life was to look: a man beside me instead of a woman—which had previously been the only option ever allowed. I had opened myself and just when I was getting a grip on the new book coming into my grasp—the one with empty pages on which I could write my story—you had vanished. Not completely gone, of course—we still had mutual friends—but gone for me.

And yet, you still encompassed me. My feelings did not die. Not for a long time. Growing up without boys around me who understood—at least, we did not make ourselves known to one another—my loneliness exacerbated my pain. I thought of you endlessly through wakefulness and sleep. I thought of you when I talked to others and when I sat in my own silence.

You. You. Everything I thought was about you. Everything I wanted to say was about you. I turned to writing music and all of my songs centered around our relationship. Melodramatic as I have always been, I could not stop writing about suffering. The years following us engendered the most music I've ever written. So too was it the most turmoil in which I've ever been. Perhaps that is why so much of my *art* was borne out of me then. I have heard people say, though, that the art is already in the artist. When I started to think clearer, years after we last spoke, I began to wonder if the pain from your absence merely gave my inner pain a conduit. Perhaps I stayed in my turmoil for so long because listening to my music gave me more pain. And so I'd write more. And so I'd feel more. I still have yet to decide for myself whether it's one way or the other—or maybe both. Suffering begets art. Art begets suffering.

Now, I acknowledge what we shared as part of my history, the good and the bad. Even if I've moved on, I know parts of us inform how I react to and feel the world around me. I never think of you, but then, I suppose, you do not need to think in order to feel.

***

The last part of our story is the only part I truly regret. Among the things which sometimes keep me up at night, my letter to you remains the most utterly repugnant. I know that I apologized before the last time we spoke, I know you told me you forgave me inasmuch as you could, and I know that my words were untrue, born out of hurt rather than hate. I know all these things, but they do not save me from remorse. If I obsess in love and pain, I obsess in regrets as well. The years since the event have brought into sharper focus the extent of the damage my words caused.

I did not understand the repercussions. I
knew publicly posting such a thing could draw a large
audience when the only souls that need be present
were ours. Still, I proceeded. In the moment, I reasoned
broadcasting to the world—or rather, our world, which is
considerably smaller and yet relatively massive to us—was
fair. You had erased me from your life. You had blocked me
in all forms of communication.

I should have sent the letter through a mutual friend. Or
better yet, I should have taken the time to calm myself, to
reflect on the reasons for your actions, and responded when I
had a level head. I was and am a quiet but passionate creature.
I smolder from within, building to enormous intensity before
erupting into flame. I did not cry; I sobbed. I was never
happy; I was elated. And though in some cases I took far too
long making simple decisions, in other instances I flew into
the fray without a sideways glance.

In the letter, I swore at you and called you names I had no
business calling you. For that I am sorry. I wished ill
things for your future, when all you had done was extricate
yourself from the constant exhibition of my heartache. For
that I am sorry. I told you to burn in hell. For that I am sorry.
Lastly, I introduced our struggle and my judgment of you
into a public setting, an invasion of your privacy. For that I
am sorry.

It took some time, but we spoke again once you had been
convinced by mutual friends. You accepted my apology, but I
understood no true reparations could be made. We would
never attain the friendship we once had, or even the
friendship we might have had. Maybe you had boarded the
boat set to sail away from my shore, but I had cut the rope
tethering you to the dock. The words we exchanged then

were shouted over the gathering distance as your vessel receded into the horizon.

Who are we now? I cannot say for you. Maybe you are an individual with family and friends. Perhaps you still have the same hobbies. I cannot say. I hope you are happy. As for me, I am a man too young to be belabored by regrets, and yet too old to escape them. I do my best day by day, though I am no stranger to mistakes. Rather than pining for perfection, I seek to atone for the grievances I've caused others. This is a better use of my time, I think. My heart is worn. My heart is not unblemished as it once was. It has been torn, it has wanted what it wants, and it has been both full to bursting and terrifyingly empty. I have listened to it, followed it, and felt with it. I have worn my heart on my sleeve, left it behind in San Francisco—though it was thankfully returned in one piece—and found it in my home. My heart has even been broken a few times and sewn again. But I do not regret these experiences, and I do not wish to forget them. I remember every stitch on my heart, both for the reasons that they're there and the means by which they mended.

EVERYTHING IS BETTER IN THE END

Dad didn't want me to go. That was mostly because he had to stay home with Mum, who was at the wrong end of a bad cold, meaning I would have to go by my lonesome. I offered to take Liza, but he said no because she was taking summer courses on account of her bad marks at the end of the last school year.

I didn't mind going on my own. In fact, I preferred it, to be honest. My family are like the wheels on a car. We're four different things, but we're all attached to the same vehicle going the same speed and always turning in the same direction. Most of the time, I don't mind it—I quite like my folks—but a girl's got to stretch her legs once in a while, you know? Become a unicycle.

Okay, so that wasn't the best extended metaphor. I'm not a linguist.

Anyway, so I opened the boot and Dad helped me get my pride and joy all loaded in. I may have had a few minor meltdowns along the way, but I think that's perfectly understandable. You can't damage the goods, otherwise what's the point in entering the competition at all? After making sure it wasn't going anywhere, I closed up the back and gave him a hug. Dad pretends to hate affection, but I know if I didn't hug him goodbye, he'd be secretly distraught. He patted the back bumper as I drove off.

I'd never noticed how rubbish the roads were between us and town until that drive. I swear, every other day I cruised along the main roads cutting through the farmlands and hit nary a pothole, but that day they were like swiss cheese. I felt like a stunt driver, dodging holes the size of my gran's Dutch oven. Meanwhile, I cringed every time things went bump in the back. There would be hell to pay if I lost because my baby'd got thrown around. I don't know who'd be paying the hell, but someone would.

The ninety-minute drive felt like a day and a half. That was the first time I'd done a trip on my own, even just a day trip. I tried to enjoy it as best I could, while grimacing whenever I took a turn too fast, but that proved a bit difficult. At long last I made it. I heaved the greatest sigh of relief when I saw the flags peeking up over the rolling hills. The car park was already half full, people climbing all over their cars, unstrapping a great assortment of vegetables or bringing out sows I could've ridden like a horse. I swallowed hard, realizing that my heart was racing. I was nervous and it'd never crossed my mind that I would be. I'd never thought the competition meant much, but I guess I really did want to win. I mean, the prize money was nothing to be scoffed at, but achieving something noteworthy for the first time in my life? You couldn't put a price on that.

I pulled into the next available spot down the row. A man was unloading ears of corn the size of my thigh and putting them in a cart. He nodded in my direction as I killed the engine.

An attendant came jogging over to me before I was fully out of the vehicle.

"Name?" she asked. She had a voice like someone who'd been smoking since the womb.

"Melanie Bell," I replied.

She cocked an eyebrow and I knew what was coming next. "Mel Bell?"

"The one and only," I said. Nobody but my parents were allowed to call me that, but I didn't know whether she was a judge or not so I let it slide.

"And what category are you in, love?"

"Vegetables."

"Right, you want to unload and take it down to that yellow-striped post, way down there. You see it? We've got wagons if you need 'em, just right there." The woman pointed as she spoke and I nodded with unnecessary enthusiasm. I couldn't help it; I probably looked like one of those prat teacher's pets on the first day of school.

She moved on to the next car pulling in and I went to get a cart. I hadn't brought one of my own, seeing as it wouldn't've fit in the car with me. There weren't many people at the cart station, but one woman did walk up at the same time as I did. I slowed to let her grab one ahead of me.

"Thanks," she said.

"It's nothing," I said. "What did you bring for the competition?"

She looked at me quizzically, and for a moment I questioned whether I was in the right place, but then her eyes lit with recognition. Her accent was faintly American, like she'd once lived there but had moved a long time ago. "Oh! I'm not here for the competition. I'll be selling at the swap meet."

I nodded. Both events were sharing the same public space this morning. I'd planned to go to the swap meet after I'd won my prize. Maybe I felt a little weird being on my own, so I wanted her to keep talking to me.

"What're you selling?" I asked.

"Eh… old items from my mom's estate that no one in the family cared to keep," she said. "Some books and boxes and things like that."

"Alright," I said, somewhat dully. Realizing that probably wasn't a very interesting response, I tried again. "Sorry about your mum."

She waved away my concern with her hand. "It's alright. Happened a few years ago and she was getting on in age. Had Alzheimer's, so I think her quality of living had really begun to suffer."

"I'm sorry to hear that." I'd dived into murky waters now. Way to go, Melanie. At least she didn't seem to mind too much.

"Yes, well," she sighed, then patted the handle of her cart. "I should be setting things out now. People are freshest when they first arrive. It was nice meeting you."

I told her the same and she walked off, the cart trundling across the grass behind her. I grabbed the next and pulled it back to my car, wishing I'd brought someone along with me. I didn't know how I was going to get my baby out of the back on my lonesome. Everyone else seemed to have someone to talk to, and it made finding someone on their own a difficult task. I didn't want to disturb anyone's conversation.

Finally, after standing like a dolt at the boot for about five minutes, I gave up on trying to ask someone to help me and just decided to do it myself. I pulled open the door and looked in on my greatest achievement.

"You need help with that, dear?" someone said.

I turned to see another elderly woman coming toward me. She was more homely than the last, with bright eyes and a face that looked as if she were always smiling. I was in no place to turn down help, especially help I hadn't plucked up the courage to ask for, so I nodded appreciatively.

"Thanks, ma'am," I said. She giggled.

"*Ma'am!* Oh, you got me laughing," she said, then got on the other side of the boot from me to help with the hoisting. "I was over there when I spotted you and thought, gosh, isn't she gonna need some help before she topples over? This is quite the specimen you got here."

I couldn't help smiling. I liked the way she talked. It was sort of soothing when you followed the rhythm of it. Plus, she was extra careful with the lifting and the both of us set my baby down perfectly in the cart.

"Where are you from?" I asked. She'd unwittingly become my latest conquest for company.

"The US, could'ja tell?" She giggled again. "I'm here with my husband Jack on vacation. We was just roaming the countryside and followed the signs here, thought it might be an interesting way to spend the morning. We're from Maine, although I talk like this 'cause I'm originally from the South."

I didn't know much about anything she'd said, but I nodded anyways.

"Speaking of my husband, I should probably find out where he got to."

"No!" I stammered. "You—you should come check out the largest crop and livestock competitions! They're happening right next door to the swap meet. Awards are going out at eleven."

"Oh, I definitely will," she said. "Looks like you've got a good chance of winning, dear."

And before I could think of something else to say, she'd gone, taking her honeyed voice with her. I turned to head toward the grass again.

Signing up was easy. They gave me a number and a lot to set up in. I could tell I was definitely the newcomer here. Although you were only supposed to present one vegetable, people had brought entire displays with them. They'd used hay bales to make stands and brought along vines and leaves as decorations. Some had even made A-frames with information about their farm or their crop. Meanwhile, I could only leave my entry in the cart, which I was fairly certain I was supposed to take back. Well, as long as nobody came along to tell me to do so, this cart would be my display. As a result of my lack of preparation, my lot looked empty by comparison, and I wondered if that would doom my entry.

I waited there for my turn to get judged, smiling at people as they walked past, feeling the effects of inadequacy set in. Twice I came close to just packing it all up and heading home. I could tell my parents I'd lost, and they'd never know I hadn't even stayed long enough to get judged. There could be no harm in that; I was used to mediocrity. Fading into the masses was something I'd done ever since I'd learned how. The prideful part of me bade me stay, though. I hadn't spent months gardening just to leave now. I did have to fight the strong urge to knock over the two-story display belonging to the tosser next door to me. If I'm being truthful, his squash wasn't all that spectacular and no amount of decoration was going to fix that.

Finally, after half the day had gone, the judge came to my

post.

She was a thin, pale woman with over-large glasses that made her seem all the more pale and thin. On her front was a pin with the acronym *IMBS*, although what that stood for, I couldn't tell you. She didn't so much wear clothes as had draped herself in fabric with exotic-looking patterns. Long beaded earrings hung down to her shoulders under wispy, unkempt brown hair. She held out a wrist to me and it took me a few moments to realize she wanted me to shake it.

"Hello, dear," she said dramatically.

"Hello."

She consulted her clipboard. "You are Melanie Bell?"

"Yes," I said, trying to sound excited and not dead nervous.

"I am Gemini. I will be judging your botanical substantiality."

I'd never heard it called that, but I supposed she knew what she was doing. While a throng of devotees looked on, the judge circled my entry. She mumbled to herself the entire time and I caught snippets like "exquisite veins" and "excellent leaf structure," which boosted my morale considerably. I will admit she was rather odd though. Before taking any physical measurements, she bent down low to get her ear near the vegetable and hummed a single note. I wouldn't have guessed that to be a metric for the competition, but what do I know about botanical substantia-whatsits?

"My husband and I once found a pincushion while on holiday in Romania that was this exact species of *varza*," Gemini said, grabbing a tape measure from her belt. "The exact same plumpness and coloring as this one as well. You haven't modeled this vegetable after it, by any chance?"

As if I could model a vegetable after
something. "No," I said, a bit flustered by that point.

A pair of blokes came along rolling a massive scale. More
roughly than I'd have liked, they hoisted my entry up onto the
platform and waited for the scale to settle. I could only
gasp as they did it, unable to tell them to be careful before the
deed was done. Gemini shimmied in anticipation.

"Ooh!" she said. "How divine!"

Then they plopped it back in my cart and moved on.

Despite their rough handling, I could feel my excitement
bubbling. The judge, strange though she had been, had said
only positive things. That had to be a good sign, right? I was
expecting tuts and looks of reproach, but she had been
ecstatic in her own off-kilter way. I was beginning to think I
had a chance. A vision of myself coming over
the rolling green hills in the car flashed into my mind. On the
hood was plastered an obscenely large blue ribbon, the tails
flapping in the wind. Dad would come running toward me,
hands outstretched.

And then, to my dismay, I watched Gemini move on to
the next entrant. Her excited peals were unmistakable. She
gushed every bit as much as she had for me and I felt my
confidence ebb. She was that way for everyone? I wasn't
special then.

Again, I had the urge to go home. I traipsed back over to
my pride and joy and plopped onto the ground. I was young.
I could come back another year. This didn't have to be it.
Who knew how many times some of these folk had come
back, how many times it had taken them before they'd won
anything. Why did I deserve to win on my first go?

I'd just had a *feeling*, you know? I started growing this and

I'd attached some bit of myself. I cared as I'd never cared for anything else in my life and I knew I had something special. I just couldn't believe that hadn't meant something. I guess it meant something to me and that should be all that mattered. If I left, if I didn't wait for the results and went home, I could still be proud to know that I'd done it.

And yet a part of me couldn't go home without staying to the end. It wouldn't be fair, realizing that all these others probably felt the same as I did.

When they called us all to the podium, I stood near the back, ready to leave the moment the names were called. The strange judge wandered up to the microphone as if by accident and stared at us all as if we were mobbing to have her home set on fire. She was a twitchy bird. I don't think I could've been friends with her were she my age.

"Cheerio," she said, as if trying to speak a foreign language. "Thank you all for your wonderful entries. I've seen some truly passable vegetation."

There was scattered applause at this pronouncement.

"We will begin with the winners of the best crop competition, and then afterwards, Miles Kilo will continue with the livestock results."

"You ready to get yourself up there, little miss?" The elderly lady who'd helped me earlier was at my side. I jumped in surprise when I heard her voice so close to me and she giggled. "You got me laughing," she said.

I smiled.

Up on the stage, Gemini unfolded the first slip of paper. "Some judges decide who's won before they've seen every entry. But I don't even think about winners until I've given them all a look, and am I glad I did. In third place, with an exquisitely girthy pumpkin, Gordon Gossamer. Yes, it has the most excellent roundness, doesn't it?"

Everyone applauded and a middle-aged man went running up to the platform, beaming at the crowd. He waved and accepted a red ribbon from one of the judge's attendants. Then he went and stood near the back of the stage.

Two more chances.

"Next"—Gemini pushed the over-large glasses up the bridge of her nose—"at first sight I thought she had no chance, but when I took a look at her entry I was blown away. I realized later that she had to be a Leo—it's the only thing that makes sense under the circumstances. Anyway, in second place, with one of the lushest cabbages I've ever seen, Melanie Bell."

"I'm an Aries," I mumbled, rolling my eyes. Like it mattered.

Then it hit me. People were applauding. The woman beside me was patting my back. Gemini had called my name; she was talking about my cabbage. *My* baby! I'd won second place!

My heart skipped about three beats. Then I screamed and began jumping up and down on the spot, excitement flooding through me.

The old woman gave me a soft push.

"You got to get going!" she said.

She was right! I needed to go up and get my ribbon!

Nearly tripping myself in the process, I stumbled out into the aisle and ambled up onto the stage. Or maybe I flew. I couldn't tell. My feet were lighter than air, my mind was soaring. I ran up to the attendant and took the white second-place ribbon with shaking hands. I didn't even take a moment to register whether this was too much excitement for a person to be feeling toward a vegetable competition. I just let the elation flood me. Gemini may have announced the first-place winner, but I didn't hear. I couldn't take my eyes off my ribbon.

It didn't matter that I hadn't got the top prize. I'd won second place. I'd done it! Me and my cabbage were prize winners for the first time. Something I'd done was worth recognition. I couldn't wait to collect my cabbage again so I could head on home, this time with happiness in me and not an ounce of apprehension. I couldn't wait to show my parents.

Imagine if I hadn't stayed. Imagine if I'd given up and gone home. All the doubt and the worry had nearly kept me from collecting my recognition.

But I had stayed, and I'm glad I did so.

Everything was better in the end.

ABOUT THE AUTHOR

Robert Pires enjoys finding stories hidden everywhere. An engineer by day and a writer by always, he happily lives in California with his husband.